THE WHITE RIBBON MAN

We gratefully acknowledge the support of the Canada Council for the Arts and the Ontario Arts Council for our publishing program. We also acknowledge the financial support of the Government of Canada through the Canada Book Fund.

Cover design: Val Fullard

The White Ribbon Man is a work of fiction. All the characters and situations portrayed in this book are fictitious and any resemblance to persons living or dead is purely coincidental.

Library and Archives Canada Cataloguing in Publication

Dickinson, Mary Lou, 1937-, author
         The white ribbon man / Mary Lou Dickinson.

(Inanna poetry & fiction series)
Issued in print and electronic formats.
ISBN 978-1-77133-473-0 (softcover).— ISBN 978-1-77133-476-1 (pdf).—
ISBN 978-1-77133-475-4 (Kindle).— ISBN 978-1-77133-474-7 (epub)

         I. Title. II. Series: Inanna poetry and fiction series

PS8607.I346W55 2018   C813'.6   C2018-901515-2
                                                                      C2018-901516-0

Printed and bound in Canada

MIX
Paper from
responsible sources
FSC® C004071

Inanna Publications and Education Inc.
210 Founders College, York University
4700 Keele Street, Toronto, Ontario, Canada M3J 1P3
Telephone: (416) 736-5356 Fax: (416) 736-5765
Email: inanna.publications@inanna.ca Website: www.inanna.ca

THE WHITE RIBBON MAN

a mystery

Mary Lou Dickinson

inanna poetry & fiction series

INANNA PUBLICATIONS AND EDUCATION INC.
TORONTO, CANADA

In memory of my brother, John Cosser

PART I

1.

Mid-November, 2000

O N A GREY MORNING IN NOVEMBER, sixty or so people, most members of the congregation as well as a few who looked like tourists, had gathered in a downtown Toronto church for the Sunday service. They sat on pews arranged in semi-circles in the nave, having arrived on bicycles or on transit or in cars from all over the city and as far away as Scarborough or Whitby or Port Credit. Some who were likely lost souls had been drawn to the church in search of a place of comfort, while others were attracted by the idea of joining a social activist community in which their voices might have an impact.

A woman in a tweed suit who had just taken a seat next to one of the regulars asked if she knew who the minister was. "No one has a collar on," the woman commented.

Rosemary Willis gestured toward a man in blue jeans who was sitting with his arm along the back of one of the pews. David Stinson was not wearing a collar and Rosemary could see why a stranger would not recognize him as the minister.

Off to the side, a man with dishevelled hair, holes in his shoes and dirty fingernails, watched a woman put cups out near a coffee urn. He reached around her to take one, filling it from the urn. Methodically, and visibly keeping his shaking hands from spilling or dropping anything, he added sugar and milk and stirred the dark liquid with a wooden stick. Then he sat back in one of two easy chairs set along the wall outside of the circle and watched. He did not speak, even when someone spoke to him. Only when another man lurched through the door and went to stand beside him, did he say anything. The two men appeared to know each other.

"Are you from out of town?" Rosemary asked, posing the question because the woman did not look familiar and asking about the minister identified her as a visitor. "I'm Rosemary."

Many tourists passed through the Church of the Holy Trinity, most vanishing at the end of the service without leaving any trace. However, Rosemary tried to remember to introduce herself and ask for names. She had learned this from watching Claire Withrow, an older woman who always made visitors welcome. Claire was friendly to everyone. She had the knack of being comfortable with strangers, something that Rosemary assumed came easily to her after the foreign postings Claire and her husband told the parish about whenever they returned to Holy Trinity between appointments abroad.

"Pennsylvania," the woman said. She was staying at the hotel next door. Later in the afternoon she would go to the last workshop of a conference on urban planning and then fly back to Philadelphia. "I thought I'd like to try one of your churches," she smiled. "This one is so close I could slip in easily."

"We're glad to have you here," Rosemary said. "As a downtown church, we have visitors from many places. Close by and far flung. Are you an urban planner?"

"Yes," the woman nodded. "The conference is an opportunity to meet people from around the world, although most of the people attending are from North America."

Rosemary was suddenly distracted by a peculiar sound. She frowned, peering around to see if anyone else had noticed. It had sounded like a strangled scream, one that was muffled because it was not coming from the large space in which the congregation waited for the service to start, but from outside or possibly the basement. The woman from Pennsylvania did not seem aware of anything unusual. Rosemary had a sense of something odd in the air now, yet no one else seemed to have heard anything. Maybe it had been her imagination. There were so many noises coming from outside. In the square next to the church, people might be chattering loudly as they clustered around the fountain and, often, young men in drooping trousers were furtively exchanging drugs. Usually, everyone in the church simply ignored the background clatter, just as she had the blasting underground when growing up in a northern mining town. But this sound that she'd just heard was different from her childhood experience of miners setting off dynamite to get at the gold in the rock. It was more like the choked voices of mothers, daughters, fathers, sons on surface when there was word of an accident underground.

Rosemary began to notice that some other people in the church did appear puzzled. The coordinator for this particular Sunday had started to greet the people, but the service had not yet begun. The coordinator looked like she had stopped suddenly, seemingly waiting for something. Although they had begun many services with assorted distractions, she appeared unable to continue.

ON THAT SAME SUNDAY MORNING when the recent days of sunshine had most people still sporting light fall jackets, almost no one wanted to think winter was around the corner. Ardith Martin arrived in her wheelchair and headed toward the side door of the church, the one that had a ramp beside the stairs. Frequently late for the service, she felt better when she saw Patsy Burke carrying her son, Sasha, and a large bag across the courtyard. Patsy had told her she could still scarcely believe she had discovered a church that was inclusive enough for her. Ardith had nodded in agreement at that statement, having felt the same way when she herself began to attend this Sunday service downtown.

Patsy was glad to be there today for the potluck the congregation had organized for Claire and Harry Withrow after the service. She was just getting to know them and was sad they were leaving for a new home in Vancouver. She always looked forward to sharing some Jamaican food and had made some rice and peas for the potluck. Eating together was such an important part of her culture. She could almost taste some of her favourites—ackee and cod, plantains, curried goat, rice and peas. And, oh, for a good Jamaican fish fry!

Ambling toward Patsy and Ardith from the other direction was a man with long, greying, curly hair and a white shirt open at the neck. Rob Hawyrluk wore a large turquoise pendant on a long silver chain and scuffed white running shoes. He looked as if he were thinking about something so intently that she wondered whether he would see or hear them. All the same, Patsy waved at him. Like her, he was late for the service that, scheduled to start ten minutes earlier, might well not yet have begun. Nonetheless, she was surprised he was not hurrying.

"Rob," she called.

He didn't hear her and seemed lost in thought.

"Rob!" She tried again, juggling Sasha on her back.

"Patsy," he said when he finally saw her. "Hey Sasha," he smiled at the toddler. "Let me take that," he added, reaching for Patsy's large bag.

"Food for the farewell celebration," she said.

He gestured at Ardith, who nodded back. He was one of Ardith's favourite people, often listening to her when others simply gave up trying to understand her. She had so much she could tell them, but if they weren't prepared to spend some time hearing her out, what could she do? She recalled the struggles she had getting the qualifications she needed to do the work she now did at the university around issues that arose in her community, issues that people with disabilities faced in every aspect of urban life.

Ardith noticed that Rob was also carrying a bag. He told them that he had brought some Asiago cheese and crackers for the farewell potluck.

"I'll miss them," Rob said. "Particularly Claire. She often stops to chat with me after the service."

Ardith knew that others frequently ignored Rob, but she also knew that even though he sometimes came across as slightly off, he was bright and funny. She wished she did not splutter so much when she wanted to say something. It was so tiresome to have her words back up in her throat and to struggle with them so hard that her face might contort and make her seem a caricature that did not reflect at all who she was inside. At City Hall, she had written and filed notes, full accounts of her petitions and presentations that were included in the records. There was no doubt that councillors knew why she was there. She had influenced much planning around making the city more accessible and was respected for that now.

Patsy smiled genially at both Rob and Ardith. She knew that others frequently seemed not to see either of them. Claire was different. Patsy could hear the older woman's soft voice with its gentle lilt asking, "How are you, Rob? Really, how are you?" She was interested in Ardith as well, always stopping to share a few words. Patsy thought both Ardith and Rob must get lonely when people did not grasp how warm and friendly they were under the outer trappings of their differences.

Rob had told Patsy about getting a cat since his partner died of AIDS the previous year. He told her he was less lonely now that he had Pilgrim to keep him company. "When I told Claire that I sometimes think I see Charles peering out through Pilgrim's eyes, she didn't flinch or ask about my medications the way my family used to when I still went to visit." Those medications addled his brain, he had told Patsy and he'd stopped taking them years ago. He was fine. If he liked to think that a cat might embody his lost lover that was his business. Patsy had nodded. If he liked to wear pendants and read about abstract, obscure subjects on theological and philosophical issues, it did not mean he had a mental illness. He might sit on a park bench and read Schopenhauer or Kierkegaard or a mystery by John le Carré—one never knew what Rob might have tucked under his arm. But he hardly seemed mentally ill, Patsy thought, only a bit eccentric. One psychiatrist had told him he was schizophrenic. Just another label.

She'd shrugged, thinking he seemed quiet, but not unhinged in any way that made her uncomfortable. She noticed Ardith wheel herself up the ramp to the south door of the church. She would catch up with her later.

The east door opened onto a small courtyard with a fountain. A man who was likely homeless sat on the edge of the fountain wearing a shapeless, grey jacket that he might have taken from a Goodwill bin. It was hanging open. Soon he might wander into the church, even if it were in the middle of the service. He probably knew where to find the coffee urn so he could get a cup. A stone building next to him now housed offices for the church as well as the fundraising headquarters for a local women's shelter. A woman read the plaque on the wall of the church and then the smaller one on the stone house before walking to the fountain and throwing a coin into the water. Small circles formed around the spot where the coin had landed and she watched it sink to the bottom to rest surrounded by a smattering of other coins.

From the west, a woman with a cane approached slowly. It was Claire Withrow. Patsy had gone to visit Claire after her hip operation and felt she had almost made a friend as she learned more about the older woman's life. Since the operation, Claire had used a cane. She was tiny, had short white hair and wore a deep green suit today. Her husband, not with her at this moment, was not very tall either, although taller than she was. Patsy thought their size belied the strength that had carried them through many changes together. They'd lived in China when Mao Tse Tung took over. One of their sons was born there. Harry was a doctor and a missionary. His work might have been like that of Doctors without Borders, but in fact he'd gone as an emissary of his church. He and Claire had lived for long periods in foreign countries yet Claire had been quick to tell Patsy this church in the centre of downtown Toronto was as much home to them as any other place in the world because they had come back to it so many times, always knowing they would be welcome.

Patsy wondered why Claire had not gone around to the entrance with the ramp, but had noticed that the older woman invariably forgot until it was too late. So, once again, she went to the door she always used and Patsy saw her struggle from the ground onto the first step. Then Rob caught up with her and took her arm. He was a man with intense blue eyes who said very little. But Patsy knew when she looked straight at him and started to talk, that the distance always fell away. A certain warmth would creep into his eyes and the corners of his mouth would rise just enough to show he was pleased.

Toward the top of the stairs, when Patsy had caught up with them, Rob mentioned that Pilgrim now rang a bell when she wanted her food. "I hung it just inside the door," Rob said. "And I showed her how to use it. Then I fed her. She picked it up quickly. Now she uses it when she wants to distract me."

Both Patsy and Claire laughed. Rob always looked vulnerable. "A cat can be wonderful company," Claire said.

Patsy remembered when Rob used to drink too much. Maybe he still did, but for a long time she had not noticed the smell of alcohol on his breath or any slight distortion in his movements. It was odd how someone she scarcely knew could be so known to her simply by being part of the same community. She thought Claire might really miss Rob. He tended to stay in the background, but was always there if needed.

"May God be with you, young man," Claire whispered.

"Where is Harry?" Rob asked.

"He had to go to Ottawa for the weekend," she added. "His brother isn't well. And he wanted to see him before we leave for Vancouver. It might be a while before we can get back east again. He should be here before the end of the service."

A FEW PEOPLE SQUIRMED AROUND to see if they could figure out where the strange sound had come from. Puzzled brows coming together, eyes darting over the space of the nave—all these gestures expressed their uncertainty about what they ought to do. Rob came through the door, but instead of going to sit in a pew, he started across the wooden floor toward the staircase to the basement. The minister was not far behind, perhaps realizing that Rob had pinpointed the sound from outside and that it was time to see where it had most likely come from. Then Linda O'Reilly, a heavy woman with dyed red hair, followed them down the stairs. Below was a wash-room for women and, a little further along the corridor, one for men. They were small washrooms, each with two cubicles. Between them, in the hall, was a water fountain. The stairs were of the same heavy wood that extended throughout the church, but the floor in the basement was tiled. As Rob made his way down into the hall, a woman emerged from the first washroom.

Upon seeing Rob, the woman began to shudder. "On the floor," she said in a shrill voice. "Feet ... sticking out. Blood." She was visibly shaken, her face was contorted, her dark leather purse had fallen or been left open. David Stinson, the minis-ter, pushed past Rob through the door. His face looked as if he had to contain his own fear so as not to frighten anyone else. Solace in crisis situations was often some form of quiet meditation for him, impossible in these circumstances. Praying silently, his eyes fell immediately on a pair of feet in red heels stretched out from under the cubicle on the right. He made a low, guttural sound and then gingerly pushed the cubicle door open to reveal a woman face down on the floor with one arm flung off to the side. He thought she must surely be dead. There was blood on the floor and wall, and he felt bile rise in his throat. He turned to tell Rob and, seeing the other man clutch at his throat, remembered that, not long ago, Rob had watched his partner die of AIDS and be carried out of the house in one of those dark bags. He could tell that Rob was reliving that memory.

"Don't let anyone else into the basement," David said. "I'll call the police."

Rob backed away, looking relieved that David seemed to have taken charge. The minister walked along the corridor, looking reassuringly at the woman who was still standing there. She was still shaking.

He looked closely at her face for the first time, not sure if he'd ever seen her before. Then it dawned on him that she was someone who came from time to time to eat in the church cafeteria and that he had smiled at her recently in the lineup for food. He reached out and put his hand on hers to comfort her. As a man who had difficulty with feelings, this was challenging for him. "Do you know her?" he asked

The woman shook her head, glancing at David's jeans as if unsure who he was. "I didn't really see her," she said. "I don't know."

David uttered some soothing words as he guided the familiar stranger down the hallway toward the stairs. He noticed the woman with the dyed red hair who had also come downstairs and he could not, in that instant, remember her name either. He did recall that she was often antagonistic toward him and questioned his stand on almost everything. She'd let him know he was completely unaware of a woman's experience, and she'd talked about the hierarchy in the church, attempting to get him to change rituals and language. Oh yes, her name was Linda O'Reilly. Yes. She was in a group working on inclusive language, and she had been adamant that he was lacking some basic understanding. Sometimes it annoyed him because he had always supported the initiatives for change raised by this congregation. Although he had not understood why she had insisted that a group to discuss women's relationship to the church be formed by women only. "How could you have such a discussion without men also?" he had asked her. "How could you work out the relationships unless everyone was at the table?" But he was not thinking about those details now, only that Linda could be difficult and that he wished she were not the one who had followed them downstairs today. Although right now she seemed to be waiting to do something —anything. Her usually loud voice was silent.

"Linda," he said as calmly as he could, trying to stop his voice from quavering slightly as he nodded to the woman next to him. "Can you look after her?"

"What's happened?"

"For now, just stay with her out here and try to comfort her. She's made a terrible discovery."

David left them together and rushed up the stairs. He was glad to be in blue jeans rather than wearing his vestments, although it occurred to him that this might not look right to the police who were, in his experience, generally a conservative bunch. He'd had lots of dealings with them. You had to if you were the rector of a large church in the core of a city. The constant exchange of drugs in the courtyard, the fights late at night, and the numerous and sundry crimes that took place on the very steps of the church sometimes meant the police were a frequent presence.

From the cafeteria door, he noticed that the service seemed to have begun. Oh good, he thought. They carry on, these people. They did not know what was happening, but they knew what to do anyway. Were they singing a hymn now? One perhaps written by a man in the congregation and set to music chosen by the young woman who was the music director. Polly Cartier could play the piano, the organ, the guitar, and the flute. The congregation was a talented one. There were times when he wondered how he had managed to secure this interim appointment. But had the bishop chosen him only because he was older, more conventional? He hated to think of ending his career as a sort of caretaker to a congregation for whom he was a mere figurehead. Occasionally they asked him to preach, but not very often. Still, this morning it was convenient, even useful, that he did not need to be concerned about more than the crisis that was unfolding.

A few people peered around, aware that the minister had left the congregation. They did not know what he had discovered downstairs but sensed that something was underway before he came up from the basement and then disappeared into the cafeteria.

At the telephone in the kitchen, David dialed 911. Once he'd had to call the fire department when darting flames with their flickering tongues had unexpectedly roused a piece of paper into a conflagration and almost consumed the cafeteria. It had been during a ceremony that was being held there. All the emergency numbers were now listed. This one, easy to remember, received the fastest response.

He visualized the body in the washroom with horror. He was fairly certain that the woman was not one of his parishioners. Had she already been dead during the earlier service that morning and gone unnoticed? He had no idea how to determine how long her body may have been there. Although he had certainly seen enough death in his day. He couldn't count all the funerals he'd presided over as a minister during the course of his lifetime, all the calls he'd made to grieving widows and widowers, to grieving children and parents. All the grieving he had shared with his congregations. Usually, he would be called in to pray with someone as they were dying. He had been present during those final moment also more times than he could remember.

This was the first time he had discovered a body or was practically first on the scene. Who could she be? So many strangers from surrounding office buildings came to eat here. The woman who had found the corpse on the washroom floor was probably one of those office workers. The dead woman could also have been an office worker, walking around in those red leather heels, flicking her head so that her long hair made a swishing sound. Now she was a lifeless form—strands of her hair stuck together with blood—lying on the beige clay tiles in the basement of his church.

THE WOMAN WHO HAD MADE THE DISCOVERY in the bowels of the church was a pale shade of white, and every so often she started to shake again. When she opened her mouth to say something, it came out in a stream of incoherent syllables. Linda stood with her lips tightly clenched, not sure what to do either. To say that everything was all right would be ludicrous. There must be something that would calm the woman. Anything. Even a strong drink.

"My name is Linda," she said, afraid that if she asked what had happened the woman would start screaming again. It seemed preposterous that accustomed as she was to dealing with emergencies and predicaments in which women found themselves, in this situation she felt helpless.

The woman looked at her blankly, but for a moment stopped shaking.

"David, the minister, has gone to call the police," Linda said gently.

"I didn't do anything," the woman said, glancing around as if looking for a way to escape. Her voice rose again.

"No." You probably didn't, Linda thought. Without a clue as to what exactly was in that washroom, she didn't think this woman would turn out to be a criminal.

"I came in to use the washroom," the woman said in what was now a low voice, starting to tremble again.

Linda noticed that she was carrying a bag with the logo of a store in the Eaton Centre and that she was dressed in a burgundy skirt with a matching jacket. She might work in an anonymous cubicle beside the water cooler of one of the office towers or more likely was downtown for the day shopping, but it was early on a Sunday morning, so neither seemed likely. Under normal circumstances she might ask, Linda thought, but suspected this woman would have to face an interrogation that would further upset her as soon as the police arrived and that it would be circumspect only to try to calm her. As someone who generally knew all the community gossip, it was difficult for Linda to restrain herself.

"The legs sticking out," the woman sputtered.

"Legs," Linda repeated.

"Shoes. Red heels."

This was bizarre, Linda thought, but she knew she could not go to look. She wondered how long she would have to wait with the woman, but also knew that it was important that both of them be here when the police arrived. You didn't watch *Homicide: Life on the Street*, her favourite television series, without knowing a lot about police investigations, she thought. She knew it was an American show and that criminal investigations in Toronto were not really like those on TV, but all the same she would like to share this piece of information with the woman. Again she restrained herself. Not a customary role for someone who delighted in telling people what she knew about a host of things. Clever Linda. So her father had said when she was very young, marvelling at her red curls, pointing them out to the men he worked with who came to play cards on the dining room table. It had pleased Linda, but at the same time it had made her think that all he saw were the superficial aspects of her. He did not know that she watched all of them closely and often considered them fools.

"I need to go home," the woman moaned.

"I don't think we can leave," Linda said. "The police will want to question both of us."

Once again, the woman began to shudder. "I should have stayed in bed," she said in a shattered voice.

Linda thought it might have been better if she had also done that. Having stepped into this day, her life seemed propelled in an entirely different direction than she could have anticipated. She felt like a skier going downhill at full speed who suddenly hits an unexpected bump and lands in an alternate reality. There must be someone dead in the washroom, she surmised, a woman in heels, otherwise there would already be a doctor or a nurse, more likely a paramedic, in attendance. Someone would be there, bending over her, checking her vital signs, offering reassurance. Who was the woman? Who would have wanted to see her dead? Somehow a body on the floor of a stall in a church washroom didn't sound like suicide to Linda. She wondered if there was blood splattered all over, something to make it convincing that this had been a murder. This woman probably knew, but Linda was afraid of setting off another bout of shuddering, even screaming, and knew better than to speculate out loud.

Maybe someone had sexually assaulted her out in the court-yard during the night and dragged her inside afterwards. But the church would have been locked then. Had the murderer followed the woman downstairs to the washroom while the early service was in progress? It would not be too difficult. Not all of the doors opened into the nave of the church. You could enter from the east and go down those stairs without being seen at all. But how could it have happened without someone hearing something? Wouldn't there have been screams from the woman? Maybe there would have been the sound of a man trying to drag a body along the hall and down the stairs, his heavy breath making a loud rasping sound.

Linda wondered if the woman was a member of the congre-gation or related to someone who was. There were many men and women who came to this church without their partners. The minister might not know her, even if one of his parish-ioners were her husband or boyfriend. The man who'd been wearing a white ribbon on his lapel flashed across her mind. An ordinary bloke who had been here on an earlier Sunday with whom she had spoken briefly. He had not come back, so he likely had absolutely zilch to do with this. And Rosemary, who had left with him that day, would never have left with someone the least bit unconventional. He must have been a friend of hers. All the things you surmise, she thought, but never ask, although she was not usually shy about doing so.

Or the murder could have happened the day before, she supposed. There were no activities in the church the previous day as far as Linda knew. This was something she had some knowledge of because of her role in the congregation as one of the wardens. In any case, the doors would have been locked. She wondered how the police would pinpoint how long the body had been there. Unless the killer had a key, it could not have happened during the night. That thought caused goose bumps on her arms. It would implicate people she knew very well. Like David. And the caretaker, Brent. She immediately rejected those possibilities.

Maybe the procedures the police used would turn up other evidence that would lead to a killer. That aspect of crime investigation intrigued her. Linda knew the methods carried out in the basement of the church would differ from those in *Homicide: Life on the Street*. There would likely not be as much drama. This was, Canada, after all, where life was more mundane. The crimes they showed on TV were not likely to be prevalent in a city and country where there were fewer guns and fewer murders than in America, even per capita.

Whenever she read an article in the paper about a woman who had been murdered, she often surmised that the husband or boyfriend would be arrested, and the press would then be full of comments from neighbours that there had been no signs, that he was such a helpful or congenial sort. How could it have been him?

Well, in any case, only after the police officers investigated this incident could it be called a murder, Linda thought. In *Homicide*, it was always a murder. That was the point. After answering crisis calls over long shifts, she always came home exhausted. Once home, she had no interest in answering her own telephone calls, so she would crash on the sofa in front of the television set. The crises she watched on TV were all fiction. The characters were not actual women whose husbands or partners had just beaten them, women whose voices she had just listened to. Nor were they women who were sexually molested as children. They were not the survivors of ritual abuse or women from war-torn countries who were tortured either. And the criminals in these TV shows were always caught and punished. Once or twice, *Homicide* had been too vivid for her and she'd turned it off. But the drama created by the exciting lives of the detectives and the politics of the police force fascinated her. She had loved that show. Maybe it was still running, maybe with different actors, but she had not watched television in months.

Now this, *this* was a nightmare—a body in the basement of her own church—and she wished she would wake up.

2.

JACK COSSER HAD JUST PICKED UP HIS CUP of coffee and was about to go to the living room with his book, a new mystery, to distract him when the telephone rang.

"Hello, Detective Sergeant," the caller said. The voice went on to tell him that a body had been discovered downtown. "The first officers on the scene called in a detective who now wants homicide there."

"Um," Cosser said, waiting for the details, knowing even before he heard all of them that this call meant he would have no time for reading, or anything else, for the remainder of that Sunday.

With his latest homicide case behind him, Cosser had hoped to enjoy the last good weather in what had been an unusually long and pleasant fall season. He had even considered driving a short distance out of Toronto to some peaceful spot for a stroll. He could not have mustered the energy to go and work out at the gym, nor to try to find someone for a fast game of squash. He picked up the phone to call his partner on the most recent case, Simon Reid. He had thought about calling him earlier that day to suggest that squash game and had decided he could hardly call an off-duty police officer and expect him to be happy to give up a quiet Sunday morning. Now it was business as usual.

Cosser glanced at himself in the mirror over the sofa. He saw a man of medium height with brown slightly wavy hair, fair reddish skin suggesting the freckles he'd had in his youth, and a short tree trunk of a neck that seemed almost to sit on top of his shoulders. In spite of everything, including being just over forty, he didn't think he looked too terrible. Except for dark circles under his eyes and a worried frown that he tried to erase by smiling. The result was a lopsided smile that did not improve his appearance.

Oh, vanity, he thought. But how would he ever get Marion to come back to him if he looked as if he were falling to pieces? And, of course, he was not. Take the recent case he had worked on, one that been cold for years. New evidence had surfaced about a year earlier and when he was assigned to follow up, he and Reid had been able to find the person who had perpetrated the crime. This had led to an arrest when the man admitted his guilt in the old rape and murder. So there had not been massive publicity that went with a trial, just a couple of articles when the man was brought in and then confessed. He was now finally in prison. Cosser felt good about that one, satisfied that one more criminal was off the streets.

He heard Reid's intake of breath when he picked up at the other end and recognized his caller's voice. "Okay, Jack," Reid said. "I get the picture."

"I'll call you after I see what it's all about. Thought I'd alert you."

"I won't leave the country," Reid quipped.

Jack hung up and changed his clothes quickly. He knew very little about Simon Reid, even after working with him for the last year or so. Marion had been right. Somehow, he had managed to take his family life, and anything outside of police work, for granted. But even within his police work he'd been absent, such as knowing what made his partner tick. He thought he knew, but did he?

"Not your daughter," Marion had acknowledged. "It's clear you love Jaime and that although you're often not around because you have to be on duty, when you are, she adores you and being with you. No. It's subtle, Jack. It's the way you scarcely see me, as if I don't exist or as if I'm a ghost. Your mind is off somewhere. It's been worse since you found that poor child, but it started before that."

The discovery of that child still plagued him. Just seeing the small, mangled body had enraged him and he did not think that anger would ever dissipate entirely.

"What do you want from me, Marion?" he had asked.

"Companionship. Love. Nothing you haven't given me in the past. It's just gradually become perfunctory."

Cosser could see that now. He wished he could do something about it. He wished that it were still possible to live a good life in a world with evil in it. He could not shake the image of the child, hair pulled back in an elastic band, naked. No child should have to suffer such indignity. Oh God, would he ever be able to deal with it? After such an experience, could one ever see the world as safe or sane, or attribute good to one's fellows? He did not know. The other officer who had been with him when they opened the plastic bag had left the force. Not long after, that same officer had attempted suicide.

Cosser shut out these thoughts as he closed the front door behind him, went down the steps and got swiftly into his car. He drove to the Church of the Holy Trinity. As he parked downtown, he thought of the drive he might have taken out beyond the tall buildings of the city and its suburbs. He had picked up his weights and put them down again, glanced momentarily at the mystery novel. And now, instead of figuring out what to do with his day of relaxation, he took the steps at the west end of the church two at a time.

The first police officers on the scene had ensured that the steps from the main floor of the church to the basement were cordoned off with yellow tape. When they discovered the body in the washroom, the officers had followed protocol and called a detective to take over the investigation. Now Detective Sergeant Cosser was taken down the stairs to view the crime scene by the police officer who had requested homicide take over the case. Immediately after inspecting the body, Cosser said he would speak to the minister. And soon he was upstairs, showing his card with his name, rank, telephone, and badge numbers to the minister of this church in downtown Toronto.

"You're the minister?"

"Yes. I'm the incumbent here," the minister said, looking up from the card, his tone implying he perhaps doubted the designation himself. "David Stinson."

Cosser nodded, thinking that this man was the unlikeliest image of a minister he had ever encountered—dressed in blue jeans with a fringe of unshaven hair on his face. What Cosser did know was that David Stinson had called 911 because of the discovery of the body of a woman on the church's premises. He thought that if this were a murder, which could not be concluded yet in spite of the blood pooled around the body, it would be the forty-seventh in Toronto for the year. That was below the average number for the middle of November, but it did not make Cosser feel better because he knew only too well that every death had tentacles that reached into families and communities. And that until the police figured out who this woman was, and what had happened to her, everyone would be on edge.

"Any sign of unlocked doors or windows pried open?" the detective asked.

"Not that I know of yet," the minister replied.

"That will all be checked out," Cosser said. "How many people have keys to the church?"

"I do. The caretaker. The wardens," the priest replied.

"How many wardens are there?"

"Two."

"I'll need their names."

"Yes, of course. Only one of them is here this morning. The woman over there with red hair. Her name is Linda O'Reilly."

Cosser nodded again. His eyes were alert, darting around the room as he talked. Now they fastened on Linda O'Reilly and another woman, standing close together, neither saying a word.

"The woman with Linda found the body. I think she's still in shock," David Stinson said. "I don't know her, although I have seen her in the cafeteria during the week. She probably came in to use the washroom. People do. If the church is open."

The church was a tall Gothic revival structure, its grey presence still imposing even though it was located in a courtyard of sorts, with the Eaton Centre towering over it on one side and a large hotel on the other. When the shopping mall was first on the drawing board, the developer had intended to demolish the church, but the resulting uproar had led to a modified design that included the church instead.

"I'll talk to them first," Cosser said. "And the other warden?"

"Claude DeBlois. He's on a cruise in the Caribbean."

"We'll have to verify that, of course, but likely that will clear him."

"I'm going to have to tell the congregation something very soon," the minister said. People in the church were watching the minister and the detective engaged in conversation. David nodded in their direction as he continued to speak to Cosser. "I've answered everything I can possibly answer," he said. "You know where to find me. I'm not going anywhere. I simply must say something now. And we need to pray. You're welcome to join us."

Cosser nodded, knowing that he and the police officers had their own work to do. Soon they would have long lists of names scrawled in their notebooks with commentary beside them. He would have to question everyone, as well as deal with the woman who had found the body. He would likely ask her to come with him to the police station. He conferred briefly with the minister, relieved at how quickly Stinson, notwithstanding appearances, grasped the essentials of the situation. Often people in potential homicide investigations were so apprehensive that they could hardly function.

"I'll get on with things," Cosser said. "You do what you need to do."

David walked over to the podium. "We're not going to be able to continue with a service today," he said, then briefly explained the situation. "I'm very sorry," he added. "The police don't want anyone to leave yet. They want to talk, at least briefly, to each person here today, so please wait to speak to them before leaving."

He then gestured toward the detective and introduced him. "This is Detective Sergeant Jack Cosser. He's in charge of the investigation."

Claire Withrow stood not far from where David spoke these few words. She limped slowly over to a spot where the minister could almost reach out and touch her. Her husband was not with her, a rare occurrence. There were shocked looks among those gathered and they glanced surreptitiously at each other. Perhaps a small gesture was exchanged or an eyebrow was raised.

People turned their heads to look at the minister who was again talking to the police officer. They could also see a woman, a stranger, with no idea who she was or what had happened, standing beside them. Her face was white and her body rigid. The warden, Linda O'Reilly, was hovering over her. There were many reasons why people came to Holy Trinity, as it was more generally known. Meetings, workshops and conferences, an endless array of activities that could be attended by anyone from anywhere were held here. Some thought the stranger might be someone a member of the congregation who only came to Sunday service might never encounter.

As a church that had always been at the centre of the community and had been built to welcome all who chose to come, many people passed through its doors. They might know the story of its origins, built with the endowment of an anonymous donation from an English woman who, at first, had chosen to remain anonymous. Mary Lambert Swale had set only one condition to her bequest, that the church be open to the public with no pews reserved. And that all the pews must be available free of charge, no matter who occupied them. So the church was built and once it was, admirers came also to see the architecture, the design of Henry Bowyer Lane, a name like the donor's that few knew. Some might come to attend a mid-week meditation. Others simply to listen to some music. All of these activities happened in this church. There was also an annual book sale to raise money for the Refugee Committee's work. For the congregation and anyone else who chose to attend it, there was a Christmas pageant.

"This is ridiculous," Linda muttered. She was not alone in wondering why David, at this critical moment, was not speaking the words that were needed to soothe the uneasiness that had crept into their sanctuary. "It's appalling that no one has provided any sort of comfort for the congregation," she continued under her breath.

Rob, the only other person who yet knew what was downstairs, looked at Linda with his lips pursed. It was apparent from his expression that he thought she was a pain. Still, there was something dreadfully wrong when you could not pray in your church. Although Linda had not said anything further, there was a general feeling gathering that the congregation needed something more than the initial cryptic comments of the minister. Otherwise, they would soon splinter up into tiny groups to gossip and reassure each other.

David surveyed the congregation from the stand in front of the altar where the microphone sat on the podium. "Gather around," he said then, aware that more was needed from him, and now ready to lead the congregation in prayer. "A woman died in the last few hours. In this church. Our church," he said. "Rest eternal grant unto her, oh Lord."

The police ignored the two men who had wandered in earlier from the street, still off to the side near the coffee pot. It appeared that the officers did not consider these men seriously as potential suspects. They had talked to them perfunctorily, as if they already knew them and how to reach them.

"And let light perpetual shine upon her," the people responded in unison to David's prayer for rest eternal.

The sun streamed through the vivid blues, reds, greens and yellows of the stained-glass windows. The two men continued to sit on the green leather chairs, occasionally glancing around them. Seldom had one of the homeless men joined the gathering so it was unexpected when one of them lurched forward. "I want to thank all of youse for what you've done for me and my buddy," he said, apparently oblivious to the tragedy unfolding within the church. "Thank you." He walked unsteadily back toward the green chairs where his buddy was now almost lying across one of them.

The prayer continued once the man had settled down again. When the minister had finished a final short prayer, the detective approached the podium and David handed him the microphone. The congregation was instructed that the whole building would be cordoned off for hours, perhaps even days, before the police had all the evidence they needed. "Nothing is to be moved. Everyone must stay away from the area that is cordoned off," Cosser said. "Everything must remain intact for as long as it takes us to gather the necessary information and evidence."

Cosser knew the investigation would cause confusion and pain to all those familiar with the victim. And also, he conceded, to the people in this church. They would be affected in ways that when they arose that morning would have seemed impossible. Individuals, families, and communities were torn apart by these tragedies. For Cosser, the most important aspect was to find the perpetrator and to ensure safety in the community. Each investigation brought to the surface disturbing memories of his own of earlier investigations, of unsolved cases he must not let intrude at this moment.

No, he thought. He must leave those thoughts alone. The

child had been hardly recognizable by the time he had found her. He could not let any of that overwhelm him now. This new case required all his attention. When he had reached the other side of it, or even the end of this day, he could let whatever wanted to surface do so. Tonight he might just crawl into his bed and watch something mindless on television; before that he would call his daughter—sweet, innocent child. He would say good night to her, reminding himself in so doing that the reason for his work had become to make a safer world for this child. That he and her mother were now divorced, possibly because of his preoccupation with such investigations, did not change how he felt about his daughter.

Cosser observed both the people and his surroundings carefully, aware that the minister was watching him. Likely everyone was watching him. This was not unusual at any crime scene. There would be many details to establish early, he knew, and many conclusions to consider. He had attended many such scenes. How long has the body been there? And fingerprints would be sought, especially on the body and in the bathroom, probably on the stairs to the basement.

"The forensic unit is on its way," he told the minister.

"Oh dear," David said. "That must mean you suspect murder."

"At the very least, that has to be ruled out," Cosser said, thinking that the blood spatter was enough to tell him that a crime had occurred. It would be important to find the weapon.

A van would arrive momentarily and police in white clothing would jump out of it and swarm through the church. They would take photographs, establish time of death, and use a brush to gather any hairs that might be on the woman's clothing or person.

The woman who had made the discovery must know the area well enough to know about the washroom in the church. Cosser also thought that during the week she might work in one of the offices in the shopping mall and come to eat lunch in the cafeteria. The minister said he might have smiled at her there once. It would have been hard not to notice her as she was an attractive woman, but Cosser had already gathered the minister was generally cordial with anyone who frequented the cafeteria. Many people must talk to him, Cosser thought, and later even take part in a service. The minister had told him that the Eucharist on Wednesday at noon seemed to provide a moment of calm for the occasional worker in the commercial empire next door. For all that anyone knew, this woman might have attended this service once or twice.

"How soon will you know?" David asked.

"It's hard to say at this point," Cosser said. "The main thing is that everyone is doing their job to find out what they can ASAP."

"Do you know who the poor woman is?" David asked.

"Not yet," Cosser said. "But more often than not there are clues of some kind that can help us identify her quickly." He certainly hoped that would turn out to be so, but did not say so out loud.

DETECTIVE SERGEANT COSSER APPROACHED Linda O'Reilly, the woman the minister had identified as one of the wardens. She stood with the woman who had discovered the body. While this woman had spoken a few nervous sentences, she still looked dazed. Rob stood near the cordon that closed off the stairs. Only someone sitting or standing on the south side of the church could see him. Every so often, a police officer went down those stairs, but otherwise no one else descended.

Soon Cosser was told that there was nothing to identify the woman and it was not long before she would be taken to the morgue. He had observed that she was around his age, dressed in an expensive dark, pinstriped suit, hair discreetly coloured ash-blonde. An empty purse on the floor near the sink likely had belonged to her. Or it could have been planted.

A man with a guitar seated in a pew not far from the altar picked out the notes of Pachelbel's *Canon*.

Through the main door that faced toward Bay Street, a reporter moved forward, together with a man carrying a large
television camera with CITY-TV on it. He picked his way around
the space toward the detective sergeant whose eyes took in this
burly ensemble approaching him.

"Excuse me," he said to Linda O'Reilly. "I'd like to ask a
few questions."

Her face reddened as her eyes followed the man with the
largest camera. Cosser thought of a cartoon animal on television
snorting in annoyance, hot air emanating from both nostrils,
which made his daughter laugh. He suspected that the church
warden wanted to know what right the media had to come in
and invade this space in the middle of what should have been
a Sunday service.

The light that shone through the stained-glass windows
was bright enough to allow him to appreciate the magnifi-
cence of this old downtown church. The stenciled ceiling also
attracted his attention, not knowing though that it had been
designed by an architect in the congregation after a fire during
the construction of the Eaton Centre had damaged the roof.
He noticed the flowers that were depicted, not realizing they
were clumps of fireweed, the first plant to grow after a forest
fire. Doves and vines added another layer of symbolism that
he might one day explore further. It was an unlikely setting
for a murder, he thought, but over the years he had seen just
about everything.

The next part of the process, he suspected, would be boring.
The questions he needed to pose to the congregation were
similar. Indeed, mainly what he wanted to establish was the
name, address and telephone number of each person present.
He also had to inform them they would likely be contacted
for more detail and he needed to know he would be able to
reach them in the next day or two.

"Was there anyone here this morning who stood out as being
unusual?" Cosser had asked the minister.

"Just the regulars, I think," David had said thoughtfully. "Although a couple of weeks ago, I recall noting a stranger with very red hair who wore a white ribbon on his lapel. A man. He hasn't returned though."

Cosser had not commented, wanting at this point only information that was directly related to the woman who was now the centre of a police investigation. Nothing thus far dismissed the possibility of murder. Someone who had not been there that day seemed an unlikely candidate for a list of possible suspects, or persons of interest who might know something about the dead woman. Especially since the minister had said that as far as he knew, she was not someone who had regularly attended the church.

When the reporter reached him, Cosser turned to shake his head. No information for the press yet.

"Murder?" the reporter asked, reaching out a microphone.

"Not yet established," Cosser said.

"ID?"

"No information for the press yet on that either."

The reporter turned his camera to the people, who were standing around as if comatose. Sooner or later, he would get his story, Cosser knew. He would persist until he had something to put on the news. The discovery of a body was enough of a story for the first broadcast, with tantalizing bits being shared as more information was uncovered. That was how these guys worked. They would hover and disappear and then hover again. At some point, the news coverage might prove useful to the police as sometimes tips would ensue, but they were not at that point yet.

Cosser asked Linda the same question he had asked the minister and would ask the caretaker, and eventually everyone who was there that morning: had she seen anyone or anything unusual that morning?

"Everything was unusual," Linda said. The woman beside her started to quiver again. He knew he would have to speak with both women again later, as he would with most people. Although he had a few additional questions for the woman who had discovered the body. As he asked them, he realized she knew nothing, other than that what she had come upon had been a complete shock for her.

"I will want to speak further with you," he said, noting her name and phone number. There was no point in taking her to the station for now, and he was reassured by Linda that the woman would be accompanied to wherever she had to go once he gave the word that people could leave.

"Can we leave now?" Linda asked.

"Not just yet," he said, looking around. "Would you point out the caretaker?"

Linda nodded toward a slim man, also in blue jeans, and Cosser made his way across the space of the nave toward Brent Matthews. In his experience, the sort of job Matthews had afforded opportunity for observations that others did not have. After the initial niceties, he asked the same question about who had been in attendance and, once again, the man wearing the white ribbon, who had not been there that morning, was described to him.

"He sticks out in my memory," Brent said. "The red hair."

"Anyone today do that?"

"I thought he'd come back," Brent said as if he had not heard the detective. "I don't know why."

It would not be unusual for someone not to have returned for any number of reasons of his own, but because he'd had an air of mystery about him, Cosser thought, those who noticed him could not quite ignore or forget him. And while he knew that anything was possible and that this stranger might play a role in the case, until he knew the identity of the victim, every one was a suspect, and everyone who was present might have an awareness of some other unusual person or an unexpected observation. He could not be certain of anything at this point.

"He wore a suit. Very few men in this congregation ever wear a suit," Brent continued. "With a white ribbon pinned to his lapel. He had striking red hair. I remember that he stayed around for a while that day. Strangers usually come for the service and then leave. Not many stick around."

"We'll get to him," Cosser said, noting that he would have to look into this in more detail sometime later.

Brent slowly scanned the room. "Trying to remember who was here," he said. "With such an overpowering distraction, I didn't pay as much attention as I usually do." He was aware now that it could be important for him to know, to remember something, he continued. Sometimes someone would come in and stand shyly toward the back. There would be greetings, but the stranger would often slip out just before or after the circle gathered for communion. "I don't think anyone left this morning. I would have noticed that, if nothing else." The word was out on the street that anyone could expect a cup of hot coffee at this church as well as some food. Even if you did not have the two dollars for lunch, someone would give you a bowl of soup and a piece of bread. When there was a potluck, you could help yourself. "I sometimes ask one of them for a first name, but no one else ever seems to."

Cosser looked toward the coffeepot where the two bedraggled men who had wandered in earlier had fallen asleep on the green chairs. One had a leg up over the back of his chair, the other was half on his and half on the floor. Neither had shaved for a while and anyone who walked near them could not escape a pungent, acrid odour. It was stale—old booze, piss.

"You never know," the caretaker said. "I've wondered, but I've never asked them where they go for a bath. It seems like a real insult to someone who likely spends the nights sleeping on sidewalks over grates and in the entrances of buildings." As they watched, one got up and moved toward the west door. He was pushing it open when a police officer stopped him, then let both men descend the stairs.

Cosser thought fleetingly that this now brilliantly sunny November day, with only a hint of frost early that morning, was a reminder that winter would soon come. One of these men could easily die of the cold out there, and to most people, he would be no more than another statistic.

3.

DAVID NOTICED THAT ARDITH, who was near the door in her wheelchair, was intently watching the two homeless men leave. They would be back the next week, he thought. He had seen Ardith try to invite them to take some of the food that had been set out on a table for Claire and Harry Withrow's farewell party. The buffet had sat untouched in the midst of the police presence, but the men had shuffled by before she could get the words out. They had looked at Ardith as they went by and she had smiled and gestured, but they likely thought she was merely acknowledging them.

Whatever Ardith might have seen, David thought, she might not get to tell the detective, Jack Cosser, because at this point he might not have had the time it would take to make out what she was saying. Even if she had observed something worthy of note, he would probably miss it. To David, the detective seemed gentle and patient, unlike many of the policemen Ardith had likely encountered, but often people gave up trying to understand her because it was so difficult. She had told him she was often mistaken for a drunk by people with little understanding of her condition. Even in her wheelchair. He'd spent enough time with her to know she was the victim of a zealous doctor who had used forceps too forcefully when he had been drinking so that she had suffered from cerebral palsy all her life. Fifty years of being locked inside with her thoughts, only rarely finding anyone with the patience to converse with her. Yet, she had earned two university degrees and now had a prominent profile among advocacy movements for the disabled. Some of the wheelchair ramps that had been placed throughout the city were there because of her efforts and advocacy.

After so many years in the ministry was he lacking in patience? David wondered, knowing that while he had occasional conversations with Ardith, he had also never really paid enough attention to her. He expected Anne, his wife, would confirm that, but he was not likely to ask her opinion about something when he already knew what she would say. He often asked whoever was in charge of the telephone tree or the Care Committee to pay a visit to Ardith, relieving himself of doing so when he felt too busy.

Coward, his judge whispered. This judge—his often unwelcome conscience—had survived his childhood and was always there with a comment when David least wanted to hear it.

David noticed two police officers closing all the doors to keep anyone else from entering as well as anyone already in the church from leaving. Moments before the back door was closed, however, an elderly man David recognized as Harry Withrow entered. David had wondered why he hadn't seen Harry at the potluck. An officer questioned him and then let him by. David saw Claire wave at her husband and he walked quickly toward her. He leaned in next to her, undoubtedly wondering what was going on. She would tell him she did not know, perhaps that she'd overheard there was a woman's body in the basement. David could almost feel her shudder. "No one has given us any details," she might tell Harry. "But the police are questioning everyone."

David turned to the congregation again. There were so many people he ought to speak with before they were all dismissed by the police. But it was Claire and Harry he must have a conversation with, he thought. It was only a couple of days before their flight to Vancouver and their new home, and this day, that had been planned for their farewell, had turned into something else entirely. More than anyone, they were likely to take it in stride, but he still felt a need to offer them some comfort. Moving would be difficult enough at their age without a morning such as this, a morning that would unsettle anyone. Still, as stalwarts, they could be counted on to remain calm in the midst of it all.

The Withrows had often been a comfort to David, an interim minister late in his career, who was filling in at Holy Trinity for a rector who had moved on to another parish. Sometimes, before a new rector was hired, the congregation needed time to reflect on the future and to get used to the absence of someone they had become accustomed to and trusted. The new hire would undoubtedly be younger than him, David thought. While he still felt capable of such a position, he knew he would not be the bishop's choice. And not the choice of this parish, either. He might even be called an old codger behind his back, he thought. No doubt this congregation thought he was not perhaps current enough with all the changes taking place in society, even though he liked to believe he had always been interested and open to new possibilities. What he hadn't bargained on was presiding at a church where a murder had happened, of being thrown into the middle of something that would disrupt the community so thoroughly.

David was about to go over and greet the Withrows when he noticed the detective speaking with Brent Matthews. Surely the caretaker had nothing to hide, although he certainly had access to Holy Trinity in off hours. Still, David did not think that Brent had whatever it might take to kill someone. At least he hoped not. He didn't know Brent that well, nor was he particularly fond of him, but he considered himself a fair judge of character and he would be disappointed to find he could be that wrong.

ALTHOUGH COSSER GOT THE IMPRESSION that Brent Matthews was someone who held back and watched, the man nonetheless quickly revealed that he was an artist. Brent made it clear to the detective that the desire to be a caretaker had never been among his ambitions, "It often strikes me as odd that I have the keys to Holy Trinity," he said.

When he started to tell the detective sergeant about the interim minister, Cosser realized that, although seemingly reticent, Brent Matthews wanted to talk about David Stinson. And while Cosser knew he had to get on with questioning others there, he felt as if this man, who seemed more observant than anyone else, might provide some information that the police needed more urgently than anything the others might reveal.

"The lights were left on here a couple weeks ago." Brent said. "When I stepped inside, it was very bright. I remember thinking that maybe David forgot to turn them off. He was likely the last to have left after the morning services. Probably he had lunch with the parishioners first. And after that he would either have gone to his office in the building next door or he would have headed home. At least, as far as I know, that's what he usually does."

Cosser did not comment, leaving the other man to ponder what else he might have to say.

"I suppose I ought to be grateful Reverend Stinson suggested me for the job here," Brent added. "But I suspect I was actually doing him a favour."

"How so?" Cosser asked.

Brent told the detective that he and David had met in a Tim Horton's coffee shop a year earlier and they started to talk as they drank their coffee. They had been the lone customers at a late hour. "He was wearing a plaid cotton shirt and blue jeans," Brent said. "He didn't have a jacket or a coat on. As if he had no idea how cold it was outside." Brent had been at a low point that evening, despairing of ever selling another painting, and he'd been silent when David first started talking to him.

"What do you do?" David had asked finally.

"I was fed up with having proposals for shows at small galleries and grant applications rejected," Brent said to Cosser. "But I wasn't sure I cared to tell anyone I was an artist."

"Jack of all trades," Brent had said to David, knowing it was not true. Still, he'd mastered a number of skills in the odd jobs he took to make enough to keep on painting.

"You know, Detective," Brent said, "he said he knew how tough it was to make a living as an artist, so I figured he wasn't so out of it after all. And then he told me he was a minister and wondered if I would be interested in a proposition. They needed someone at the church, he told me. A sort of caretaker, he said, but he figured I would still have time to paint. There were certain things that had to be done, of course, but the hours were fairly flexible.

"I told him I didn't think I was interested," Brent said. "I moved away from him, wondering if the man had fabricated his whole story. He sure didn't look like any minister I had ever encountered. I think he could tell how dubious I was because he said, 'I hope you're not insulted.'"

Brent had told the minister that he preferred to do almost anything else. "I'd rather drive a bus," is what he'd added, as though to emphasize his point.

Cosser waited. He did not know what he expected to hear from this man, the caretaker of this church, but, for some reason, it was not what he was hearing at the moment.

"David chuckled," Brent said. "Then he said, 'Don't you need some kind of special license? I wouldn't think anyone would let you drive a bus if you just went in and said that was what you wanted to do.'

"What kind of fool did the man take me for?" Brent asked the detective now, rhetorically. "I always thought priests were naive in the ways of the world, but surely not that naive.

"'Of course, I have a license,' I told him."

"'Oh well, I'm glad to hear it,' David had replied, laughing. And then he said, 'If you change your mind, here's my card.'

A week or so later, I sold another painting," Brent said. "But I knew the payment would not carry me more than a month or two. And I had to do something, but I really had no interest in driving a bus again. So I called the number on his card," he continued. "I was a bit embarrassed about it," he went on, "only to discover that David didn't know what I was talking about."

"I don't recall that conversation," was what the minister had said when Brent phoned. But later he suggested that Brent drop by anyway.

"I turned up at his office to find that not only did he not recall our conversation," Brent said, "but he didn't recognize me either. I suppose he meets a lot of people in his line of work, but it struck me as odd anyway. Still, he was polite and referred me to the hiring committee for the church, even though I could tell from his baffled frown that he had no recollection of our previous encounter."

This did not seem as unusual to Jack Cosser as it did to the caretaker. The detective was aware that people who were very preoccupied could easily forget inconsequential encounters. He frowned and tried to steer the conversation back to the incidents of that morning. He still did not know the identity of the woman, and he needed whatever information this man could give him.

"I found the door to the church unlocked a couple of weeks ago," the caretaker continued. "When I went inside I could hear music. It startled me and I wondered who was in the nave."

Cosser was surprised that his inquiries seemed to have unleashed something in this man, as if Brent, too, had something he needed to investigate. It was as if he were watching everyone in the parish, not just watching out for them.

"I walked quickly down the hall," Brent added, telling his story. "When I reached the side of the altar, I could see beyond to where Polly Cartier was running her fingers up and down the keyboard. Of course, it would be Polly. Although occasionally I did come upon one or another of the wardens playing the notes as they sang the words of some modern hymn." Polly's head was bent over the ivories, the light from one of the stained-glass windows shining on her tawny hair. Rather than interrupt her, Brent had turned to go back down the hall, but she'd already seen him. He had been worried that she might not have been safe with the door open when there was no one else in the church, though she would likely have rejected this.

"Oh, Brent," she'd said, looking up. "You startled me." A gentle smile crossed her face.

She was wearing a light green smock that night, he told Cosser. "Like an old surgical gown my girlfriend once brought home from the hospital for me to use while painting."

"I would have liked to talk to her then," he said to Cosser. "Since we both work here, our paths cross fairly often, but we've never shared anything more than casual greetings and conversations." He shrugged and added, "She's quite young actually. Although I guess she's only about five or so years younger than me."

"How old is that?" Cosser asked.

"Thirty-six," Brent said, continuing as if he had not been interrupted. "There's a boyfriend, I think, though I'm guessing. I don't actually know for sure. I've never asked her. Nor what she thinks of David. As the person who plays the piano, and sometimes the organ, she has a lot of contact with him. That evening she was practising the music for the next week's hymns. At least, that's what she told me. I told her that I was impressed by how organized she seemed. Preparing well in advance."

Her reply had surprised the caretaker. "She indicated that she had to prepare in advance because she worked somewhere else during the week. That she'd thought this might become a job with more hours. Then she said, 'But I guess David forgot.'

"I thought she might ask one of the wardens about it," Brent said. "But she said she wasn't sure how much she could handle and still manage the other job." Brent had not asked her what that was, still considering whether to tell her the story of how he'd come to work for the church. "Her comment about David forgetting to extend her hours reminded me of how he did not know who I was when I called him about the job he'd offered me that night at the coffee shop.

"It's been okay working here," he said pensively. "Most of the time. I like that Holy Trinity has always welcomed everyone. It's not unusual for strangers to wander in."

Cosser could well imagine a stranger making this central space a part of their exploration of downtown.

"Someone who knows that lunch is served in the cafeteria during the week might use the washrooms, too," Brent said. "It's decent food and not too expensive."

Cosser nodded in agreement.

"By now, I expect to see people I don't recognize. And it's just as true at the two regular services on Sunday mornings as it is at any other time."

"You must know more about the people who come to this place than anyone else does," Cosser said, hoping this encouragement might spur the man to reveal unexpected pieces of information. "Maybe even more than the minister."

Brent smiled. "I might," he said. "It's actually fascinating at times. I can watch them all from the periphery. It's odd how difficult it seems for new people to become a part of this community. Even though the congregation is tightly knit, everyone seems to be on the edge to some extent. It's a bit of a paradox. It took a long time for me to figure out who was who, and I have the advantage of working here. Once I heard a woman ask the minister how you got to belong."

"'You just keep coming,' David replied."

"Is that what it takes?" Cosser muttered, but Brent did not seem to hear him and the detective thought he had better be careful what he interjected into this conversation when he was attempting to get some perspective for the investigation.

"And then there are the street people who come in and help themselves to coffee. Although they are outside the fringe of the community, to me they are still a part of it," Brent said. "I guess the broader church community feels that way too or they wouldn't set up the large coffee urn every Sunday before the services."

Cosser nodded, looking up at the ceiling, once again admiring the height and the stencilled design of flowers and doves and vines in different colours. Brent, looking up momentarily also, said that after an earlier fire, the interior walls of the church and the organ had been restored.

All before his time, Cosser thought.

Brent continued to talk, now telling the detective that the night he had found Polly practising, they had both been startled by a loud, lurching sound. They whirled around and saw a man in a ripped jacket staggering toward them. Brent wondered if he had forgotten to lock the door when he came in.

"I moved toward the man. 'Looking for something?' I asked him. 'Coffee,' the man said.

"I took his arm to guide him gently back toward the door. I told him the coffee was all gone. At which point, the man uttered some profanity in slurred words that I was just as happy not to be able to decipher. I told him I'd get something for him and urged him to follow me next door. But the man shrugged his shoulders, muttered some more foul words, and stumbled out the door onto the steps to the courtyard."

Brent had turned toward Polly again who had been watching him intently. "'What about you?' I asked."

"What about me?" Polly said. She seemed startled.

"Want a coffee?"

"I still have work to do." She gestured toward the sheets of music on the piano. "But thanks, Brent. Another time?"

"'Sure,' I said, thinking I ought to get some more work done while I was there, too. At the very least, I needed to see if everything had been put away so I went to the small kitchen off the nave," Brent said to the detective. "After lunch, there are people who stay to do the dishes. Even so, if they're distracted I might find a couple of unwashed cups or some garbage that has been overlooked."

That day, he told Cosser, he'd picked up some rolled up napkins from the floor and put them in the green garbage bag next to the sink.

"And this morning?" Cosser asked, thinking that Brent was more fastidious than he would have supposed given his relative disinterest in the caretaking work itself.

"I haven't even had a chance to look around," Brent said. "That last time, Polly was still here when I was ready to leave, and I told her I had made sure that all the doors were locked. I asked her to double check the one she left by. I was even more cautious about the doors that day because of the man who had stumbled in. I've been like that ever since.

"I wasn't sure Polly had heard me. But I was almost sure it wasn't her who'd left the door ajar earlier that night. Polly is so responsible."

Cosser had let him carry on even though by now Brent Matthews was rambling. The man was more talkative than he had surmised, and he had spent far more time with this possible witness than he had intended. There were many others that needed to be questioned before he could let them leave the church.

"I opened the door as quietly as I could so as not to disturb her and walked out the side door," Brent continued.

"'Hey, Mister,' a man sprawled on the steps outside stopped me. I looked down and saw an outstretched hand begging for change. It was the same man who had come into the church earlier. I gave him some coins from my pocket, knowing it would likely end up being spent on cigarettes or booze.

"It was the least I could do," he added apologetically, as if the detective might care about that.

Cosser nodded as he finished scribbling in his note pad. He

handed Brent his card. "What I need to know is how I can reach you. And if you think of anything else, particularly about this morning, I'd like you to contact me."

DAVID WAS AMAZED THAT THE PARISHIONERS were carrying on again even though the basement was crawling with police and there were more police coming and going through the main doors of the church. There were many dressed in white jumpsuits who had arrived all at once and swarmed the interior of the church, taking photos of the windows, of the doors, and likely of the dead woman below, from every conceivable angle. And of the blood, too. The parishioners, on the other hand, were gathering around Claire and Harry, continuing with the plans for the farewell lunch. They were shielding the older couple. Not everyone could stay now that it was almost three o'clock, but many did. They lined up, took plates, and filled them with sliced beef and ham, which had been refrigerated during the delay. They took bits of different salads with bread, rolls, and butter. They stood and talked quietly, but it was clear from their subdued tones and worried faces that there was a pall on the occasion.

Harry walked over to the microphone. "Claire and I appreciate your friendship," he said. "We hope you'll come to visit us if you're ever in Vancouver. And we hope to come back from time to time. Thank you for building and sustaining this community through thick and thin. Today is a new challenge, but you as a community have what it takes to get through it. This place has been a home for us for so long, and we'll miss it. In some sense, though, we will also take it with us."

"We picked up a cake at St. Lawrence Market yesterday," a woman announced. The cake, had been iced with a design of a plane flying over blue, green, and brown mountains on a white background. The woman placed it on a nearby table and invited Claire to make the first cut. Harry stood beside her. They said they could not remain much longer as there was still packing to do. But they seemed reluctant to leave also, as if haunted by the events of the day. David thought they might be waiting for the body to be carried out, and for the police to leave so they could all purify this place again.

"We'd like to sing a song for you," Polly, the music director, said. She was quickly surrounded by a small group of people—the unofficial choir of the church who met weekly to sing.

The song was one that Harry and Claire had brought back from their travels—a few words in Swahili, a few in Mandarin. When it ended, a slim man with dark skin and hair came forward and presented Claire with a gift and a card that had been circulated and signed by most everyone who was there that morning. Almost everyone there knew Claire and Harry personally. This man, originally from an island off the coast of Africa, had been welcomed into the church community some time ago by them. *Bon Voyage!* was printed on the front of the card. *We will all miss you* was on the inside.

Rosemary had invited the woman from Philadelphia, who was in the city attending a conference, to join them at the potluck as she too had been questioned by the police. When she was at last told she could leave, she turned to Rosemary and said, "Thanks for making me feel welcome here. I'm sorry about what happened this morning, sorry for the woman, sorry for all of you who belong to this church. It's such a wonderful sanctuary and it won't be the same again, at least not for quite a while."

"No," Rosemary said.

David overheard this exchange and wondered what conversation had taken place between the two women earlier. The woman was right. It would soon be clear to everyone that this place would not, or could not, be the same again, he thought. This community would carry the fear and pain of this death for a very long time.

4.

BRENT MATTHEWS WATCHED AS PEOPLE gradually streamed out of the church, everyone subdued. A family of two women with their children, a boy of ten and a younger girl of six or so, were uncharacteristically quiet as they left. Both children, who had grown up in this church, clung closely to their mothers.

It was as if he watched an entire pageant every Sunday, Brent thought. There were times when he felt a bit like a voyeur. Actually that was what he was, he'd decided. A voyeur. How could he be otherwise?

A man caught his eye. *The ancient mariner*, Brent thought, knowing that if he said hello to Jim he would go on talking forever. Even so, he was an interesting man. His wife had a rather round face framed by honey-coloured curls with streaks of grey in them. She wore glasses with light blue rims and had on a pair of small gold earrings shaped like seashells. She smiled easily at those around her. Her husband, whose face was framed by a bushy white beard and mustache, was older and shorter than she was.

After a recent bypass operation—"quadruple, by the way"—Jim was often heard to say that he had finally learned how to sit back and relax more, and how to listen to others. Though Brent found it hard to extract himself from a conversation with Jim, all the same, he was a wealth of information backed up by a lifetime of experience.

"Hello," Jim said. Yes, he was doing very well, he said. He'd had to pick up some nitroglycerine because he should not be without it. He said that he did not want to panic because he did not have the pills on hand should he need them. "Better not to live with that much stress," Jim said. "The doctor told me I was a light breather and that stress classes might help."

Exercise also helped, Brent thought, but he did not think this was the time to say so. "But, you're feeling all right after this morning, I take it," Brent said.

"Oh, I'm upset. Imagine. In our church," Jim said. "But I know how to meditate now and I also exercise and that helps me cope with stress." He breathed deeply and seemed proud of himself. In an earlier period of his life, he would have imagined himself as a sort of sleuth, as a person who could figure all this out before even the police could. Now he moved with the crowd. Detective Sergeant Jack Cosser had questioned him. "I did my part," Jim said. "If they call to ask more questions, I'll answer them."

Brent walked around the inside of the church, avoiding the cordoned-off areas, thinking about the people he had watched leave. He knew these folks well now, observing them as he moved around the edges of the church, making sure that things were in order. They did not know him particularly well, but that was how it had always been for him. He had been a watcher, an observer, a listener. To create and make art on the side had been his ambition, to travel, perhaps to live in some foreign country. Mexico. Thailand. He did not know. It could be Uganda now that it was safe to go there again. So all of his jobs had been of the kind that allowed him to leave them behind. It had led colleagues, friends, and family to make comments about "not living up to his potential," but he had taken pride in never allowing himself to be defined by easy labels and standards. He supposed he would be under suspicion now, merely because he was less known than the others were and because he had more access to the church. After all, he and David and the wardens, Linda and Claude—but Claude was away on vacation—were the only ones with keys to the church. He imagined Linda would be ruled out rather quickly. Polly probably had a key, too, it occurred to him, but he could rest on that one. It would have nothing to do with her. So it was David or him. Either one of them could have come into the church at any time. Suddenly he remembered suggesting to Rosemary that she write a mystery novel set in Holy Trinity. From conversations with her, he'd learned that she wanted to be a writer; maybe she had even started to write her book.

He'd forgotten all about that conversation with Rosemary until now. When they had talked that morning, it had never crossed his mind that there might be a real body found in the church one day. What would Rosemary tell the police? It would sound very suspicious. He thought of his girlfriend, Gisele, and began to perspire when he realized even she would not be able to vouch for all his time during the previous night because, although they lived together now, she was in Montreal visiting her family for the weekend. Her sister had just had a baby.

Life and death. The birth of this baby, like all births, was a miracle. And death … well he knew about desperation and poverty from working at the food bank, and for a time, answering the distress line. He knew about death from working with AIDS patients and from volunteering at hospices. Life and death were often juxtaposed.

Who was the woman they had found dead in the basement? No one seemed to know, but it did not usually take long to figure something like that out. Somebody somewhere would notice that she, someone's girlfriend or mother or sister or friend, who sang in the shower or walked down the sidewalk inserting small dance steps, was missing.

When he checked the tiny kitchen off the back of the church, he found that someone from the congregation had done all the dishes and put them back on the shelves above the sink. Any leftover food had been removed. He was usually spared this chore, thanks to a few willing volunteers. He checked the doors in the parts of the church he could access and went outside to sit by the fountain. He was not sure when all the police would leave, but David had asked to see him. He had arranged for an appointment the previous Sunday, only the time was later in the day now, changed by the unexpected events of that morning. So Brent waited for the hour to arrive when they would go over whatever David was bothered by now. He did not like the minister much. He seemed so nervous and suspicious, and the way he looked around through heavy eyebrows drawn together seemed almost sinister at times. With his appearance, David would have made a better detective or small-time criminal than a minister. But underneath it all, he was a kind man, Brent supposed. Albeit somewhat out of his element in this church. A little old to change now as quickly as this congregation, on the forefront of social activism, required. But that was not a caretaker's business.

It's not up to you to have opinions here, he thought. You know that even though they treat you well and like you, you are still an employee.

But he was actually tired of it. Even one year as caretaker of a church was longer than he had envisioned. Someone was going to buy a load of his paintings, or at least one of the recent ones that were infused with bright colours. Something was going to come together and he was going to go somewhere else to live. But there had not been even a nibble on anything, not a commission either, and no other exciting opportunities had emerged. Even Montreal would be a change. Maybe he would be inspired by the style and atmosphere there and he could create something no one could resist buying. And Gisele had started talking about moving there. He would not mind. He could speak French well enough and it would give him the opportunity to become truly fluent and prepare himself to go to France or one of the French-speaking countries in Africa.

He thought about the dead woman in the basement and

how, by not going into the women's washroom this morning, he had missed her. He had told Detective Sergeant Cosser that. Yesterday he had checked the washroom before he locked the church for the night. Around five. She had not been there then. Of that he was certain. But how did she get there? When?

"Hello, Brent," David said.

"Hello, David."

Brent was aware that he had not heard the prayers of the people today. He liked best the ones that invoked prayers for the suffering of whoever had been experiencing injustice whether at home or abroad, for other parishes, or for the loved ones of the individual parishioners. There was something particularly moving about the way someone who seemed ordinarily very quiet would stand and pray for a dying relative or give information about a parent or sibling who had died in some far-off city and speak about the ordeal of caring for them at that distance. "I was glad to be able to help, though," one man had said. "I became much closer to my mother as she faded away from the large woman she had been with a loud, cheery voice to someone more like a bird with a hoarse or high-pitched squeal." It struck Brent though that these people were not very good at supporting each other directly. They made public statements about their pain, but if you talked to them they would rather discuss the plight of the victims of ethnic cleansing in Bosnia. Or the collapse of the Russian economy. Or just about anything else but the way they were feeling. As if the loss of a parent were insignificant when set against the perils of *The World at Six*. He himself was no stranger to working with and for good causes while keeping an icy silence around his own innermost thoughts and feelings.

He considered that this place was not a sanctuary from the world's pain; it was not a place to come to meditate for most of the congregation. And now it would be even less so. Although during the week he sometimes noticed someone wander in, a stranger perhaps, who stood and looked at the altar or at the stained-glass windows, who seemed to be seeking some inner tranquility. Perhaps they also went over to the cathedral on King Street for the music. Or to the fountain outside the church to spend a peaceful moment under blue sky next to the sound of water.

"The woman who found the body was in the cafeteria on Friday," David said.

Brent did not reply. David had asked for this meeting before Friday, before today when the body was discovered.

"I expect you told the police," Brent said finally. And, "Did you have something particular in mind you wanted to talk about?"

"Yes," David said. "Of course." His mind often seemed to be off in some other place, almost as if he were daydreaming. Then suddenly he would say something that sounded profound or else was entirely irrelevant. "But before that, I want you to know that the police could be in the church all evening. They said it might take all night. And they mentioned, by the way, that there are professional services that will clean up the washroom after. I wanted to give you that information." He searched in his pocket and pulled out a card.

"Thanks," Brent said. He had wondered if he would have to do it. It was the one time he had thought of refusing, so he was relieved.

"We wanted to ask if you would extend your contract for another year," David said. "The members of the Personnel Committee are very pleased with your work."

Brent let out a long breath. It was a living. It was a place with a fascination all its own. But he had never been a churchgoer and this job had not convinced him he would ever want to be. He did not want to remain too long here. But another year? It would be reassuring to know he could count on an income for that long. It could be a goal to have something else on the platter before that year was up.

"We can offer you a slight raise in salary," David said.

"What about six months?" Brent did not know where the thought came from. It simply sprang forth when he opened his mouth.

"Well, I guess that's better than saying no," David said. He smiled slightly. "Perhaps in six months we'll be able to persuade you to stay another."

Brent wanted to say he doubted that, but he nodded ever so slightly.

5.

WHEN DAVID LEFT HOLY TRINITY, only a handful of police officers were still there. And Brent was also in the church, of course, where he would spend at least another hour moving the pews back to their regular location and putting the table where food had been set up over to the side again. He was glad Brent would not have to clean up the washroom in the basement when the police were finished. The body would have been removed by then, but he would not want to have to mop up whatever was left after that either. And Cosser had said they might leave the scene intact for at least a couple more days while the police made sure they had all the evidence. The thought of the woman dying a violent death in his church had left David shaken. As the subway train crossed over the Don Valley Parkway, he could see cars in long rows streaming along the highways below and he tried to rid himself of the earlier images of limbs strewn across a tile floor, bloodied hair and clothing, tiles. All of it. It seemed more a nightmare now than something he had actually seen. It would take more than a ride across the Bloor Viaduct to change the scenery of this unfortunate day. As soon as the police were finished, whatever that meant, he would have to return to the church. If he did not hear anything from them before the morning, he would go anyway.

At Broadview, he left the train, climbed the stairs to the street and walked east. He needed both the air and the exercise. Besides he liked this area where he often heard the hearty laughter of someone going into a Greek restaurant, and the babble of children walking home from school. There was also the Carrot Common where vegetables and fruits were piled in neat stacks of organic produce – reds, yellows, greens. As you went further east on the Danforth, the talk around you became more and more spirited. He had moved to the area before it had become so lively, and he was glad to be there. It reminded him of Montreal, of the way the sound of another language and the vivacity of the French-Canadian culture was the subtle background that had crept into his dreams. Although he spoke fluent French and even gestured differently then, somewhere deep inside was an Anglo reserve he had never been able to dispel. Anne said he was more natural with his gestures in Montreal, speaking with his hands when he spoke French. He was not the staid person the congregation assumed him to be, he thought. He knew the bishop had chosen him for this church because he seemed staid—quiet and also well-grounded in the liturgy and history of the Church of England. His mind wandered to whether he would go to the support group for sleep disorders the next evening. He had not told anyone except his doctor that he had insomnia, although his wife knew. How could she not? He had never asked her how much she actually knew. The insomnia had been his secret for such a long time that he felt almost as if this support group that he had recently found was also something to be hidden. As he thought he might hide participation in Alcoholics Anonymous were he an alcoholic. He was relieved to have found some aid from one of the drugs prescribed by a doctor after a sleep study at a downtown hospital. But he kept going back to the support group to hear different speakers in the hope of finding some natural way to conquer his problems. He was about to undergo a series of acupuncture sessions and would likely go the next day to hear the woman who had been invited to speak about nutrition. Unless the police asked him for something, there were no pressing matters in the parish that required him to stay for the evening.

At the last meeting of the sleep group, the woman who had met him at the door and had checked his name off a list had been asleep in her chair as soon as the speech had begun. Early into the presentation, she had fallen onto the floor in a slow roll and slept there for the full hour. Everyone knew that she organized the meetings, made sure they began on time, and then fell asleep. Although the first time he saw her fall, David jumped up ready to help her until someone near him put a hand on his arm to stop him. Now he knew she had a technique of going limp that cushioned her fall. The only time she ever hurt herself was when her shoulder hit the edge of another chair as she tumbled forward. The speaker commented that he had been warned that this might happen so he had not stopped speaking. Nor had anyone else budged, although David saw a woman near him shudder for a moment until she realized who it was lying there on the floor between two rows of chairs, not hearing the speech at all. Not even the questions and answers.

"Narcolepsy," the woman next to David said.

He nodded as if he knew what she was talking about, but he did not lose his sense of horror when to him the woman on the floor had momentarily been a dead body. Here lay a whole mysterious world, that of sleep and sleeplessness. Earlier a man had talked a lot about sleep apnea and restless legs. His wife was at the meeting with him so she could see he was not all that unusual.

"He has so many problems," his wife said to David. "He takes drugs for all of them so you never know what's going on." She said it was not only the sleep disorders, but also manic depression, loss of motivation, memory lapses. "We have to have separate rooms now."

As David wondered about mentioning his pastoral work, he reminded himself that he was not there to take care of others.

He was not even sure he was taking care of himself. For him, it was such a rare experience even to think about self-care. Sometimes as a minister he felt that his work ought to go on around the clock.

It bothered him though that there were parts of most twenty-four hour periods that he could not account for because he occasionally walked in his sleep. As he strode along the Danforth on his way back to the house, he was not sure if he had done so the previous night or not. He was almost afraid to ask Anne. But suppose the police began to question his whereabouts. Could even he be sure he had been at home in his own bed? A month or so ago, he had awakened up to his armpits in the Humber River.

The weather was still balmy a month ago, David thought. But it isn't any longer.

He could see bits of paper blowing in the wind along the sidewalks and the grey sky hugged down into the landscape. Some night soon the rain would turn to snow and in the morning, for a brief moment before grey slush took over, there would be a soft cover of feathery white. It would be winter.

And even more than the weather that would be cold and bleak, so would the thoughts of his parishioners as they thought inevitably of the woman who had died in their basement. There would soon be stories on radio and television. It would be splashed across the newspapers. For the next few weeks, the church would get endless publicity and what good would come of it? It would likely be impossible to at least turn the interviews he would have to endure to the vulnerability of women, to the plight of the homeless Although this woman, dressed in a tailored skirt as he recalled from the glimpse he had seen of her, had not been poor. It was the shoes he remembered clearly, stylish heels made of red leather. Expensive. However privileged her life may have been, she's dead, he thought. And he imagined her soul as troubled, aware of her attacker, still terrified.

The prayers of the people are needed, he thought. *Rest eternal grant unto her, oh Lord. And let light perpetual shine upon her.*

There was solace in his faith. There was hope in the salvation granted by Jesus and the resurrection. He fingered the cross he wore around his neck, touching the place just below his Adam's apple where the collar would stop were he wearing it. Blue jeans did not seem quite the right apparel for a minister. He had seen it in one of the police officer's eyes. But sometimes he wore them to help him keep from rushing in at every juncture in the service. Sometimes his only role was to make an announcement that clarified something about church activity or informed those in attendance that he was the parish priest. Today it had fallen upon his shoulders to orchestrate the proceedings while saying very little. Once the police had taken over, he had just waited.

6.

ROSEMARY WALKED OUT OF THE FAR DOOR of the church alone, leaving a few parishioners behind still chatting with Claire and Harry. At the end of her interview with the detective, she had almost mentioned the man with the white ribbon, but what could that have to do with anything? What did she know about him that would either implicate or exonerate him? Nothing really. She had answered the ad he had placed in the paper, and when he called, she suggested he come to the service at the church. When they met that Sunday, Rosemary had left the church with him, suggesting they walk over to the Art Gallery and afterwards to a Chinese restaurant where they had a light lunch. He showed her some photographs of large, brightly coloured hot air balloons taken in New Mexico. Red, yellow, and blue stripes and circles formed designs on the balloons floating over a desert. He said he had been married for a long time and that his wife had left him.

"I don't understand why," he said.

Especially since she still called and asked him to fix things. One week it was the washer, another a hinge on the back door. One of his daughters did not want to see him at all. Rosemary did not think there was anything memorable about him and had decided not to see him again. She need not have worried as he did not call her again right away. Then, on the preceding Friday night, he left a message on her telephone, repeating that he was Mr. Almost, the anonymous moniker he had used in the newspaper ad she had answered. She did not return his call. She felt apprehensive for the first time. What if he had murdered the woman? Maybe she, Rosemary, was on some hit list he had started with names from respondents to his ad. She could have told the police officer she had met him that way. Instead she had not said anything about him. She had not lied that they'd met through a mutual acquaintance. Nor that she had suggested meeting him at the church, embarrassed about answering the ad even though it was common to meet people that way these days. She should probably have let the police officer know about him. But what connection could there possibly be between her and that woman? Although she supposed the murder victim might have been one of many women he'd met as a result of that ad. However uncomfortable she felt about it, she ought not to conceal anything from the police. Even though the detective had not been asking about any other Sunday. And that Sunday, it had been his first time at the church, so why would she even remotely think he might somehow be involved in the events of this day.

As she walked through the Eaton Centre, loud music pounded, making it impossible to think. She went into a store, browsed half-heartedly, and stopped to look at a pair of khaki pants on sale. She tried them on. This was how she shopped, on the move. Sometimes she was lucky and found something at a discounted price. More often she frequented the second-hand stores for bargains. Today, it was sheer distraction.

An hour or so later, she arrived at the subway platform to wait for a train. There was a busker at the entry, playing a guitar, and she remembered once doing a dance step on this very platform. Jive, swing, or something like that, late at night when the station was almost empty. Now there were too many people around. You had to draw the line somewhere. And she was shaky.

"Rosemary," a man's voice called out.

She jumped, startled, and then smiled when she noticed it was Brent.

"This is a nice surprise," he said. "I thought by now you'd be long out of this area."

"Hi, Brent," she said. "On your way home, finally?"

"Yes, finally. With all the commotion, I didn't have a chance to talk to you today. David wanted to see me and then I had to finish a few things in the church after everyone left. By then I'd missed you"

Something flitted across his face that she could not fathom, but she let it pass. "Well, here I am," she said.

"Want to go for a coffee?"

"Sure."

"Let's get on the train and get off at Spadina."

"Right." They would head south and go around the loop and up to Bloor Street. From previous conversations, he must have remembered that she lived in that area where there were coffee shops galore along the strip west from Spadina. She was not sure where he lived, but it did not matter. Most of the time, they talked about books. Brent was a good listener and always wanted to know what she thought about whatever came up. Eventually he talked, too—long discursive responses. It was a mystery to her that they could maintain a conversation when they did not like the same books and held widely divergent ideas on many topics. When the train came in, they found seats easily.

"The church won't be the same," Brent said.

"No," Rosemary said. "It's sad for the woman, but it's sad for the church, too. What a thing to happen on Claire and Harry's last Sunday." She was about to say more, then realized that while she trusted him, she knew next to nothing about him. And he had access to the church when most others did not. She felt momentary panic. What if he had...? No, no, no. That's impossible. Anyway, they were in a public place. She needn't worry.

They walked along Bloor Street, settling on a coffee shop that had become a popular spot in the neighbourhood. She often saw a columnist from the morning newspaper sitting there. Sometimes she also saw someone she might have seen on television. Other times, the place was full of familiar faces she often passed on the street. Rosemary now smiled at the columnist and he smiled back. They had never spoken, but they had crossed paths innumerable times. She often thought she might one day comment on one of his articles, that it might lend some sanity to an otherwise one-sided discussion. He was invariably critical of the media, even his own newspaper. She liked that the newspaper could be so entrenched in a set of political assumptions and yet publish a critique by him on those same pages.

Brent ordered café latte and Rosemary asked for an espresso. "A double," she said. "Straight up."

Brent did not look surprised any more when she ordered. He knew by now she did not smoke or drink alcohol, ate a vegetarian diet, and worked out regularly at a gym in the Manulife Centre. He didn't know that she thought walking on a machine while watching television was about the most boring thing you could do. He'd often seen her on her bicycle. He wished he could sustain that kind of motivation.

"I've signed on for another six months at the church," he said. "They wanted me to commit myself for a year. But I can't. I keep thinking I might get things together and go to Bangkok."

"Why Bangkok?"

"Oh, it could be anywhere. I just needed a concrete name."

"Why?"

"I'd like to go some place where I could live in another language."

"Any particular language?"

"Spanish, I think. Although I speak French quite fluently."

"Sounds like a start," Rosemary said. "Only it won't be Bangkok then."

"Yeah, a start, but if I'm still thinking of Bangkok, it hardly constitutes a plan."

"Well, you could get to that with another couple of steps."

"Let's say Mexico, then."

"That sounds interesting," Rosemary said.

"There are places you can live quite cheaply there."

"What would you do?"

"Probably teach English to the locals." He sipped his latte. "Tell me about the guy with the white ribbon. Do you think he could be involved somehow in what happened in the church?"

Rosemary was startled. "I can't imagine how. He was a bore essentially." Just another lonely heart trying to find romance through the personals, she thought. "I don't know enough about him even to guess if he knew the woman. I didn't tell the police that I'd met him or how I had. I suppose I could have told them it was through someone I know. But that isn't true. I met him through an ad."

"On the internet?"

"No. The newspaper."

"Are you nervous?"

"Yes, of course. He knows my phone number. Although I was careful not to give him a last name or an address. All the same, people can be tracked down through the tiniest bits of information."

"Be careful," he said. "And tell the cops the truth."

She sighed.

"Gisele is in Montreal again," he said. "I'm not sure she'd want to go to Mexico. Sometimes I think, why set goals that are impossible when I could go to Montreal. She'd love that."

"Montreal is a great city. I love the ambience there. It creeps in under your skin. The potholes don't seem to matter there."

"I didn't know you knew Montreal."

"University days. And I go back often. I go to Quebec City, too, sometimes by myself so I have to speak French. I walked on the Plains of Abraham last fall when the leaves were golden.

I wish it wasn't so cold in winter. I might have moved there."

"Really? You're full of surprises today."

"I don't intend to be. We just haven't spoken about it before."

"You know," he said. "I'm really glad you're on this earth."

Rosemary laughed. Sometimes Brent made the most unexpected comments. They always caught her by surprise and they often made her chuckle.

"I mean it."

"I know you do. I'm not laughing because I think it's funny. I guess because I'm flattered and because you said it so unexpectedly. It reminds me of a chap at the dance club who came over to ask for a dance and said, very formally, 'May I have your hand in marriage?'"

"What did you say?"

"Same thing. I laughed. You know, when something delights you and you have no words because you're also surprised."

Brent sighed. "Yes," he said. "I know."

"What's the matter?"

"Well, at the same time as we're talking, someone is likely identifying the body of that woman."

"Yes," she said. "I remember when you suggested a little while ago that I might write a mystery set in the church. It's sort of odd that life is happening as it might have unfolded in that novel." She noticed that Brent looked nervous, as if he'd forgotten what he'd said to her. Or as if he wished she had not remembered that comment.

He nodded, but did not say anything.

"I remember what I thought. Who, me? Stodgy librarian writes novel. I don't think so."

"I don't think you're stodgy," he said, ignoring her comment. "You have a good mind. You could write a novel set anywhere and about anything."

"Oh sure," Rosemary said. "You know what, Brent. I'm too lazy. I lack the discipline. Besides I like my job. I have no burning passion to be a writer, it's just a fantasy."

"I thought the passion was there, too." His voice was stronger now, but she'd noticed he had not specifically mentioned the church again.

"Don't you think if it were I would have done something about it before now?" Rosemary asked.

"Not necessarily," he said.

"Why not?"

"Maybe it's too scary."

"I can't imagine why," she said.

He shrugged.

7

POLLY PUT ON HER DARK BLUE HELMET and unlocked her bicycle from the rack outside the east door of the church. The detective had not asked more than routine questions and she had nothing to add. She had Cosser's card and instructions to call if she thought of anything else. It did not seem likely that she could provide clues, but of course she would get in touch with him if anything occurred to her. She noticed Rob in the restaurant window across from her and considered joining him, but she was anxious to get over to the island where Eric would be waiting for her. She also knew that anyone who had been in the church that morning would have only one topic of conversation. Had there not been that morbid discovery, they would all be preoccupied with the departure of Claire and Harry. Instead the church had turned into what at times had seemed like a surreal movie set.

She hoped the community did not list and capsize like a large ship on the shoals. The church meant so much to everyone who came there. Even the strangers who visited only once on their way through Toronto took something from it. The element of danger made Polly nervous as well. She was often at the church until late. It was not easy to leave or arrive without feeling as if you could be followed or attacked.

She supposed she could ask Eric to meet her on evenings when it would be dark before she left. And Eric would, she knew that. The thought of their wedding in a church where a murder had occurred bothered her. She wondered if in the spring, everything would feel different. The criminal would long since have been caught. People would forget. There would be tiny green buds on the trees.

She did not want to get caught up in the materialistic world of the mall just behind the church. She thought of Mother Theresa, of Gandhi, people she admired. Both were dead now, but were devoted to peace in their lifetimes. There were also the great composers who had created the music she played. Sometimes she played a flute in one of the subway stations—chosen these past two years by a committee that assessed buskers—with her backpack open to receive the coins of passersby.

She looked up and saw Rob, aware that he was watching her. As she started to cycle toward Bay Street, she waved. Heading south to the docks to catch the ferry over to Wards Island, she thought of Eric with his collar up in the wind, waiting for her on the other side of the short ride. Soon she would be giving up her apartment and moving into his house. She caught the same ferry almost every Sunday and, when she arrived, there was always a meal ready that he had prepared. His house looked out toward the large green space where children played in the summer. When she saw him, he would hug her then take her bike and walk it for her. But this time would be different. This time as they walked, she would tell him about the woman in the basement of the church. And she wondered how she could keep him from worrying too much at the same time as she wanted to talk about precautions she ought to take. She had not called him because she would arrive at the same time she always did. Unlike most of the other parishioners, on Sundays she usually did not get away from the church until late as she liked to confer with David about the music for upcoming services. This Sunday everyone had been there late, not only because of the farewell for Claire and Harry, but because of the police investigation. Polly thought the difficulty of being in the building that day, knowing the body was still there, still in the basement washroom, had been offset by the presence of those same police.

When she saw Eric as she walked off the ferry, she could see that he was distracted. His dog had run after something. "Come on, Butterball," he called, although that was not the dog's name. It was just a name he answered to when nothing else seemed to work.

"Hi, Eric," Polly called. "Hi, sweetheart."

Eric turned and suddenly she was engulfed in a huge hug. "Thought you might have gone off with the sleepwalking minister."

"No one's supposed to know about that," Polly said. Eric did because once he had run into David in a Tim Horton's, eating a jelly doughnut.

"Either he was sound asleep, or he has a twin out there," he had told Polly at the time.

It was their little joke about David who was otherwise, they had agreed, a rather conventional and staid man. Although sometimes Polly doubted it had really been David, since Eric had only rarely come to the church and he might have mistaken some other man for the minister. But Eric had insisted.

"He was even wearing his clerical collar," he'd said. "But when I called him by name, he said that wasn't his name. He even talked in his sleep."

What Polly had wanted to know was how Eric could be sure the person he had spoken to had been asleep. But, from the bit of research she'd done afterward, it seemed it was entirely possible.

"I heard something on the radio," Eric said. "About a woman found in the basement of the church."

Polly shuddered. "So, it's on the news already," she said. "It was awful. We heard a shriek just as the service was about to begin. Apparently a woman went downstairs to use the washroom and found the body. The police came and questioned everyone."

"How are you, sweetheart?" Eric asked.

"Really shaky," Polly said. "But I feel better now I'm here."

Eric hugged her. They walked along the path away from the dock, exchanging greetings with a woman pulling a small, fair boy in a red wagon behind her. Otherwise, unlike when it was warmer, or even colder and snowing, there was no one else around. The days were short now and dusk began to fall before five o'clock. Polly would stay over tonight, and perhaps the night after. Usually she did not work on Mondays.

"I wonder if the police know that the minister sleepwalks."

"I don't know," Polly said, "but what difference would that make?"

"Well, he might do something in his sleep that he would never do when awake. Maybe it isn't sleepwalking. Maybe he's some sort of Jekyll and Hyde creature."

"Oh, I hardly think so," Polly said. "Anyway, he didn't do it."

"Do what? "

"Kill anyone. He's as gentle as can be. He wouldn't."

"Oh well," Eric said. "We all have sides no one else knows about."

Every so often, Eric made one of these mysterious comments that left her wondering. It was as if there was something he wanted to tell her and then could not find the words or perhaps the courage. Once she had asked him about it, but he had feigned confusion. If Eric turned out not to be the kind and caring person he had been to her for the two years she'd known him, she did not think her music would be enough for her all on its own

"Are you trying to tell me something?" Polly asked.

"No," Eric said. "Just the ordinary surprises in store for us when people we know well and love do some unexpected thing or tell us stories about themselves that shock us."

A word surfaced in her mind from a long ago television series, *Star Trek*. Both of them had watched it as children. It was the name for some creatures who looked like humans, but who did not have any emotions. "Well, just as long as you don't turn out to be a Vulcan."

"Not a chance," he laughed.

Let him keep his little secret or secrets, she thought. Some day he would tell her. And it would turn out to be something so inconsequential that she would laugh then also.

8.

A COOL BREEZE SWEPT UP THE LANE WAY from Queen Street where Old City Hall with the clock tower on top sat on the corner. It housed courts now, while across Bay Street the new city hall awaited its newest identity as the home of the megacity. Some said the changes in Toronto from a staid bastion of British colonialism began around the time that Henry Moore's "Archer" was set down in Nathan Phillips Square. Somehow the cultural sensibility that allowed for that modern piece of curved sculpture marked something underlying that was seeking expression. It was from that moment that many thought Toronto became a more interesting and exciting city. Now it was a vibrant city with the diversity of cultures intermingling, and unless you lived in Toronto before the arrival of Moore's "Archer," you wouldn't know that there had been a split second in time when things had shifted.

In the restaurant across from the church, Rob sipped his coffee near a window that looked out on the square. He saw David wander through the door to the Eaton Centre and Rob figured he was about to take the subway to his home out on the Danforth. He could still see police cars around the church and the yellow strips barring entrance to the east door. He supposed they would call David when they were ready to leave. Some arrangements would have to have been made.

Ardith wheeled her chair through the main door of the restaurant and waved at him. He looked forward to seeing her because when he took the time to listen, her perspective often gave him new understanding. Poor Ardith, he thought, locked inside a body that betrayed her, lacking the ability to voice intelligibly the wisdom and insight that through patient listening one could garner from her. He thought of how happy she was when she sat and listened to Polly play the piano or sing, seemingly mesmerized by the music, clapping at the end, a luminous smile on her face.

He beckoned and moved a chair so she could sit at the table, placing a menu directly in front of her so she could read it easily. She pointed with a wobbling finger at a milkshake.

"What flavour?" he asked.

"Chocolate," she grinned, each syllable emerging slowly.

"Chocolate was Charles's favourite flavour," he said. His partner had been a boy from a small prairie town who had come to love all the opportunities in or near the large urban centre. They had often gone to concerts, ballet, and opera performances as well as to the theatre.

Rob signalled to the waiter. "My friend is ready to order."

"Did you see the crowd down on Queen Street?" the waiter asked. "Do you know what was going on?"

"My friend wants to order something," Rob said. "And, no, I don't know what was going on."

Ardith gestured, trying to answer the waiter. Both men let her struggle to continue, even when she started to flail her arms with the effort

"Car," she said, her tone determined. "Crash," she added. "BOOM."

The waiter looked at her blankly. Then his eyebrows came together in the middle as he puzzled over these two sounds. "Oh," he said. "You mean an accident."

She nodded vigorously and smiled. Rob knew this was a victory that occurred only occasionally, that a stranger suddenly comprehended what she was saying. And finally she also managed to convey that someone rushing the light at Bay Street had slammed into an oncoming car. An ambulance had arrived on the scene by the time she had decided to come back to the restaurant and see if anyone from church was there. She was glad to see Rob through the window because he always had time for her, she slowly told them. They both listened carefully and nodded.

Ardith looked up at the waiter, her brows suddenly furrowed and her eyes focused on his. She pointed at the menu, her finger swaying over the chocolate milkshake. "Chocolate," she said in the long drawn out way she had first said it to Rob.

"Chocolate," the waiter smiled. "Chocolate milkshake?" He turned to Rob to ask if he wanted anything else. "Fill your coffee?" As he turned to go, he spun around toward them again. "You go to the church across the way, don't you?" he asked. "I've never been inside it myself, but I watch the people. They're sort of different. I see some of you so often, I almost feel like I know you." The church set in the centre of stores and hotels and huge commercial buildings intrigued him, he said. Even if you never went inside, it lent a special aura to the courtyard the restaurant overlooked.

Rob thought the waiter must be a writer, he was so articulate. Artists and writers often made their living waiting tables, he thought. Or like Brent, found part-time jobs that left them time to practice their art as well.

"Just think, a lot of people had to fight to keep it here when this development was proposed. Hard to imagine now." This always astounded Rob.

"What were the police doing at the church?" the waiter asked. "Did someone have a heart attack or something?"

"Actually," Rob said. "There was a body in one of the washrooms."

"A body?"

"Yeah."

"Whose?"

"I don't know. I don't think anyone knows yet. Maybe it

will be on the news and on television later. And probably in all the newspapers tomorrow."

The waiter looked worried as he glanced down at their order and checked something off with his pencil. Then he slipped away.

"It's too bad it had to happen on the last day for Claire and Harry," Rob said.

Tears trickled down Ardith's face. It was quite likely she would never see Claire and Harry again, Rob thought. Not unless they came back for a visit and at their ages anything could happen. Claire was already having trouble walking or climbing the stairs. He knew Ardith was concerned about her. She'd said it must be difficult to find that you could not do the things you had always been able to do, acknowledging that she herself had never been able to do many of those taken-for-granted abilities. Ardith had commented that able-bodied people ignored her, and she thought it was because they were fearful of one day being consigned to a wheelchair themselves.

Rob could see how upset Ardith was. She was probably thinking about the events of that morning. He was surprised when she began to write some almost illegible words on the other side of the paper placemat. After both their orders had come, Rob thought he'd figured out part of what she was trying to convey. She had seen something early that morning when she was dropped off near the church by the transport van for the disabled. But he was unable to make out what precisely she had seen. Something about two people. And that it was early. The very early morning service would have been going on then, he thought.

He scratched the top of his head, trying to grasp the details of what Ardith was saying. He knew she would be worried that people would become suspicious of each other, and the one place where they felt safe and accepted would change. No one had come right out and said that the woman had been murdered, but if she hadn't, then why had the police asked so many questions? And if she had been, there were many people who could be under suspicion. Ardith was probably one of the few who would not be suspected. Unable to go down the stairs, she could only use the large accessible washroom on the main floor. Although there would be innumerable people who would likely be able to prove that they had been somewhere else during the time frame of the death's occurrence, whenever that had actually happened. Ardith said something else, but Rob could not make it out. Nonetheless, she continued, by then seemingly desperate that he understand her words. She looked at him pleadingly and tried to get the words out again. He wished he knew what she was trying so hard to convey to him so he would have some idea of how to respond. She seemed increasingly agitated and he felt more and more helpless.

"I think forensic investigation can establish some things quite accurately," he said, thinking that might calm her down a bit, not even sure what he himself was referring to. Then he acknowledged that he had not understood everything she had said, and that he knew that she was upset and that everyone there that morning was also upset. And they were all upset about Claire and Harry leaving, too. "You've been coming to this church for a long time. It won't be the same without them."

Indeed, over time the departure of the Withrows might create more of an ongoing difference than the events of that morning. This seemed to distract Ardith momentarily. He watched her struggle to speak again, assuming she would say something to the effect that the church would not be the same for a long time. And it might never be again.

"Yes," he said. "I guess everyone who was there this morning feels that way."

She nodded with the look of satisfaction she occasionally wore when someone grasped what she was attempting to communicate. He was glad he'd guessed at least that much correctly, but he felt uneasy that he had missed something more important that she had really wanted him to know.

What neither of them really knew, and could not yet know,

was how the church community and the individuals who formed it would be affected. Life has a way of surprising us, he thought, with roadblocks and unpredictable events that come barrelling in from left field. He felt sorry for David as the minister and for Polly who, as an employee of the church, could not avoid the politics either. For some reason, he forgot about Brent, the caretaker. He imagined Brent as someone outside of the community who would probably not be touched by the tragedy. Although he had to admit to himself that Brent seemed to be there not only to do his job, but also to watch the people who gathered there. Rob would be happier if he understood the reason Brent watched as carefully as he did, but he did not expect to understand because it seemed to him that Brent did not know either. For some reason, though, Rob sensed that Brent might understand Ardith better than he did. It was not because he though Brent could understand her words more clearly, but because there was something about him that suggested he could read thoughts without having all the information spelled out that most people required. Maybe Brent would be able to tell Ardith that what she had seen that morning, whatever it was, had a simple explanation. If the church doors were open, Brent or David must have been there. Or perhaps Polly had been. Rob wondered if Polly also had a key.

As he looked at Ardith, it finally dawned on Rob that she might have unwittingly seen the woman in the bathroom arrive alive that morning. And unless she made a colossal fuss about it, no one would talk to her long enough to allow her to explain. No one would ever imagine that she might know enough to avert some of the mistrust and suspicion that was inevitable otherwise and had, indeed, already begun. But surely she could not know something that no one else did.

"Do you need to talk to the police?" he asked as he continued to mull over this possibility, though, at the same time, he thought he might simply be jumping to conclusions.

She nodded.

"They're going to interview everyone," he said. "Did they say when they were coming to see you?"

She shook her head in the negative

"They'll call you soon," he said, speaking as if he knew what would happen, although, in fact, he had no idea.

He finished his coffee, anxious now to get back to his apartment. Some slight sense that he ought to do more niggled at him, but he managed to ignore it. As he began to stand up, he thought about his cat, waiting for him. It was a lengthy walk to where he lived near a trendy area with an abundance of bookstores and coffee shops. Pilgrim, a black cat with splotches of white around her nose and on two of her paws, would be sitting at the window of his small apartment on the third floor of a house on Brunswick, south of Bloor Street, looking down onto the street watching for his approach. The outline of her shape at dusk these days was almost eerie, like a ghost cat on Halloween. It took a special cat to listen to him talk about Charles. "You must think I'm silly," he would say to the cat and Pilgrim would tip her black head at an angle, seeming to listen even more carefully. He remembered when Charles had had to be in bed all the time, wanting so badly to die at home. With the help of a few friends and some volunteers from the hospice, he had been able to. Rob knew his own life might have been cut short, but he was not HIV-positive and for some reason, unbeknownst to him, he had been spared that fate. Unlike Charles, the dead woman at the church had not had to go through months of a debilitating illness, her life instead ending abruptly and unexpectedly.

"I'm going to walk home now," he said, lips pursed.

Ardith looked less agitated, he thought, but then he noticed that she was disappointed. She leaned toward Rob and he bent over and touched his cheek to hers in the French way, first on one side and then on the other. She would know the words, he thought, but not be able to say them.

"The police will figure it all out," he said, not realizing that he was reassuring himself rather than her. Then he started to clear the way so she could manipulate her wheelchair out of the restaurant. "See you soon," he said as she started toward the street to wait for the van that would take her home.

9

BY THE TIME HE LEFT THE CHURCH, Detective Sergeant Cosser had interviewed everyone who had been there. He would start contacting many of them to get more details the next day. The officers in the cordoned-off area, and then the forensics team, had checked over everything on and around the body, but their actual reports would follow after they returned to the lab and completed their part of the investigation there. They had shown Cosser a piece of paper that had been in the purse of the deceased woman. He noted the address that had been scribbled there, aware that this was an avenue with at least some promise of providing useful information—one he would follow up immediately. There had been initial disappointment when the purse on the floor near the woman was found to be empty. The piece of paper, tucked away inside a pocket of the purse, the first piece of information that might lead to her identity, had raised his spirits.

There was a name on the scrap of paper —Sandra—followed by a telephone number and an address scrawled in large, dramatic letters. He recognized the address as being in the High Park area.

Cosser returned to the station, just a short distance north of the church, where he looked for his partner, Simon Reid, so he could fill him in on the case. As was customary, he had a cop working with him who was newer on the force than himself and who would spend a couple of years learning what was involved in homicide investigations. Detective Constable Reid had almost completed that time, but at Cosser's request, Reid had been called to work with him. He had wanted Reid at his side. When he did not immediately find Reid, he decided to go to his office and call the number scribbled on the crumpled piece of paper that had been retrieved from the murder victim's purse. He suspected he would get an answering machine. Instead it was a male voice that came across the wires.

"May I speak to Sandra," Cosser asked.

"Just a moment," the man said.

Cosser heard the man call Sandra's name and waited while the woman picked up at the other end. It seemed that she was in a different room, or on another floor, as he heard the click of the first caller disconnecting.

"Yes, hello," a woman's voice said.

"Sandra?"

"Yes?"

"This is Detective Sergeant Jack Cosser of the Toronto Police. I'd like to come by. You might be able to help us."

"I don't understand."

"The police are conducting a homicide investigation and I would like to speak with you.

"My goodness. Why?"

"You may have some information that would be helpful to us."

"When?"

"Right now, actually. I can be there in twenty minutes."

He heard an intake of breath before the woman responded. "I have no idea, Sergeant Cosser, of anything I would know that could help you. I haven't heard anything about anyone."

"No, you wouldn't have. What I'm looking for is information you might realize you do have when I give you a few facts about the circumstances. It would be better to speak to you in person."

Cosser knew that this was when the situation would become more difficult for this woman because it was extremely likely that Sandra would turn out to be someone who knew the victim. It was not the kind of news he wanted to deliver on the telephone.

As soon as the woman agreed to his visit, he hopped into his car and drove out to the address on Indian Trail. She had confirmed that this was indeed where she lived. It was raining hard, and water from puddles splashed up toward the sidewalk where a pedestrian jumped back to avoid the spray. Willfully splattering people was not an offence, he thought, but maybe ought to be.

He drove through the intersection of Bloor and Dundas, and took the first turn to the left, then another turn shortly afterward onto a tree-lined street. The houses were old, and solid brick, iconic structures that suggested stability. The one he stopped at had a new roof with chocolate brown shingles. There was a light over the door and as he climbed the steps to the porch under the light's glow, he could see shapes moving in the room to the left of the door. He hoped that this Sandra would be able to identify the victim. At the same time, he hoped the victim would not be someone particularly close to her. It was always a difficult situation, but one he had experience in handling.

A woman with short, dark hair and designer glasses, seemingly in her thirties, answered the door. After Cosser said his name and showed her his ID, she stood back slightly and invited him into the house. In the living room, she offered him a seat on a low, upholstered, light-green sofa and sat down across from him on a wooden chair with a cushioned seat. He could hear someone putting dishes away in the kitchen and wondered if that might be the man who had answered the telephone earlier.

"It's an unfortunate situation," Cosser explained. "The victim's purse was empty and no one at the church where she was found knew her."

Sandra's hand went to her mouth in a gesture of horror. "Was she murdered?" Sandra asked. "Did someone kill her?"

"We don't know that yet," he said. "What we do know is

that the only clue to her identity is this slip of paper with your name, telephone number, and address on it."

"I see," Sandra said.

"Did you give this information to anyone recently?"

"Well, yes," Sandra said. "I gave it to Margaret."

"Margaret? Do you have a surname for her?"

"No, I'm sorry, I don't. That must seem odd, but she's someone I met in the library while we were both doing research in the Business Department. We talked about getting together for coffee some time and she took my phone number. She seemed more comfortable with that than exchanging them. Seemed a bit odd to me, but I liked her so I said okay. I told her to feel free to call me anytime."

"Are you able to give me her address?" Cosser asked, but it was more a statement than a question. As if he expected she would do so without any hesitation.

"Well, she did tell me, but since she preferred to contact me, I didn't write it down. I think I can give you an idea though." She wrote down a midtown address. "I think it's near Grace or Clinton or something like that."

"That's still a bit vague," Cosser said. "You're sure you don't remember a last name."

"Atkinson. Atchison. Something like that. I didn't write that down either. I don't know for sure."

"Well, thank you for your help," Cosser said. He would have to search those two names and similar ones and then find an address that fit what Sandra had told him. After leaving the house on Indian Trail, he decided to try to reach Reid again and bring the constable up to speed. At the same time, he could ask him to start the search on their database. "I'm on my way to pick you up," he said when he finally did reach him. He wanted his partner to accompany him to what he assumed would be the home of the victim.

"I can meet you at the station," Reid said. "Easier all round."

Dark descended early and it was already pitch black except

for the street lights when he arrived at the station downtown where Reid was waiting for him. He had brought him up to speed on the phone and Reid had already done the work to find the address.

"I got lucky," Reid said. "I have the info! Thought it might take much longer."

Cosser nodded. "Well done!"

"Any suspects yet, Jack?" Reid asked.

He and Detective Sergeant Cosser had worked together for over a year, and by now they knew each other's strengths, such as Reid's irreverent sense of humour. Cosser knew that Reid would find a way to be funny when they would be deep in the midst of a discussion afterwards; he would make some unexpected comment that would immediately make the tense muscles in his forehead relax. Reid had a woman in his life, who was quite a few years younger than him. Cosser had teased him about this once or twice, but more often Reid would be the one to make a slightly self-deprecating remark about his relationship.

"Blind to my faults," he might say. "Too young to notice maybe."

"A handful of people who were there this morning," Cosser said in answer to Reid's query about any suspects he might have identified at the church. "Can't say so yet, but none really seem likely. The minister. The caretaker. One of the wardens. Oh, and the music director. An unlikely bunch to have murdered the woman, especially since apparently no one there actually knew our victim. As far as anyone knows. The woman who found her had wandered in, apparently to use the washroom. But she didn't see the woman's face, only her feet. And blood."

When they parked at the curb and looked toward the house that Reid had deduced was where Margaret Atchison lived, or had lived, Cosser hung his head briefly. He felt incredibly tired, not surprising after such a long day, he supposed. Too early to let go of vigilance and become sleepy though, he thought.

"Okay," he said. "Let's see what we can find out." As they approached the semi-detached house, Cosser nodded toward the one on the other side. "Let's try that one first, see if her neighbour knows anything."

He rang a bell beside the door and saw a shape approach in the barely lit hall inside.

"Yes?" A woman was speaking through what Cosser assumed was a locked door. Perhaps she had noticed the police cruiser parked in the space on the street. A hand moved the curtain in the door and a woman's face appeared.

He lifted up his badge so she could see it through the glass. "I'm Detective Sergeant Jack Cosser," he said, surprised to see someone he recognized. "I met you at the church downtown earlier. My colleague is Detective Simon Reid. We're looking for your neighbour, Margaret Atchison."

She opened the door. "Oh," she said. "I didn't recognize you at first."

Cosser nodded, waiting for her to continue.

"Margaret Atchison?" she repeated, seeming puzzled. "I don't know anyone by that name. But I do know there is no connection between my neighbour and the church. The woman who lives next door is Marni. Why would the police be looking for her?" She stood back so both officers could come into the hall.

"At least, I know her as Marni," she continued. "Margaret might be her given name. I don't know where she is today. Only that I expected to see her earlier and I don't think she's back yet. But she may have gone away for the weekend."

"I'm sorry, Miss...?" Cosser paused. He did not remember her name.

"Burke," she said. "Patsy Burke. Why are you looking for Marni?"

"This is difficult, Miss Burke," the detective said, catching the lilt of the islands in her inflection. She seemed nervous of the police presence. She had reason to be, he thought, knowing the rate at which black people were arrested compared to their counterparts in the city. "We don't know if your neighbour is the person we are looking for until we ask you a few questions. We don't mean to frighten you. "

"Would she usually have told you that she was going away for the weekend?" Reid asked.

"Yes, usually," Patsy said, her gaze now moving beyond Cosser to meet the glance of the other detective. "But not always."

"Does your friend have fair hair? Of medium length? About five foot six inches tall?" Cosser continued to describe the woman he now knew as Marni.

"Yes, but…"

"Well, we may have found her," Cosser said. "But we need someone who knows her to positively identify her."

"Identify Marni?" Patsy said, shock registering on her face and in her voice. "What about her sons?" she whispered. "They live with her. Maybe they know where their mother is."

For a moment, she sounded hopeful and Cosser thought she would like, not surprisingly, to find that this was all part of a bad dream.

"We have reason to suppose that a body found earlier is that of Mrs. Atchison," he said as kindly as it was possible to convey this sort of news. "We're not sure, of course. But the description we've been given of Mrs. Atchison matches."

"Well," Patsy said, seeming to have recovered her equilibrium. "If I were hit by a car or fell onto the subway tracks or keeled over dead somewhere, it wouldn't be hard to figure out who I am. Someone would only have to pick up Marni's purse to find her driver's license. Marni always carried her purse, a small, wine-coloured leather one. I don't get it; it must be someone else."

Cosser nodded. What she said was true. If the purse had not been emptied at some point—and it was hardly likely that the woman would have been carrying an empty one (Reid had been the first to comment on that)—there would likely have been a credit card, maybe her health card. Any or all of these.

"The purse we found was empty," he said. "It was a small purse that she would have worn over her shoulder."

"What about Chris and Dean?" Patsy said. "They must be wondering why their mother hasn't come home. They were just dropped off by their father and I saw them clomping up the front steps and roughhousing with each other. Their father and Marni are separated, and they spent the weekend with him."

The cops looked at each other. "We should talk to the father," Cosser said. "Do you know his phone number? We don't want to alarm her children."

"I'm afraid not," Patsy said. "Except Marni did give me an emergency number once to call about the boys if for any reason she could not be reached. About anything at all that might affect them. I think their father has a cell as well—Marni told me."

The two policemen turned around.

"Just a moment," she said, her voice rising slightly. "I think I do have that phone number somewhere."

Cosser looked at Constable Reid and nodded slightly. Sometimes there were breaks that lead to information that made it possible to push an investigation along more quickly. And it was certain that the husband would have to have an alibi; if the victim was indeed his ex-wife, he would most certainly be a person of interest.

Patsy came back into the room with the number written on the back of a used envelope. "I found it," she said.

"Thanks, "Cosser said.

At that moment, the sound of a child crying interrupted them.

"Ah," he said. "Children."

"One. Sasha. My son, a toddler."

Too young to be in any trouble, Cosser thought, but what could happen to him as an adult male in this society must frighten his mother. He realized he had not asked Patsy Burke anything about herself, but why would he have done so? At this point, it would have been irrelevant, even intrusive. But he did think of young black women he knew who had thought of moving back to Jamaica when confronted yet again with some experience of racism.

Patsy sighed. "And what about the boys next door? How long do I leave them if an adult doesn't come soon?"

"Are they left alone at other times?"

"Yes," she said. "They *are* teenagers. But if—"

"We'll see that they have someone with them within a couple of hours. Could you have them here until then?"

"And tell them what?"

Cosser shrugged. "I guess anything to keep them calm for the time being. I want to speak to them briefly before we leave so we'll let them know you are at home."

Patsy nodded. At another whoop from Sasha, she looked upwards and poised herself to take the stairs the moment the police officers left. "It doesn't feel quite as secure here any more," she said. "I like the neighbourhood and I thought it was a safe place to raise my son, but now, with all of this, I feel very uneasy."

"I understand that," Cosser nodded, noticing that her voice had become slightly shaky. "We're trying to move forward as quickly as we can. Find out who this woman is and then expand our search for anyone who might have wanted to hurt her."

"Probably you'll find that there are plenty," Patsy said, but then the crying overhead grew louder.

"I know you have to go to your son," Constable Reid said. "But could you tell us what you meant by that remark."

Patsy looked torn between running up the stairs and providing some kind of answer. She started to take a step and then said, "Well, there's the ex: he used to hit her. And there's also her family, Jehovah's Witnesses, who rejected her when she left the community. Occasionally she would notice someone following her and she thought it was probably one of them. She's a good person though and she doesn't have any real enemies or anything like that. Not that I know of anyway. Unless you would call persistent Jehovah's Witnesses enemies."

"How long have you known her?"

"Since she moved into this semi about two years ago."

When the toddler's cries escalated again, Cosser thanked her and turned to leave. As he opened the door, Patsy was already half way up the stairs.

"We'll likely have reason to get back to you," he said, but thought she had probably not heard him.

Outside, he and Reid went down one set of stairs of the semi-detached houses and Reid went up the other to the porch on the Atchison side. "I'm going to give Atchison a call first," Cosser said. "Hang on a minute." He took out his cell and dialed the number Patsy had given him.

"Richard Atchison?" Cosser asked when a man answered.

When the man confirmed that he was indeed Richard Atchison, Cosser introduced himself and indicated he was investigating a case that might involve this man's ex-wife. When he asked for his address, Cosser noted that the man seemed apprehensive about giving it to him, but he relented when Cosser assured him he was a Toronto police detective and he needed to verify the identity of the victim.

"I'm on my way over," Cosser said, noting once again the man's fearful tone, and wondering why he sounded so nervous.

He joined Reid at the door of the semi where Cosser knew Marni's boys were inside. Reid pressed the bell on the brick wall. A boy came to the door within seconds and peered out through a window at eye level.

"We're from the Toronto police," Cosser said. "We would like to talk to you for a moment." He showed his badge.

The boy nodded and opened the door.

"Is your mother here?"

"No."

When do you think she'll be back?"

He shrugged. "Don't know," he said.

"Do you know where she is?"

"No."

"I would like to leave you a number," Cosser said, taking out his card. "When she comes home, I would like you to ask her to call me."

A second boy hovered in the background. He appeared to be younger than his brother. The older boy took the card. "Okay," he said.

"We were just talking to your neighbour," Cosser said. "If your mother takes very long to come home, Mrs. Burke will look in on you. If you want to, I think you know her well enough to knock on her door before that."

"Yeah," the boy said.

10.

D AVID WONDERED IF HIS WIFE was feeling better. Anne had a bad case of the flu, but that was not why she had not been at Holy Trinity that morning. She rarely attended his church and had found another place to worship. The strong involvement of the congregation offended her. She did not want to be there only to see him sidelined, she said. Times had changed since they had their first parish in a small town where they lived in the rectory and the congregation expected her to be a part of everything. In that town, the minister and his family's every step were carefully scrutinized.

It's a wonder our marriage survived, he thought.

Fortunately for his reputation, the sleepwalking seemed to have begun only in later years. Although he'd had insomnia for as long as he could remember. At university, on the nights before exams in particular, he had scarcely slept at all. He had walked the halls sometimes. When he had run into the floor fellow, he had pretended to be restless. And he had drunk the odd beer, sometimes coffee.

David passed a sign on the sidewalk, pointing up an alley to an organic market. He made his way through the covered stalls and bought a bag of green apples. Then he passed the church on the corner, crossed the street, and, after walking east past a few buildings, he reached the Carrot Common. At the next street, he turned north toward the large brick house he and Anne rented. He did not know if they would remain in Toronto after he finished with this church. It might be time to retire, although he was not planning on that quite yet. The bishop had encouraged him to consider it though, and ultimately it would be the bishop's decision. Perhaps he would be able to help out at another church somewhere in the diocese.

As he climbed the wooden steps up to the porch, David wondered how much he would tell Anne about the events at the church. He knew Anne would greet him before he even opened the front door. He could see her eyes gaze heavenward disdainfully. At this church, anything could happen, they seemed to say. But when he went inside, he saw that she was fast asleep on the sofa in the living room. It looked as if she had lain down for a moment and before she had known it, had fallen asleep. He tiptoed past her and entered the kitchen.

"David," she murmured. "Is that you?"

"Yes, my dear."

"I was up almost the whole night," she said.

"I'm sorry," he said. "I must have slept right through. Did I?"

"Well, if you didn't wake up, you must have."

She knew about his insomnia, but she did not know about the strange places he sometimes found himself when he walked out the door. Indeed, he hoped she thought he had simply decided to go for a stroll, quite intentionally.

"Not even any strolls," he said.

"No, you scarcely moved a limb."

Thank God for that, he thought. He did not want to tell her that she might have to be his alibi. But he decided he'd better tell her that the police might drop by.

"Why?"

"Most unfortunately," he said, "down in the cavern of the church this morning, we found a dead woman in the washroom and it seems likely that she was murdered."

"Good Lord," she said.

"Yes," he said, "indeed." What could the good Lord have been thinking? Although what better place to die than in a church? On the other hand, he had always thought he would like to die in his own bed, surrounded by his wife and children and all the people who loved him.

"Do they have any idea what happened?" she asked. "The police?"

"They aren't saying yet."

"Well, thank heavens you weren't sleepwalking last night."

"So you know."

"Of course, I know" she said. "Do you remember the time your wallet turned up a week after you couldn't find it? Well, some man brought it over. He said he had enjoyed chatting with you in a doughnut shop and that you'd left the wallet on the counter there. I know you never go into doughnut shops. I know you hate them. I know from what he said that you wouldn't even have known you were having the conversation."

So she knows everything, he thought. In some ways, she knew more than he did. He wondered why he had been visited with this particular affliction. Insomnia was one thing, but living a separate life in one's sleep was another. He had no idea about what he had done then. But he was very grateful that now he could be certain that he had nothing to do with the woman in the basement of the church.

"What about Friday night?" he asked.

"I couldn't tell you," she said. "I slept through. But I suspect you did, too, because there were none of the telltale signs that are there when you've been out somewhere."

"Like what?"

"Crumbs in the kitchen. A Tim Horton's bag in the garbage. Jam jar on the counter. The front door unlocked. Lights on I know I turned off the night before. The television or radio on."

"Oh," he said. "So all this time, you've known and not said anything. Why not?"

"I don't know," she said. "I think I kept hoping I was dreaming."

11.

SITTING IN THE FRONT SEAT OF THE CAR, Cosser looked over at his colleague as Reid took out a notepad and pen. Cosser sighed. He thought this might prove to be a positive identification and while it made him feel relieved as a police officer getting on with his work, on a human level it was always difficult. Okay, Mr. Nice Guy, his inner voice said. Toughen up. What kind of cop are you? He wanted to tell himself to shut up, but knew better. He needed to hear this message even if the voice was some version of his own. Before starting the engine, he pulled out his cell and called the forensics department. These results need to be rushed, he told them. "I want as much informatioin as you can provide on my desk first thing in the morning. And your timing around the rest of it."

He sighed again. There were so many situations in which he knew people were going to be upset. He was good in such circumstances and able to reassure them if that was what they needed. He was also skilful in drawing information, even confessions, out of them. But that knowledge did not offset the extreme difficulty of witnessing such distress and sometimes it was hard not to absorb some of it. When he did, he would not show it, instead waiting until he was alone to breathe deeply and try to empty his mind. He used every trick he knew so as not to become so cynical or depressed that he would become angry. That was where jogging and swimming lengths came in, restoring his balance. He found that listening to music also helped. Especially now that he lived alone. Marion would not be there when he eventually found his way back to the small apartment he had rented after the breakup.

"You're not saying much tonight," Reid said. "But those sighs tell me that this is a tough one for you. Not that it wouldn't be for anyone and obviously it is for me, too. But something's on your mind, Jack."

"Mhm." Cosser simply shook his head.

Reid would not be shocked to hear about his domestic situation, Cosser thought. He considered telling his colleague about his unease, which had not diminished in the days and weeks since he and his wife, Marion, had separated. Nothing made up for that. He did not like it and he was lonely—a gnawing feeling that overtook him the minute he left work and returned to his empty apartment. A trial separation, Marion had said. Then there was no end to the trial, just the ongoing reality of his existence in a tiny apartment in an old brick house just a few blocks from the house where they had lived together. When the divorce papers arrived, he had wanted to tear them up, but he had resisted. If divorce was what Marion wanted, he thought he ought to go through with it. After all, what point was there in trying to preserve a sterile relationship with someone you did not even live with any longer? But suppose she still loved him? Suppose...? He shook his head again. He had to stop the incessant, pointless chatter in his mind. He had to get some rest.

"You can talk about it if you want."

"It's all right," Cosser said. "Just tired."

Reid did not pursue it, leaving his superior to mull over his thoughts and keep them to himself. Cosser appreciated that his colleague did not intrude and yet could express just enough concern to be a good team player. Perhaps he would talk to Reid at another time, but this was not it. And what was it he would talk about anyway? His thoughts and feelings were so diffuse that he would scarcely know where to begin. Although he thought probably at the core was something he hesitated to mention because next to the work they did it somehow seemed trivial. To call it loneliness would probably be accurate, but it was the kind of label that no one wanted to hear about. It marked one as weak, he thought, and perhaps suggested that someone else needed to take over. All he wanted was to say the word out loud because—as he had learned in the years of being married to Marion—to speak such a loaded word would begin to remove some of its power.

"There it is," he said as he pulled the car next to the curb in front of a house in Etobicoke. "Sort of a long way for the kids." Beside a black door, there was a light on the porch that made the number underneath it visible from the street.

"This could become complicated," Cosser said, "when he realizes our victim could be his wife, or ex really. Keep your eyes open for signs that he may be more than distressed. That he could be the one who killed her."

"Yes, of course," Reid said, not as if he were offended, but simply in agreement.

They both got out of the car at the same time and moved up the walk toward the porch where the door opened as they approached. A man in a dark T-shirt, jeans, and slippers stood there, waiting. He was tall and his expression was inscrutable—no smile, no welcome, not even curiosity.

"Richard Atchison?" Cosser said. Did the man look resigned? Or was he reading too much into it? Probably just mild confusion as to why the police would be on his porch late on a Sunday evening. He would know he had delivered the boys safely.

"Yes." He backed up, gesturing for them to come inside.

The two police officers followed the man into the hall and then into the living room. It looked like what Marion had often referred to as a "guy place"—clothes piled on the couch and books on the floor, with no discernible hint that it had been planned or decorated. It was a functional space. Cosser supposed that after a brief separation the man scarcely had his life together. Did he resent the breakup of his marriage? Had he taken it out on his wife and murdered her? It happened more often than Cosser would like to contemplate.

"This is not something that I like to have to do," the detective said. "But we have the body of a woman at the morgue and she hasn't been identified yet. Following up on the meagre material we have, we suspect it might be your wife."

"Ex-wife," the man said.

"Yes, I gather. But Mr. Atchison, this is a serious matter."

Richard's shoulders sagged. Having seemed somewhat hostile, he now became quite quiet. "Yes," he said. "I know, and I hope it isn't Marni."

Cosser gave him a description.

"Well, all of that is true of Marni, but surely such a general description could fit any number of people."

"That's why we would like you to come to the morgue," Reid said. "You may find it isn't your ex-wife and that will end it for you. Or you may be able to provide us with a positive identification."

Richard looked down at his blue jeans and slippers.

"You have time to find some shoes," Cosser said. "We can wait outside and you can join us when you're ready." He thought the man looked befuddled and he rather hoped Richard Atchison had an alibi for the time of the victim's death. Even though it would make his life as a police officer a lot easier if this man were to confess to something.

When Richard came out and approached the car, Cosser felt almost sorry for him. This would change his life entirely. Even the trip to the morgue and seeing the body would be hard, but if it were his ex, the man would be faced suddenly with a different future. If he were the perpetrator, he would be tried and end up in jail. Either way, he would have to change his life to take care of two sons who would likely be distraught and resentful.

He watched the man bend down to fit his tall frame into the back seat. They drove directly to the downtown morgue where Cosser got out of the car at the same time as his colleague. Richard sat, head down, seemingly waiting to be given his instructions. Cosser opened his door for him and Richard leaned over to avoid hitting his head as he stepped out onto the pavement.

Inside, with the sheet drawn back to reveal only the head of the woman who had been found that morning, Richard Atchison gasped and turned away. It did not take more than that for the police officers to tell that he had known instantly that this was his ex-wife. Cosser was now ready to begin the process of asking all the necessary questions. He was relieved to have the victim's identity confirmed, but he also felt a brief wave of sadness for a family that might never recover. Now the questions he would have to ask would add to the man's grief and confusion.

Watching the man register his shock, and noting that Richard had seemed altogether surprised, Cosser knew that he would now have to confront the supposition that this man might not be the killer.

"Mr. Atchison," the detective said. "I think you are able to verify the identity. We don't have to stay here, but I do have a few questions to ask you."

Richard Atchison seemed dazed, but he nodded. He was so quiet, almost like a large puppet, waiting for someone holding the strings to move him. It did not seem the man's normal stance at all, but every time he witnessed a similar scenario, Cosser marvelled at the different ways people took in bad news. Richard walked slowly toward the exit, turning once to look back at the covered body on the table as one of the lab assistants lifted the sheet to cover the woman's face again.

"I need to tell you that you will be considered a suspect, so our questions are mainly regarding where you were at the likely time of the murder," Cosser said as they stood in the vestibule. "So we'll have to take you into the station to conduct the interview."

Cosser and his partner led the man outside. They stood as Reid opened the door for the man, who suddenly became quite agitated. "Oh my God, my kids," he said. "Oh my God," he said, articulating each word distinctly. "What will I tell them?"

"We will drive you over there after you answer a few questions for us at the station," Cosser said

"I need to go back to my place to get my car."

"We can drive you there."

"Thanks," Richard mumbled.

Cosser gestured at Reid to get in on the driver's side and to take the wheel. He sat in the passenger seat and as Reid started the car, Cosser turned to face Richard with his left elbow over the back of the front seat. He wondered if the man could actually be guilty, but knew that to assume so could postpone the arrest of someone who was the real perpetrator. At the moment, this man simply looked as if he still could not believe what he had just seen.

"There will be a list of possible suspects within hours," Cosser said when they reached the station and settled into a room where the interview was recorded. "I expect you realize as the former husband of the victim, you will be a prime suspect. So the questions I am about to ask relate to what you were doing during the hours she was presumed to have been killed."

"Yes," Richard said. "And whatever you may ask or think, I didn't do it."

"Can you account for your whereabouts between about noon yesterday and early morning—say eight or nine—today?"

"I picked my boys up at noon yesterday," Richard said. "I was with them up until I returned them to Marni." He stopped. "I mean to where she lives. Lived. I have to figure out what to tell them. I have to go and get them." He started to sound frantic, almost to hyperventilate.

"We'll go get your car now," Cosser said.

Richard stood up with a heavy sigh, and followed the police officers out to the street.

"Can you tell us anything about your former wife?" Reid asked as he parked in front of the house where the two officers had been only an hour or so earlier.

Richard stared blankly at Reid.

"Is there anyone else in the family who ought to be informed, for instance?" Reid asked.

"Well, I don't know them," he said. "But I guess I'll have to call her parents."

"We can do that. Can you give us the information?"

"I think I need to call them myself."

"We still need the information. The police will inform them officially."

He looked befuddled. "I hope it's at Marni's. I don't know them or where to find out how to reach them. I never met them."

"Any reason?"

"Oh yeah," Richard said with more conviction than he'd displayed since the visit to the morgue. "They're holy rollers. You know, Jehovah's Witnesses. Marni was disowned by them. I don't remember the word they use for it. She left her family, and the Jehovah's Witnesses, before I met her. They said she had rejected the true path to salvation."

They would probably say that now too, Cosser thought, but did not comment. He had no love for any form of fundamentalism, and he wondered if this was about to create a very complicated web of circumstances surrounding the crime.

"Did they ever do her any harm?"

"Not really, but for all the time we were married she often seemed to be looking over her shoulder."

Jack Cosser looked at his colleague and they exchanged a glance indicating this would also require follow-up. "Did they take an interest in their grandchildren?" Cosser asked.

"No sir," Richard said emphatically. "She didn't want them

to, but I would have forbidden it."

It seemed as if the man's strongest emotions were roused by the thought of these in-laws he had never met. There were often many webs of feelings surrounding any case and Cosser figured these ones would be as complex as any others he had encountered. Not convinced that they would find any reason to arrest a suspect in Marni's family, he nonetheless kept an open mind about it.

"Their last name is Miller," Richard said. "Victor Miller. That's her father. I don't remember her mother's name. They're on a farm somewhere near London."

"Thanks, we can follow up. That's enough for us to find them. Unless you remember more. In the meantime, do you want a police escort over to the house to pick up your sons?"

"Oh my God," Richard said. "They're there alone aren't they?" He looked horrified as the realization dawned on him.

"Their neighbour was going to keep an eye on them until..."

"I think I'd rather go there myself. I don't want to alarm them any more than I have to right away."

"Yeah," Cosser said. "Nor do we. Although we will have to question them at some point."

"I see," Richard said, but only as if registering yet another bit of difficult information. Not as if he feared what might emerge from such a conversation. "When?"

"We'll be in touch," Cosser said. "There are bound to be further questions for you also."

He kept his eye on Richard Atchison. as he went up the walk toward his car.

"Looks as if he's going right away," Reid said.

"Do you have any contacts in the area the woman's parents live in?" Cosser asked, meaning police ones. He wanted to go out to question the parents himself, but they had to be told tonight. If it waited any longer, the identity of the woman could be released, or discovered, and that was not the way they ought to hear about the murder of their daughter.

"Yes," Reid said. "I can take care of that."

"Thanks, Simon. I hope your young woman won't mind a new case."

"That's police work," Reid said. "But she won't mind because we broke up a few months ago. She has a new guy in her life."

"Oh, I'm sorry to hear that."

Cosser noted the shrug beside him and thought he was glad to be working with this detective constable again. When they'd first been paired, it was after he'd had a woman cop as partner for quite a while. He'd worked well with Jenny, too, but it had taken him a long time to figure out what her expectations were when they talked about anything personal. How she often just wanted to talk, not expecting him to come up with solutions. As far as work was concerned, she'd been as tough as anyone he'd worked with and usually receptive to anything that might solve a problem.

But with Reid it was different. They were both men with some common understandings of what that meant: the ways in which men went after what they wanted with a certain underlying sense of, yes, even entitlement. They might try not to show it, but acted upon it anyway. That made it easier to work through situations at times, he thought, recalling how Jenny had often second-guessed or even ignored him, leaving him to pull rank on her. He'd never liked doing that. Even so, there was something about Reid that unnerved him every so often. He had never figured out what it was exactly, and sometimes thought he was likely simply envious of the way younger women fawned over him. Jack had never wanted to cheat on Marion, his now ex-wife, but there had been times when it had bothered him that women found his partner so attractive. Not that Reid had ever responded to those over-tures, not in his presence anyway. A blonde at the Christmas party spilled something on Reid's suit and then offered to take it to the cleaners. But Simon had merely shrugged, seemingly devoted to his own younger very attractive partner, Kim. Kim

was now with a new partner. What a shame, although Cosser
supposed Reid would sooner or later introduce him to yet another beautiful young woman. So, Cosser did not know why
whenever he saw his colleague, he had the uncomfortable sense
that there was something about him that he did not know.

"What do you think, Jack?" Reid asked. "Any doubts about
the ex's innocence?"

"I think there have to be, but I hope for the boys' sake he
isn't guilty. He seems to have an alibi." He had to base his
assumptions on that, but he had not questioned the sons yet.
"I'm going to take a run out to visit her parents in the morning.
And try to see the church warden right before I leave. Linda
something."

"O'Reilly," Reid said. "Want company?"

"I would, yes, but I think there's so much ground to cover
that you could stay here and deal with some of it."

"What did you have in mind?"

"All the reports that will be coming in. I'll have a quick look
at them before I leave, but it would help if you could go over
them and keep in touch with me while I'm on the road."

Reid's face brightened. "And a background on Richard
Atchison. Credit card checks on both of them. Telephone calls.
And what about the boys?"

"Yes, we need to question them. Perhaps even tonight."

Reid nodded.

"Although let's have a look at test results we get back first.
And someone has to get in touch with her parents, so could
you rouse that contact?"

"Right, I'm onto that as soon as we get back to the station."

"Thanks."

The police had to deal with taking the unpleasant news to
family members before it became public knowledge, so it would
not be left to journalists. In some circumstances, they would
have left it to someone like Marni's husband, but in light of
the recent separation that would not suffice.

"Charlie?" he asked now, wondering if the person Reid would call was the police chief in London—that was the closest larger city. And knowing that Reid knew the chief well.

"Yeah, I may have to go down the chain a bit, but he'll know who to call."

SOON AFTER HE ARRIVED AT HIS APARTMENT that night, Cosser lay down on the floor and started to do push ups. Afterwards he had a shower and went to sleep. He woke up more than once during the night and when he finally got up it was only five a.m. He sat down at the kitchen table, wearing the bottoms of a pair of striped flannel pyjamas, thinking that even if the odds were slim, some time soon he would ask to talk to Marion on her own. From the window across from him, he could see a small park in the Annex where Jaime still went to play at times. She was too young to go on her own, so either he or Marion took her there. He loved the delight on his daughter's round, chubby face when he pushed her on the swings or she slid down a slide. This strengthened his resolve. He would ask Marion if she would consider trying again. After all, he thought, it would not be the first time that a couple married for a second time.

Slightly more relaxed at this thought, he picked up a book, lying open on the floor beside him, and went over to the sofa where he started to read where he had left off the last time. It was a mystery novel. You would think in his line of work he would read something else and often he did. Matthew Fox's *Original Blessing* and some of the books that had come after it. And heaven knew how he even knew about the books he picked up, but he had liked *Invisible Man* by an American called Ellison. Early in the morning, with an hour before he would dress and leave, his distraction was a mystery called *The Last Detective*. He liked the curmudgeon in charge of the investigation, a British cop who eschewed computer technology. You could not last long in this business these days without using a computer, but he liked the way this cop was able to focus differently because he had come from another era. Not one replete with cell phones and faxes and all the gimmicks that the last twenty or so years had given to the world and to police investigations. Not that Cosser did not use all of that same gimmickry himself, it was just that there had to be a place for human ingenuity. And, he thought, also for the human spirit.

He knew his work would never deter all crime or wipe out evil. Still, there must be a place on a police force for someone who was concerned about moral and philosophical questions. He had advocated for more humane treatment for victims, for a more sensitive response to family violence. As he had never done it by criticizing his fellow officers, but through channels and avenues that had arisen at different times, he had not been ostracized. Not like others he'd seen spurned for taking what some perceived as the moral high ground. It annoyed him that this could happen. Wasn't the reason for a police force captured in the police motto? To serve and protect. If so, it was actually immoral for police officers not to look for more effective, responsible, and sympathetic ways to do that. He had enjoyed being on task forces, working with people from across the city, and believed strongly in community policing. It had been satisfying to see some change as a result of information that the police alone could not have accumulated. Take the task force on race relations. There was a long way to go still, but more officers with different racial and cultural backgrounds had been hired and some of the actual protocols had indeed started to change.

His eyes started to flutter and close and the book fell first onto his stomach and then onto the bed as he dozed off to sleep again. Not long after, he was awakened by the shrill ring of his alarm clock.

PART II

12.

Two Weeks Earlier

AT THE BEGINNING OF NOVEMBER, Marni Atchison contacted her parents and they immediately invited her to return to their community. When she refused, they offered to come to visit her in Toronto. She waited for them nervously, twisting a strand of fair hair around her fingers and twirling it above her head. It surprised her that she felt grateful about the imminent arrival of both her mother and father. She realized then how much she longed to talk with them. But what could she say that she had not thought better of during almost twenty years of silence?

Beyond the window, her eyes traced the length of the grey branches of a tree at the edge of the yard; that sombre almost lack of colour was indicative of the passage into a darker season; at least until the snow fell, and brightened everything up for a day or two. Or more. At the sound of the doorbell, Marni jumped up and went to the front of the house where she caught a glimpse of her neighbour going up the steps next door. She shared a common wall with Patsy in a semi-detached house with identical layouts on either side of that partition. Marni loved the bright colours Patsy used, so different from those in her own more muted surroundings. Her décor consisted of black-and-white units purchased at Ikea with a few bright knick-knacks displayed on their shelves and surfaces. Maybe she could change things now that she and Richard had separated and he had moved out.

At the small window in the entry, she saw her father's face peering through the glass. He and her mother were standing there expectantly as she opened the door. If she did not know these two elderly people were Caroline and Victor Miller, she might well have imagined them as a pair of Jehovah's Witnesses callers. Something at almost any other door they would have been. Taking in a deep breath, Marni noticed her mother's grim expression as she turned to watch Patsy. Her parents would see her neighbour as a potential convert, Marni thought. Or would be suspicious of her, as they had always been of anyone who did not belong to the Jehovah's Witnesses.

Attitudes that deep-rooted would not have changed, Marni thought. Unlike the physical changes she could see, deep lines on her mother's face and hair that was now grey. Her father was almost bald and his cheeks seemed to have sunk, as if he had lost his teeth and not replaced them. She thought of the previous day's conversation on the telephone.

"It's Marni," was what she'd finally said when her mother answered. It was as simple as that, her name, an announcement that would have been quite unexpected.

There'd been a long pause while Marni listened to the sound of jagged breathing over the wires. Twisting the telephone cord between her long, slim fingers, she'd waited for her mother to speak.

"Marni," her mother finally said in a polite, yet cautious, tone Marni remembered so well. "Is it really you?"

"I'm not with Richard any more," Marni said softly, knowing this news was something her mother had expected to hear much sooner. Years sooner.

"So you'll come back now," her mother had said. As if all those years had not intervened. As if they had spoken only days or weeks earlier. "And bring your children."

"I don't know," Marni said. This hesitation, a slight hint that she might, was the best she could do. And while she did not like to lie, sometimes for brief moments she was not sure herself any more. She'd left home for the city when she was not much older than her sons were now and she'd never returned. The boys did not know their grandparents. Nor had their father wanted them to.

"I don't want my sons involved in a fundamentalist religion," were the exact words Richard had spoken.

Well, neither had Marni. Why did he think she'd left the Jehovah's Witnesses? But she'd often avoided quarrels by staying quiet. She'd also maintained silence after her mother and father had disowned her. But they'd been right, after all; her marriage had ended in disaster.

"We'll come to visit you," her mother had said. "Your father and I."

"All right," Marni replied before she could change her mind.

"We'll come tomorrow."

Marni was shocked at how quickly her mother wanted to see her, as if she felt she had to pounce before Marni relented.

"We'll catch an early train into the city."

"I look forward to seeing you," Marni replied and, however apprehensive she'd felt, that was true.

Then they had both hung up.

MARNI LOOKED INTENTLY AT THESE PEOPLE standing in her doorway, the parents who had raised her. "Come in," she said, her voice as welcoming as she could make it while still attempting to come to terms with how much they had aged since she'd last seen them. Fearing her words sounded forced, she smiled to allay that impression.

"Who is *she*?" Marni's mother asked, glancing over toward the house where Patsy had by now disappeared through the door.

"Who?"

"The woman who went in next door."

"She's my neighbour," Marni said. "My friend, Patsy."

Marni's mother frowned and Marni wondered if she thought Patsy had filled her daughter's head with what the Jehovah's

Witnesses would consider wrong ideas. She conveyed enough with a glance for Marni to know that she could never turn her back on friends like Patsy who were open to possibility and cared about her as a person and not a follower of some religion.

"When will the boys be home?" her father asked.

"They're with Richard." She'd decided to have this meeting alone to prepare for the possibility of Chris and Dean meeting their grandparents. Neither they nor Richard knew about it.

"That's simply not acceptable," her father said, his mouth firmly set. He pulled at the knot in his tie, as if it were choking him. "After all this time, of course we expected they'd be here today. We came all this way to meet them."

"I didn't mislead you," Marni said, glancing down for a brief moment, not wanting to see her father's disapproval written across his face. "You'll just have to wait." She picked a piece of white thread from her dark skirt and rolled it between her fingers before looking up again.

"Will you bring them back with you to…?"

"I can't answer that now," Marni said, turning her eyes away. Although she'd hoped that when they met the boys, something would change. Maybe that she could be a part of their community and have family in her life. But then there would be the question of meetings. They would not be able to accept her as she was now, and they would expect her to attend at the Kingdom Hall with their community. Three times a week in a setting where so many expectant faces would be scrutinizing her was daunting. There was no use pretending she could do that and continue with how she lived now. It was an illusory hope that people hung onto, she knew that, when something was so unpalatable that they needed to fool themselves to bear it.

"You must have known what we would want," her father said. "You were raised to know the Truth and surely you appreciate your children ought to know it, too."

Marni's throat tightened and she felt tears somewhere behind her eyes. She knew that everything was coloured by the strength of their convictions. The thought that grandchildren might not soften them seemed inconceivable.

"Is that more important than seeing and getting to know them?" she asked.

There was a deep frown on her father's face, that same disapproval she'd feared as a child. She did not dare to look at her mother. She could imagine how wonderful it would be for her sons to have another set of grandparents, but how could she subject them to the kind of upbringing she'd had? Instead, she'd let them know they had choices. She would never let them believe that they would be judged and found wanting, that the end of the world was always imminent.

Marni sighed, realizing that she would have to let her parents know she would not return. And that saying so would leave her without even the minimal contact she'd hoped for.

"Marni," her mother said, uncharacteristically softly. "We want you back in the family. We do miss you."

Marni raised her eyebrows slightly, but gave no other indication of hearing her mother's words. "I made some lunch for you," she said, noticing they had nodded at each other at these words.

"All right," her father said, his heavy brows hanging almost into his eyes. The dark hairs now had many grey strands that sprouted out beyond the fullness of his brow. This acquiescence seemed to Marni a sign that he had not given up hope of succeeding at convincing her that his convictions were right, and that she ought to accept that she had made a mistake in leaving. Smiling through tightened lips, she disappeared into the kitchen where she took a large green salad with croutons from the refrigerator. Then some simple sandwiches she knew they had enjoyed. Salmon, lightly dressed, and mixed with a bit of chopped celery and cucumber. When she put these offerings on the dining table, she saw her father's face light up and the lines in her mother's relax.

"Thank you, dear," her mother said.

They gulped down their food, as if they had not eaten for a while. Afterward Marni placed a tray of cookies on the table and poured them each some tea.

"Would you like to see some pictures of Chris and Dean?" she asked.

"Of course," her mother said.

Marni went to get the albums she had taken out in anticipation of this visit. Her parents opened a recent one and studied the photographs. When she saw their eyes meet with a knowing smile, she felt suddenly dizzy. Reaching out, she grasped the side of her chair to steady herself.

"Are you all right?" her mother asked.

Marni nodded. She took in a long, deep breath. This had been a terrible mistake. But how else would she have known for sure?

"Could we come back some time to meet the boys?" her mother asked.

Her father was quiet, but he did not voice any opposition.

"I'll let you know," Marni said, holding her breath momentarily so as not to show her surprise. She'd thought when the time came for them to say goodbye, and after her parents had acknowledged the failure of their mission, she would never see either of them again.

"Don't take too long, Marni," her mother said as she picked up her purse and headed out the front door. "We'd like to meet our grandsons."

Her father was already half way out and down the steps when he turned toward the door on Patsy's side of the house. Up on her deck, he took out a pamphlet from his briefcase and stuck it through the mail slot.

Marni sighed, hoping Patsy would not be offended.

THE NEWSPAPER LAY JUST INSIDE THE RAIL on the porch across from the door so Marni had to step out in her bare feet onto the wooden floor to reach it. A balmy breeze wrapped around her, harbinger of another unseasonably warm day for November. She wondered what the boys were doing, what Richard would buy for them this time. Would it be another expensive game? Something that appeared to be trying to win their favour?

After she made coffee, Marni sat at the kitchen table with her mug, still too hot to drink, and began to read the editorial section. Then afterwards she skipped to the horoscopes and finally to the personals. There were only a couple ads and she imagined there were fewer now with online sites making inroads on the role of newspapers. Usually she was skeptical, but every so often she would inadvertently see an ad that intrigued her. The thought of what her parents would think occurred to her because of their recent visit, but on this particular morning as she continued to read, that awareness evaporated. Her eyes fell on an ad that began "ALMOST intelligent gent," and she suddenly burst out laughing.

Imagine anyone writing that, Marni thought, nonetheless attracted by the underlying humour, the slightly bizarre.

Mid-40s, the ad continued. *Fit, walks horses, dances the salsa, cycles, travels, homes in* TO & FLA, *boat, non-smoker,* TSX ADDICT. *Two left feet and a computer would be assets. Send picture of computer.*

Without any experience in the world of dating, this struck Marni as an odd request, but maybe such requests were commonplace. Or were intended to elicit questions and conversation. The man also expressed a preference for a woman who was unbelievably patient.

That's not me, Marni thought, but she was intrigued. Would she respond? If so, where would she suggest meeting? It would have to be somewhere with plenty of people around. Maybe over near Honest Ed's, the huge store with uneven floors and bargains overflowing on display tables, or at the Second Cup just before Bathurst. It always had people sitting at tables near the windows and was an easy walk from where she lived near the supermarket. She tried to think of a place a bit further away, perhaps in the opposite direction, and an image of the open central area of the main library with its curving carpeted stairs that led from floor to floor struck her. When she rode the elevators there, she could survey the entire five floors of the library from the rear curved glass section. She went there most often when doing research for the small firm that employed her.

No, she thought, the Second Cup was likely the best bet for a first encounter. Marni read the ad again, chuckling at the image of tripping over her feet while dancing. And why would he consider a computer an asset? Maybe he was a programmer with a particular language he'd want a woman to grasp. Since she worked with computers, she took having one of her own for granted. She decided to write to him and reached for a box of blank cards in the drawer of the desk under her computer. The painting on the front of the cards was of two cardinals, a flaming red male and a more muted female. The house seemed so empty without Chris and Dean throwing a ball around while she ducked and told them repeatedly to take it outside. Or with their books scattered on the dining room table that had wooden benches on both sides as if built for outdoor picnics. This would give her something to do.

Sitting down on one of these benches, Marni began to write.

Dear Almost Intelligent Sir,

I have never responded to an ad before and I may never do so again, but as I happen to have a rather splendid photograph of my computer on hand, I thought I would take this opportunity to share it with you. Although I fear two left feet would not help with the salsa, I do possess such feet and would likely be prone to tripping on them on the dance floor. My two teenaged sons would encourage me to respond to your ad and would love it if I took off for FLA and left them with a house to themselves. And I would love to go out

for an evening to dance and leave them to cook their
own meal, likely Kraft dinner.
    So if you think you can stomach the patient mother
of teenagers and are willing to endure their piercing
looks and pointed questions, do call.
Sincerely,
Marni

Not sure where the words came from, she surprised herself
by sliding the note into an envelope, addressing it, and then
placing a stamp in the upper right hand corner. In a city
the size of Toronto, she imagined the man would receive
many replies from women touched by his humour and slight
self-mockery. Twenty or thirty others? Even forty or fifty. She
had no idea that at this very moment there would be many
more than that all across Toronto chuckling as she had as
they browsed through their newspapers. One who worked
for Canada Post was amused, then moved on to read the
sports section. Anyone who wanted a photo of her computer
probably wanted to steal it, she thought. Another, at a call
centre, thought the man must be a Luddite to advertise in the
newspaper instead of online, but still mused that she might
have answered were there a telephone number. Or maybe
not. What did she need with a man who thought he was
no more than an almost? A woman from Holy Trinity, the
downtown church that Marni's neighbour, Patsy, attended,
was among those who did actually reply to this ad. Although
Patsy talked to Marni from time to time about the different
members of the congregation, she had never mentioned this
particular woman.

    "They're friendly," Patsy had said. "You'll have to come
sometime."

    "I can't," Marni had said, unable to imagine that the God
underlying this church's faith would be any different from
the cold, stern, and judgmental one that she'd grown up with

in her Jehovah's Witness family and community. A memory surfaced of the young girls and boys she'd met on the street when she ran away from her family, telling her she might find free coffee and food at Holy Trinity. No one had told her the name of the church then, but it had not been hard to find. She had never told Patsy that she'd already been to the church in the downtown courtyard behind the Eaton Centre.

She took the note out of the envelope and read it again as she pondered whether to walk to the mailbox. It was not something she had prepared herself for: dancing and laughing and travelling.

"MR. ALMOST SPEAKING," the voice on the answering machine said. "This is the almost intelligent gent who advertised in the *Globe and Mail*. You can call me Mr. Almost, although my name is Patrick."

A week after replying to the ad, this was the message that the women who had responded heard. As did Marni, who had not really anticipated a reply. The man had called, said a few words about himself to the answering machine, and then left his phone number. She now faced another dilemma: would she or would she not respond? The Witnesses and her parents would say she would be annihilated. Although after her days of living on the street, she worried more about robberies and the threat of rape, recalling recent alerts that Toronto police were looking for a serial rapist. It seemed a bad omen for someone responding to an ad in the personals.

When she saw Patsy on the sidewalk later, she called out to her. They exchanged the usual pleasantries and then Marni asked the question she'd been contemplating since listening to the message. "Do you think it would be a mistake to reply?"

"Do you?"

"Well, I remember the Scarborough rapist. Could he be a predator like him? And I guess I am having trouble deciding because it's different from anything I've been raised to think was acceptable. I don't worry as much about the nonsense that my head was filled with as a child and teenager, but dating's new after being married for so long. Do you really think it would be okay?"

"Why not?" Patsy asked. "Just be sure to meet him on neutral territory, a place where there are other people around. And don't give him your address or your last name. You never know. You can screen out most people that way. And I'm sure it won't mean Armageddon."

Patsy knew the lingo of the Witnesses by now. She even made Marni laugh sometimes, although she never made any comments that might seem disrespectful.

"I had some literature in my door the other day," she added.

"That was my father," Marni said. "He saw you go into the house when they arrived and he never passes up an opportunity for a new convert. I guess he didn't go the whole way and knock because they had a train to catch. I'm sorry I didn't tell you they were coming, although I would have eventually. It's the first time I've seen them since I left home in my teens. It never dawned on me he would jump onto your doorstep with those pamphlets."

"Not a problem," Patsy assured her. She knew it had nothing to do with Marni who would never proselytize about anything. "I read a bit of it," she said. "Interesting that you came out of that background."

Marni nodded. As a child, she'd sat at meetings because her parents said she had to. Otherwise she would not be saved. It was what she'd heard all her life, yet she was never able to imagine that her presence at those meetings made all that much difference. Most of the time she was thinking about being somewhere else anyway. And, from a very young age, she knew that one day she would leave. Even though she'd always been told that a teenaged girl who left would destroy herself with drug abuse, prostitution, and bad relationships. But Marni was determined.

"One day you'll be judged," her father had often said. "When Armageddon comes, if you haven't done what's right, you'll die."

The often-quoted verse from Thessalonians that states when people are saying that everything is "peaceful and secure," then "destruction" will surely follow, was always offered as proof. The verse said that disaster would fall suddenly on those who would not be saved, "as labour pains on a pregnant woman." And there would be no escape for those not saved. The Jehovahs also talked about judgment and she feared the knowledge that deep in her heart she wanted to get away from the Jehovah's Witnesses would be revealed. Even so, she loved her family and knew they loved her. Especially Gramma, who might have believed everything her parents said, after all she'd raised her father, but Marni never had to do anything to make Gramma love her, Gramma just did.

So as a child, Marni watched the news on television and when there was war, she was not frightened. What frightened her was when there were peace talks. As soon as she was old enough, she was determined to find out if everyone lived like that. Now she knew they did not.

She thanked Patsy. "I'll call this Mr. Almost and see if he's worth meeting," she said.

Inside, putting her purse down, she picked up the telephone. When a man answered, he told her his name was Patrick. A good enough name, she thought. It was a solid one. His voice seemed to have a slight lilt. She wondered if he was Irish, but did not ask. After a brief chat, they agreed to meet at the reference library.

"I have red hair," the man said. "You won't be able to miss me."

"Well," she said. "I'll be wearing a dark brown leather jacket and cords." She also told him that she was tall and slender, had fair hair, and that she would wear a pair of mismatched earrings.

When she stepped onto Bloor Street, Marni looked around

to see if she were being followed and was comforted to see only throngs of people rushing in all directions. This main street in Toronto was often like that, but sometimes she ran into someone she knew among the throng. Meeting someone familiar on the street like that had a pleasant neighbourhood feel about it, something that as someone who came from a small country town in southwestern Ontario she appreciated, even if she might also occasionally worry about being followed.

As a breeze blew her hair around her ears, Marni was relieved her world was entirely different now. It was a long time since the spectre of being poor had haunted her. Even memories from the time she lived on the streets had faded. Nor did she think she needed to keep looking over her shoulder, but she did, so thoroughly was it engrained in her. So, glancing back every so often, she made her way toward the spot where she would meet this man who had placed the ad. Patrick Sloane. Mr. Almost. The reference library, always teeming with people, felt like a safe place to her, even safer than the coffee shop she'd been considering as well.

Marni walked north and approached the library from the other side of Yonge Street. Her preoccupations did not often touch on the fear of imminent danger any more. Although the anonymity of city life had mostly suited her, even though by now, after many years of living in Toronto, it was not unusual for her to encounter familiar faces that were friendly.

She thought of the gossip—more unlikely in her urban milieu—that had been one of the disadvantages of a small community. Never would she forget suddenly spotting a boy from her bedroom window who had climbed up the TV aerial to peer in her window while she was undressing. Since he had disappeared by the time she rushed downstairs to tell her parents, they had not been able to confront him.

It turned out that no one in the town would admit to it, though it quickly seemed the whole town knew about it and someone must have known who the culprit was. So nothing had happened to the peeping tom because for any kind of punishment to be meted out in the Jehovah's Witnesses community, there had to be two witnesses. Without two witnesses, it was as if a transgression had never happened. Two people having an affair could be disfellowshipped if someone knew about the affair and one of the errant couple admitted to it. Hearing about neighbours in this situation had been used to indoctrinate Marni with the fear of what could happen if she ever stepped out of line. But nothing happened to the boy *she knew* had peeped at her that evening, leaving Marni outraged that he had gotten away with it because of some silly rules that meant no one would believe her story.

A car honked as she stepped out to cross Yonge Street and she hopped backward onto the sidewalk, aware that she had not been paying attention. A part of her still felt she could be punished for what she was doing and it had set off a flood of memories. She could not be disfellowshipped, of course, as that had already happened. So, she shrugged her shoulders to get rid of the tension and after checking the traffic, carefully stepped out again. How embarrassed she'd felt, Marni recalled, then annoyed, as her mother questioned why she had not had her blinds drawn.

"It wasn't my fault," she'd said, stung by the tone of accusation in her mother's line of inquiry. They lived so far out in the country, without any neighbours nearby, so closing her blinds had never even crossed her mind.

Her girlfriend was the one person she had confided in and that had lead them to decide it was time to talk more seriously about running away. They had a pact not to tell anyone about what they shared. By the time they reached the age of sixteen, they would regularly sneak behind the high school to smoke joints and talk. The pot was not hard to come by as they could always find some boy who would sell them small amounts. Where the boys got it didn't concern them. At times, Marni's mother seemed suspicious, but Marni did not miss meetings and she still went from door to door with them, so her parents ignored what little clues she might unwittingly have left for them.

Then, one day, when both girls had some money saved, they ran away. The pot gave Marni the courage to get as far as Toronto. It not only calmed her, but later helped both of them to stay in the city because they could make money delivering the pot to customers of a dealer they had met on the streets. It was summer and they mostly slept on park benches or under a blanket on a beach. Then one day her girlfriend said she was afraid of the coming winter, and of being stuck on the streets. She decided to go back home, leaving Marni to cope on her own. More than once, she went into that downtown church Patsy talked about now and helped herself to coffee, and one Sunday found she could also line up for soup and bread. She avoided talking with anyone, figuring they would get around to the subject of God, and the only God she knew about was one she wanted to get as far away from as was possible. Without making any friends in Toronto, when the cold weather did arrive in late October and the evenings became darker, she became discouraged and also returned home.

"God told me you would come back," her mother had said, her eyes filled with tears. Marni could tell her mother had missed her and that she was both relieved and hurt. After a week or two, her parents said she would have to go to meetings again and Marni quickly understood that nothing was going to change. She would have to leave for good as soon as she felt stronger. This time, she was determined to find a job somewhere and a room to live in. No more standing on the street asking people for money. No more sleeping on park benches and under bridges. The following spring she would make her final break.

When she reached the library people were milling around as Marni had anticipated. It did not cross her mind that danger might be lurking around the corner. And that soon a whole city would be wondering about the identity of a woman found in the basement of a church. The police might well surmise someone in the church had something to do with her murder and they might be right. But no one would have actually figured out anything that could have provided a warning to her. In any case, there would have been no reason beforehand to think any threat would come from the man she was about to meet any more than it might have come from her husband from whom she was recently separated. Although the proximity of the date of her death to the encounter at the library might arouse suspicion if it became known. But just before that rendezvous, what Marni was acutely aware of, was how lonely she felt, and that what drove her to meet this stranger was precisely that loneliness. It was that simple. She chuckled under her breath at how ridiculous that seemed. Instead of tapping into fears that might have led to a different outcome, she let the humour wash over her.

I'll have something to tell Patsy later, she thought. This situation was ludicrous enough to warrant that. And maybe she would also tell her new friend, Sandra, whom she had met recently browsing through business magazines in this same library.

As Marni approached the door of the library, her mouth became suddenly dry. She looked around at the people clustered around the entrance and did not see anyone who matched the description Patrick Sloane had given to her. She also looked at people she did not recognize to ensure there was no one from that long ago Jehovah's Witnesses community following her. It was always a relief to find there was no one who seemed even remotely interested in her.

Pushing the next door open, she broke out in a cold sweat. She took in a deep breath and moved toward the turnstile that led into the main space of the building with its ceiling five floors above. Just as she went through it, she spotted a man with red hair coming toward her.

"You will know me," he'd said. "Red hair. Debonair. I'll be wearing a grey jacket."

Still fearful of running into someone she knew, she was even more uneasy than she'd suspected she would be. She might be expected to introduce the man and how would she do that? Meet Mr. Almost. Hardly.

He reached out his hand. "Patrick," he said.

"Hi, Patrick. I'm Marni."

They both stood, awkwardly groping for words.

Finally he cleared his throat and said, "Coffee?" and she nodded. Simultaneously, they turned toward the door again and walked out onto the sidewalk. He pointed to a small coffee shop across the street, and it did not take them long to agree on this place and to settle in at a counter with high bar stools.

"I brought pictures," he said, opening an envelope. He took out some colour photographs and arranged them on the counter in front of them, one of vivid yellow flowers, another of a pelican.

"Stunning," she said.

He pointed to one that showed a small, clapboard house close to water, and said that was where he went in the winter to get away for a while. "The house is close to a canal that leads to a river that flows out into the gulf," he said. In the photograph, the water shone emerald in the bright southern sun.

"I thought since you said you didn't like Florida, I'd show you how beautiful it can be," he said.

That was not me, Marni thought. I did not say anything like that. She refrained from telling him he might consider a filing system.

"It's Nick's place," he said. "I get to use it."

"Nick," Marni said. "Should I know who that is?"

"He's my boss," the man said, as if she ought indeed to know.

"Oh," Marni said. "Well, whoever owns it, it looks like a winner."

Patrick seemed to relax again. He flipped through the photos until he found one he said was of Nick and showed it to her. She shrugged, no longer showing any interest.

"I was on the other side once," Marni said. "Near Cape Canaveral. Or at least near enough to be able to see a spaceship take off." She had taken the boys there one winter for a week and left her husband at home in Toronto. I make a good living working in computers, she'd thought and she'd wanted to treat her boys to something special. Money was one thing Richard was never any good at. She was relieved now that she'd kept a separate bank account.

"Oh," Patrick said. "I love walking along the beach, looking for shells, and listening to the waves crash against the shore."

She sighed, recalling the moon shining down on the long grasses growing in the sand.

He took a sip of his coffee, and then started to tell her about his last girlfriend.

Why is he doing this? she wondered. She did not intend to tell him anything personal. As he droned on about his past relationship, she realized that she did not want to see him again if he happened to ask her. She imagined her parents in their kitchen with the faded curtains and dark wood cupboards. They had always worn clothes in dull colours, though neatly pressed. What would they think of this man's bright red hair? But it no longer felt that any decision she might make about Patrick had anything to do with them.

"It will arrive this Sunday, Mother," her father might have said. And it would have taken Marni a moment to remember her mother's name was Caroline because her father never referred to her that way.

Marni knew by then that what would arrive was not a special parcel. Their home was stark, nothing like those of her new kindergarten schoolmates. There were no books in the house except the Bible. And there was never candy or music or anything very amusing, only the insistence that she believe something without questioning it. "No Room For Doubt" was what she named it as she grew older. There was no room to have a dialogue or conversation. When she tried, their glowering looks silenced her. They had been talking about Armageddon for weeks. And now her father proclaimed that the coming Sunday would be the day.

Marni was startled by Patrick's voice as it rose higher and higher. She suddenly realized she had stopped listening entirely. What was he saying? She did not feel the slightest interest in this man who went on about matters irrelevant to her. As she looked intently at Patrick Sloane, trying to focus on what he was saying, she started to wonder if her loneliness had actually led to something so foolhardy as this moment? To such a waste of time? She realized the answer was yes, but she was nonetheless clear that she would not let that loneliness cloud her judgment again. She needed to put an end to this.

"Hey," he said, suddenly smiling and reaching for her hand. "How about you and me go get a little drink somewhere? I like you. You're just the girl I'm looking for."

Marni eyed him, aghast. Her mind had drifted as he droned on and he must have thought she was listening. Now that he had possibly bared his soul, she was suddenly Ms. Right.

"No," she said, pulling her hand away sharply. "You're mistaken."

"No I am not," he said. "I can tell."

"How?"

"Great vibes. Great vibes between us."

Marni shook her head. "I don't feel them."

"Give it a chance."

She sighed. Not likely!

"I'll call," he said.

Marni nodded and stood up, putting on her jacket. When she slipped her bag over her shoulder, he started to rise also. "Please, finish your coffee," she said. "I'll head out on my own." She could feel him continue to watch her as she moved away, relieved at least that he did not attempt to follow her.

As soon as she was outside, she moved quickly to get out of his line of vision. Walking west on a tree-lined street north of Bloor, she was relieved to have escaped from what seemed a bizarre fantasy world this man inhabited. The further she walked, the more the encounter receded from her mind. Instead she began to wonder about her older brother, Leonard, whom she had not seen or heard from since she'd left home. When he was eleven, still very much in thrall to their father, she'd watched him in awe. She'd wondered why he did not see what she saw. But no one had paid any attention to Marni, and she often sat reading labels on boxes in the kitchen when they started talking about Armageddon for the nth time that day. As she'd hugged her sweater tightly around her to ward off draughts that the plastic window covers did not keep out, her arms and legs would start to tremble. Would Armageddon be like an earthquake and swallow them as the house came crumbling down around them? She pushed back her chair quietly and slipped up the stairs to her room to play with the little doll her aunt had given to her secretly. It might be the last time. If Armageddon came, her room would be gone, her doll, and everything else.

"Margaret." Her father's stern voice echoed up the staircase. It was never Marni. "Come and set the table." When she went down, he was waiting at the bottom. "Your mother needs help."

Her parents believed they would be among those saved because they had followed Christ and tried to spread the news. They said they did this so people could repent in time. Even though many doors were slammed in their faces, they persisted. If you knew the Truth, you had to do that her mother told her, just as Christ's disciples had.

At the table her father said grace and then her mother served the food. Marni hurriedly gobbled down some chicken, trying to eat a lot in case she made it through Armageddon and there was not any food left. Since her parents had this power to predict what would happen, she didn't understand why they did not make plans.

"Child," her mother scolded. "Not so quickly."

For two days, Marni worried. When everything was calm on Monday morning, her doll sitting quietly on the chair and her clothes hanging in the closet, she got ready for school. She took a pair of socks from her drawer, expecting everything to be in turmoil. Once she was dressed, she was almost afraid to go downstairs, wondering if she'd slept through everything. But when she reached the kitchen, she found her parents at the table as usual, sipping their coffee and packing their pamphlets into cases. Leonard was eating his toast, his cereal bowl and juice glass already empty.

"Where is Armageddon?" she asked. ""You said—"

"Oh well, we got the dates wrong," her mother said.

From that day on, Marni was not sure about anything they said. But even at the age of five, almost six, she had known better than to say so.

13.

PATSY SAT WITH THE NEWSPAPER OPEN to the business section, but instead of reading the latest news on the stock market, she watched for Marni through the front window. With the trees almost bare, she would see her neighbour when she approached. When she and Marni had met on the street on the day Marni and her family had moved in, the large van parked across both driveways, Patsy had been relieved that her new neighbours were a young family. And it was not long before she and Marni had become friends.

Earlier, two fair-haired boys, Chris and Dean, Marni's boys, got out of a Ford Taurus at the curb, the blue one Patsy recognized as their father's, and hurtled up the walk. They jostled with each other as they thumped up the steps to the porch. Chris, a lock of hair falling over his forehead, saw Patsy and waved. Dean was at the door by now, out of her vision, inserting a key into the lock.

It was not like Marni to be this late and Patsy did not think she had come in at all the previous night. If her friend stayed out overnight, that was her business, but she had said she would be around this weekend. She'd even suggested they have coffee on Sunday morning before Patsy went to church. When she had not yet turned up, it worried Patsy. She thought about what Marni had told her about the date she was pondering. Not only that, but Patsy recalled the earlier stories of being watched by unfamiliar people in different places. Rarely had it been anyone

Marni could identify. But she had known somehow that word got back to her family about what she was doing. They had disowned her, disfellowshipped was what Marni called it, but they never let up on their efforts to know about her movements. Marni had said her whole upbringing had programmed her for self-destruction if she ever left, and sometimes she became very strained at the thought that her marriage had fallen apart for that reason. She had told Patsy what she knew from the inside of the Jehovah's Witness community and that it was not a pretty picture. Even so, she'd still blamed herself for her situation. While Patsy had never encountered anyone with an experience like Marni's, she believed her. But certainly not the part that insisted that everything harmful that happened around her was somehow caused by her actions, or inaction, for that matter.

Patsy had a more unclouded view of life and were she on the island now, she would order a Margarita. Many years back, she'd moved to Toronto and at this time of year, she still could not help but dream of being on a beach in the Caribbean. As the leaves fell from the trees and she was reminded of the cold season on the horizon, she shivered. She had never become acclimatized to winter, never become a lover of skating or skiing, and she longed for the heat and the sea breeze.

Oh, to be there now. Maybe Aloha would go with her. She was intrigued by Aloha, in love with her even, a lovely woman also from the Caribbean, who had what sounded like a Hawaiian name. She'd told Patsy that her father had nicknamed her Aloha when she'd become obsessed with a hula hoop as a young child. The name had stuck. Patsy hoped that her lover, this woman with a lilting voice and light brown skin, would move in with her sooner rather than later. They had some common understandings—about slavery, for instance. Patsy and Aloha had not travelled together yet, but they planned to some day visit Ghana, where so many black people had been taken forcibly to become slaves in the New World. This was not something she talked about with Marni. Her friend of light hair and white skin understood many things more than most people who had always lived with a privilege they were not aware of, but Patsy had observed limits to that comprehension.

Where was Marni?

There was no sign of her yet. So Patsy's thoughts drifted off again, dreaming of her island where she could put her feet up and chat endlessly with one of her cousins. Or Lenore, the girl she had discovered when Patsy was eleven, and who was also going to visit her father

"I'm going to see my Dad," the other girl, slightly older than Patsy, had said, when they ran into each other in a large apartment building.

"Me, too," Patsy said. She got cold all over when they both walked down the hall and stopped at the same door. Patsy had heard stories when she was not supposed to be listening, but she had never heard about another child. Later she discovered there were five or six others. Lenore was the only one she had ever gotten to know though. They talked often after that day, accepting that they were half-sisters. Gradually they had acknowledged they rather liked doing things together, sometimes talking about their Dad as well. They even laughed at how silent their father had been when he had opened the door to find both of them waiting for him there.

"What a guy," Patsy heard Lenore say. "Not the kind of guy I want when I get older. But he sure knows how to get around."

Patsy learned about sex from Lenore, and how to wear makeup and how to dance. She could tell Lenore liked the way Patsy asked her questions, the way she believed everything Lenore said. Why shouldn't she? Lenore was her older sister and she was smart. Lenore also told her it was important to get an education. Her mother had told her that, too, but she often did not listen to her mother. Why did her mother stay with a man who went around having children with so many other women? Her mother was finally leaving him now, years and years later, but all the same she was doing it, and Patsy was happy.

She was roused from her reverie by the sight of Marni, who waved at her, then tapped at the door.

"As soon as I've seen the boys, how about coming over for a coffee," she said. "In half an hour?"

"Or you come here. Sasha's sleeping and I won't have to disturb him. Where have you been?"

"On a sort of date," Marni laughed. "Mr. Almost. It's a good name for him. He doesn't make the cut, for sure."

"I don't mean to pry. But were you gone all night?"

"Oh, that's okay," Marni said. "No, I was here. I must have been very quiet and I went to bed early. This morning I went for a walk and stayed out. Then I met this man just after the library opened at one thirty."

"I guess I was a little worried, thinking that you'd said we'd get together."

"I'm sorry. I forgot to tell you I'd be late."

An hour later, Marni sipped on her coffee as they sat at Patsy's table that overlooked the back deck. She described Patrick Sloane: tall, slim, bright red hair, blue eyes, well dressed. "He had an accent," Marni said. "Came from Ireland. The south, I think. Roman Catholic. I didn't tell him about the Witnesses. But he was a wealth of information, far too personal for a first date. Also, he wore a white ribbon on his lapel," she added conversationally. Marni had not asked him why, she said, "It struck me as peculiar."

When Patsy frowned, Marni asked, "What's the matter?"

"Nothing," Patsy said, but she was struck by the similarities to a man she'd spotted in church the previous Sunday. He was talking to Linda when she'd noticed him. It had been just before she left the church that day, in a rush to get home in time to meet with Marni—as she often did on Sunday afternoons, and as they'd arranged. She wondered if Linda had answered the same ad. Patsy thought she would go to the morning service again the following Sunday to see if the man came back, whether he'd be on his own or, more likely, with Linda. There was no point in telling Marni. It was far too nebulous to be useful information.

Marni went on. "I don't know what it is about men that they think they have to tell you so much and in such detail. He just went on talking. Occasionally he'd ask a question, but he didn't seem all that interested in anything I had to say. So I listened, for the most part, though I confess to tuning him out after a while. You'd think that would give him very little to base an impression on, but he wanted to arrange another get together. I said I wasn't interested."

"Glad you said no," Patsy said.

"I'd rather be lonely. Maybe it would be even lonelier with someone like him. Like listening to a husband go on and on and marvel after fifteen years that he doesn't know very much about you. Oh, he knows what you do with the toothpaste tube and what you like to eat and where you work and all that daily stuff, but he doesn't know what you dream about or even what you think about. Mine didn't even know what my favourite flowers were. He bought me bouquets sometimes, but always yellow roses because he liked them. I think I once told him how much I loved irises, but I don't think he was paying attention. I used to like yellow roses, too, although not anywhere near as much as irises and wild flowers and daisies. Now I dislike them intensely. My yellow rose marriage, a symbol of impending disaster."

"Oh well," Patsy said. "There's got to be something. Mine's bruises."

"Well, yellow roses and bruises, except the bruises came first, then the roses."

Patsy nodded. They had this understanding that came from being on the fringes, women who had sustained bruises, single women with children, one escaped from a Jehovah's Witnesses family, the other a woman of colour. Sometimes you did not need words, you only needed to sit together, Patsy thought. And in this way, they sipped their coffee wordlessly, until Chris came in. The door was not locked and when Marni visited, the boys often went back and forth between the two houses. They climbed around the divider in the middle of the porch without using the steps as Marni and Patsy did.

"Where's my striped T-shirt, Ma?" Chris asked. "The one with the sailboat on it."

AFTER THE BOYS WENT TO THEIR UPSTAIRS BEDROOM, Marni watched the news in the living room. Peter Mansbridge was the anchor. It was almost eleven and she was surprised when the telephone rang.

"Hi, Marni," a man's voice said. "It's Patrick."

She was indignant that he would call so late, but waited. After all, she was awake and watching television.

"What about it?" he asked.

"What about what?"

"You know," he said. "Getting together again some time."

"I'm sorry, Patrick. I'd rather not. I told you this before."

"Aw c'mon, Babe."

"There really isn't any point."

"Okay," he sighed. "But you're a classy chick."

Marni hung up and shook her head. Some nerve! What did he mean by saying she was a classy chick? It did not matter. She knew she did not want to see the jerk again and it had nothing to do with what her parents might or might not think about it. Although for a long time, she had believed in Jesus and she had cared about what He might have thought. Her parents might have been wrong about the date of Armageddon, but she had thought that surely Jesus knew. Until she stopped believing in anything. Until she reached her teens and talked about going away to study at some university.

"No," her father had said. "We won't have our children

going anywhere where they'll try to teach you that your religion is wrong."

Marni had gone on rounds with her mother, a present but silent witness, all the while planning how she would get away. She had not told them until she was about to leave.

"You know the rules," her father had said. "If you leave, you won't ever be able to set foot on our doorstep again. You'll be rejecting the teachings of Christ and—"

Marni was incredulous each time she heard this assertion, but she managed not to say so, just nodded. She knew the rules, but as soon as she was ready she would indeed leave.

So when she was seventeen, Marni left home for the second time to start a new life in Toronto. At first, she lived in a hostel, then in a rented room. She got jobs in restaurants and bars and saved as much from her tips as she could. She took a course to learn how to use computers. Although she knew this was what she had to do, she was still torn by the desire to see her family, by the knowledge that they would only contact her if someone died or if something terrible happened. At first, Gramma phoned her and asked Marni to call when she wanted to, but when the family found out about the calls, her grandmother had to get a new telephone number. All because of a stupid religion, Marni thought, one that had her father in thrall to the extent that he had repudiated her, and her mother had not disputed him. It was hard to believe that her mother could do that. And now that she had children of her own, it was beyond Marni's comprehension. She went upstairs and looked into the boys' room, a small room with bunks that took up less space than twin beds would have. The boys were almost the same height now. Chris liked the top bunk and that was fine with Dean who was still uneasy climbing down in the dark. Dean had always been the shy one.

"Good night," she whispered.

But they were both asleep.

PART III

14.

Mid-November

OVER THE SOUND OF HER SON CRYING, Patsy was aware of the two police officers heading out to their car. As her front door closed behind them, she was left with the image of an unidentified woman's body that might be anyone. It could not be Marni, she thought. That was not possible. Her friend would turn up any minute. If Sasha did not need her, she thought she might call one of the women at the church, but distracted by the cries that had become louder, she continued up the stairs in his direction. As she approached the door of his room, she was aware that the cries had turned into crooning noises. She was surprised; a few moments earlier Sasha had sounded determined to let her know he needed attention. It was fascinating how a baby's mood could change quickly if they noticed something else that intrigued them.

When she entered his room, Sasha was cooing at the birds in a mobile strung from the ceiling over his crib. As soon as he saw his mother, he stretched out his arms toward her, ready to play. He started to make the sounds that meant he wanted her to pick him up. She changed him, and cuddled him, then whispered, "Sasha, Sasha, little angel, Mommy's buddy," as she tucked him back into his crib. When he dozed off, she tiptoed out of his room and went down to the kitchen again.

She could hear the television through the wall, probably the voice of a sportscaster. Was it time for her to go over to see what Chris and Dean were doing? By now they were probably wondering where their mother was. Or maybe they were glad to have an hour or two to themselves, and assumed Marni would walk in the door just in time to start dinner. But Patsy had told the police officers she would check on the boys and she tried to think of how to do so without alarming them. When she knocked, they came to the door right away. She asked if they were alone and they nodded. Would they like to come to her place? she asked. No, it was okay. Chris told her they would watch television until their mother arrived.

An hour or so later, Patsy, who had been listening for any unusual sounds, saw the Taurus park on the street again. Shortly after, through the wall, she could hear a man talking to the boys in a low voice. If something had happened to Marni, Richard Atchinson, Marni's ex-husband, might be under suspicion. Patsy was aware of the bruises Marni had lived with during the marriage, but she had not been told of anything more recent other than the arguing about access visits with the boys. She felt certain that Marni would have told her if there had been threats or anything like that.

As she watched out the front window, it was not long before Patsy spotted Richard, whom she had only said hello to occasionally, go down the front steps with Chris and Dean. He was carrying an old brown suitcase and a navy backpack. She wanted to know what was happening, but she did not want to upset the boys, so she restrained herself from rushing out the door. But she sat in the window seat and continued to watch. It was not until she heard the report on the radio about the body in the church that she thought the unthinkable, that the woman discovered that morning might have been Marni, even though that did not make any sense. Marni would never have gone to a church. She might have been lured there, Patsy supposed. But why? How? She wondered if she could call the police and ask questions, but the brief announcement on the radio made it clear that a positive identification was still pending.

The visit from the police officers had disturbed her. She was deeply worried about Marni. Although she had chosen her house with care in a neighbourhood she felt was safe, the news about Marni left her feeling that maybe nothing was safe any more. Still, it was safer in Canada then in Jamaica, she thought, and as much as she missed the country where she was born, this city was now her home.

Patsy had broken through some barriers in Toronto, both as a black woman and as a lesbian. Although she had not come out at work, or told any of her colleagues about Aloha. Not even her former husband. One of the reasons she went to the church downtown was because being "out" there was comfortable. She wished that her friend Marni had come to Holy Trinity with her, but Marni was not interested in visiting any church at all. So, she couldn't fathom how or why Marni might have ended up murdered in the basement of Holy Trinity.

"I didn't trade the Witnesses for some other brand of Christianity," Marni had said. She was taking a course in Buddhist meditation and wanted to go to India to visit an Ashram. That was about as spiritual as she felt comfortable with.

Marni knew Patsy was lesbian, but it had been hard for Patsy to reach the point where she felt she could be open with her.

"It's all right," Marni had said. "I figured maybe. It wouldn't be the first time someone has come out to me either. I'm often approached. Why, do you suppose?"

"Oh, you're a good person," Patsy said, then teased a little. "And attractive."

"I wondered if that was why," Marni said. "The attractive bit. Too bad. I'm about as straight as they come. Even though men haven't treated me that well. Not my father, my brother, my uncle, or ex-husband. None of them. But you know, I was born this way and that's how it is with me. I just need to pick my men better. They can't all be that bad. Although, when I was disfellowshipped, I was told to expect any number of bad experiences to punish me for leaving the church."

Patsy thought of the other day when Marni had returned home later than expected. She'd been on a date, Patsy recalled, with the man who had placed the ad in the newspaper. It was not as if Marni was obligated to tell her anything. They led quite separate lives, but they were also friends and neighbours and they had begun to share some of the intimate details of their lives. Patsy was grateful for how helpful Marni had been with Sasha, having had Chris and Dean, both teenagers now. Marni knew something about toddlers and their needs.

It felt too late to call anyone, but surely someone would have contacted her by now had they known the woman they discovered in the basement of the church was someone she knew well. What a foolish thought, she realized, as no one at the church would have known Marni was her neighbour. She went into the kitchen and turned on the radio, hoping she might hear something on the news.

15.

WITHOUT KNOWING IT, Rosemary Willis had laughed at the same ad at almost the same time as Marni had. When it was her time to be questioned by the detective, it was no longer a laughing matter. Nor did she tell him about her encounter with the man who had placed the ad; it had not seemed relevant. But that day remained vivid in her memory. She could still see herself, sitting at a small table in her kitchen, wearing her pale blue dressing gown, her bare feet tapping on the dark ceramic tiled floor. Through the opening to the living area, she'd been aware of the books on her shelves. Row after row of them. Also visible were the photographs on the walls of places she had visited: The Eiffel Tower, streets in small hill towns in Provence with flowers cascading from window boxes, the deep blue of the Mediterranean, and the white cliffs of Santorini.

Rosemary had selected some of her favourite photographs and framed them. She looked at them longingly now as she recalled drinking ouzo and sleeping on one of the beaches on Santorini, sheltered under those white cliffs next to a young man from Istanbul she'd met at a hostel. Their campsite was on a black sand beach formed from the lava of a nearby volcano. They'd stayed there for two weeks before leaving for the northern islands and Mt. Olympus. The thought of Deniz's warm skin made her tingle. Was it time for another trip? She and Deniz had met an old Greek man on the island of Paros who invited them back to his house for coffee. The old man had played his guitar for them and after that he'd played backgammon with Deniz.

As she sipped her coffee and scanned the newspaper, the memory of those carefree days of meeting people in different places lent sparkle to her day. Deniz had written to her for a while, but after a few months the letters had stopped. On this day, until she saw the ad, time had stretched out gloomily ahead of her. She could not resist reading the personals, although she did not usually respond to them. When she did, mainly it was as a challenge to see if she could write something that would elicit a reply. She figured her average at better than ninety percent, although rarely was she interested beyond a first meeting. This is the last time, she often told herself. But sooner or later she would see something she could not resist, something that would intrigue her enough to spend fifteen or so minutes reinventing herself—massage the information to fit; aim at getting a meeting. She'd found she was adept at it.

Hi! She typed. There was no name to append to this. She had rejected "Hello, Mister," and several other salutations. Just "Hi!

> *Almost lacking in judgment and intelligence to be answering an ad, but yours wins the award for the most unique one that I recall seeing in the "Globe Personals." Straight from the hip or right up front, as you will ... I don't fit your criteria. If I had a second home, I think I'd prefer Provence or Tuscany to Florida. Also, I'm not unbelievably patient, but then that would likely bore you anyway. How's that for two left feet?*
> *I am fit, in my early forties. I walk, skate, do yoga, swing dance (would like to learn to salsa, although you might need patience at first). I have a bicycle that I haven't been riding as much as I'd like to for the past year or two, but I still enjoy it when I do ride.*

I like to travel. Am a non-smoker. No addictions. No, that's not true. It seems I'm addicted to my computer and I'm in contact with people near and far on e-mail. I surf the internet looking for what? Information on the TSX perhaps Still, an addiction to something other than the Toronto Stock Exchange might be more attractive, e.g., possibly works of art or cabinet-making or even poker, but if you make money at it, what a preoccupation! And I do know enough about investing or speculating or just following the markets to be able to carry on a relatively coherent conversation.

Unfortunately, I don't have a picture of my computer and no camera at the moment. So I'll draw it for you. It's attractive and state of the art and only a year old, so not obsolete quite yet.

If you care to contact me, I'd be pleased to hear from you. You can reach me at the following telephone number and/or e-mail address:
Best wishes,
Rosemary

She turned on the radio and listened to a discussion on the CBC about the incidence of mercury in certain kinds of fish. She decided to go out for a walk, knowing she would feel better afterward. The mailbox at the corner, where she would drop the envelope in the slot and then likely forget about it, would provide this morning's destination. So when she was dressed in jeans and jacket, she headed in the direction of the red box, located in front of a small store she often frequented. After checking to make sure the letter disappeared into the mailbox, she went inside and scooped some raisins from one of the bulk bins and filled a plastic bag.

"Hello, Rosemary," said the woman at the counter.

Kunim and her husband had come from Korea and taken over from the last owners, who had also been from Korea.

When they arrived, none of them had known much English. But they could figure out what the items were and how much to charge for them.

"Hello, Kunim," Rosemary said.

The woman held up a children's book. "For the English." She pointed out a word, *fragile*, and asked how to say it.

Fitting that she, a librarian, should be called on this way, Rosemary thought. She enunciated "fra-jile" and Kunim repeated it after her. Usually it took three or four repetitions to get an approximate pronunciation. Sometimes she would also find herself explaining the meaning when Kunim asked. A nod, and a smile, would indicate she'd grasped it.

After those exchanges, Rosemary sometimes asked questions. "What did you do in Korea?" Things like that.

She imagined that she might one day write the short story these people conjured up for her. She had no idea where to start or what the hook that drew people in would be. Figuring it out, asking the questions to elicit the information, then assessing it must be a bit like the work of a private investigator. A sleuth of some kind.

"Hoover them in," she had read in a book on writing that budding authors often asked for at the library. The books on how to write and how to get published were among those most frequently requested at the reference desk in the literature department.

There was a story in that store, Rosemary was sure of it. She could see the title in a small literary periodical. *The Bulk Food Store,* by Rosemary Willis. One of the small, prestigious magazines. *Grain. Descant. Fiddlehead.* She had some of them on her shelves at home and the ones she did not have, she often indulged her fantasy life by skimming while working at the library.

Rosemary Willis, the writer, she thought. You know the one. She was reviewed in the *Globe and Mail* on the weekend, by that man who reviews first novels.

Of course, it had not happened yet. She did not have a finished book that could be reviewed, much less published. But who knew? Most days she thought sooner or later it would all come about. And Brent believed she could do it. Maybe he was right.

ROSEMARY ALSO RECEIVED A TELEPHONE CALL from the mysterious man who placed the ad in the newspaper. "Hi, sweetheart," the man had said. "This is Mr. Almost."

"Pardon?" Rosemary asked, annoyed that anyone would be presumptuous enough to refer to her as "sweetheart."

"Mr. Almost," he repeated. "From the newspaper ad."

"Oh," she said. "Of course. What's your real name?"

"Michael," he said. "Sloane."

As they talked about his ad and then his computer, Rosemary fiddled with the pages of a calendar on the table in front of her. There were photographs of wild flowers on each page. The trillium, Ontario's official flower, was on the cover.

"Why did you want a photograph of my computer?" she asked.

"Why not?" he replied. "You have a nifty one. Or you can really draw."

"I see," she said, but she did not.

"So," Michael Sloane said. "Where can we meet?"

She thought if she had a coin she would toss it and thus decide whether to go on a date with him. If the coin came up heads, she'd go. Or she could choose tails. Did she really want a date with him? No, probably not, but although she was irritated by him, she was also curious. "Why don't you come to the Sunday service at my church?" She thought that would be a safe place to meet him. She described the downtown location of Holy Trinity where she attended the late service on Sunday mornings. They could get to know each other over the lunch afterwards.

"In behind the Eaton Centre?" he said.

It was almost a statement rather than a question. So Rosemary left it at that and did not feel it appropriate or necessary to allude to her reasons for going there. But had he asked, she would have told him she liked that the community that belonged to Holy Trinity was drawn from across the city, and you could expect to see people of many races and different sexual orientations as well as small children participating in the service. It was not always obvious who the minister was as someone from the congregation might just as well be officiating.

"You could wear a white ribbon on your lapel," she said. "So that I will know who you are."

"Sure. Any colour you like," he said, making it apparent he was not aware that men who worked to end violence against women typically sported white ribbons.

It was a way of screening, she thought, although surely not foolproof since she could not decide if he had passed or failed her first test. In any case, she could watch him and decide whether she would bother to introduce herself afterwards. Of course, he knew her first name so he could find her if he wanted to, but she suspected if he thought no one was looking for him, he would leave quickly. And that would be the end of it.

On the prearranged Sunday morning, Rosemary saw the man with a white ribbon come into the nave and sit in a pew toward the back. It surprised her when Linda was the first one to greet him. And when he stood awkwardly in the line-up for lunch, Linda appeared as if by coincidence at his side. Rosemary should have known Linda, who managed to occupy the centre of any discussion and seemed to know everything that was going on in the community, would have noticed the man. Not only because of the white ribbon, but because of his bright red hair, not unlike Linda's hairdresser-induced colour, and he was also almost handsome. And, of course, a stranger.

So there Linda was, once again engaging him in conversation. She was a solid woman always dressed in bright colours, with similarly bright red hair that had for a while been almost purple. Rosemary wondered how she might interrupt them. She had worn a pair of woollen trousers with a black sweater and jacket, instead of her usual blue jeans, to inspire more confidence, but she realized her finery did not make any difference. She felt as shy as ever.

Looking over at Brent Matthews, Rosemary noticed the caretaker was also aware of this interplay and seemed to be watching the two with discreet interest. Likely all he knew was that the man was new to the church and was amused that Linda was taking more than a passing interest in him. He would probably be surprised to see her interrupt them. Usually if Linda defined territory, no other woman, nor man for that matter, was likely to cross her. Least of all me, Rosemary thought. But why not me? Brent always talked to her as if he sensed she had some spunk in her, even knew that she dreamed of being a writer.

"You could set a story in this church," he'd said one day.

"Like what?" she asked.

"I don't know," he said. "Maybe a mystery. Maybe someone gets murdered in the church."

"Good heavens," she said. "Can you imagine the furor here if I dared to write something like that?"

But she had liked what he had to say. Once she ran into him at St. Lawrence Market and they had talked over coffee. Brent described the members of the congregation as radical Anglicans. Rosemary suspected that he admired the social justice stands taken by this eclectic group of people. Individuals all. There were a number of ordained priests and ministers who had made this place home. A community of gay people also found the environment comfortable. She liked that children wandered about during the church service and that it was not uncommon for a child to crawl or run across the floor in the middle of the homily. And certainly when the circle gathered for the Eucharist, there was a lot of interaction between the adults and the children. Rosemary thought Brent was right and that it would be interesting to set a novel in this church. The community seemed to be an analogy for life, a small microcosm of the larger whole. So many people came and went to meetings, concerts, church services, and choir practice, that there was endless room for speculation. Yet another idea bouncing around in her head that she would likely never put down on paper, she thought and sighed audibly. Although Brent took her ideas seriously and she was reminded he seemed to be able to conjure up an image of her as a published author.

"So?" he said. "Why not? It would be fiction. Anyway, they'd probably be really excited by it. Just think of all the interest in the church it would cause. You could run mystery tours to the place the body is discovered. Put yellow police tape across the scene, like on television."

Rosemary had laughed out loud. She had completely forgotten about the conversation until this very moment. Once again, she almost dismissed the thought out loud with a sneering guffaw, but instead looked once more over at the man who'd placed the ad, still engrossed in a tête-à-tête with Linda. Rosemary walked around behind the pews, unsure what to do. His red hair stood out, as did the stark white ribbon awkwardly pinned to the lapel of his jacket. It seemed odd that he would not have mentioned his most obvious feature, by which anyone would easily recognize him. She also found it odd that his and Linda's heads almost matched, although his colour was obviously not from a bottle. Rosemary lined up behind them, but it was not until they reached the soup pot that she was able to break into their conversation.

"Michael," she said. "I'm Rosemary."

"How do you do?" he said.

Linda nodded at her, and then quickly ladled out some soup and went to find a spot on the bench running along one side of the room.

"Are you going to have some soup?" Rosemary asked.

"What about if we go somewhere else?"

"Where?"

Maybe she could use him as the prototype for the victim in her novel. For a moment, she thought she might ask Brent's opinion, but she did not want to draw attention to what she was doing with this stranger. And in the church! My goodness, she thought, he could be studying people there with some dubious criminal intent. He was more apt to be the murderer than the victim. Oh, for heaven's sake, she thought. I'm making up a story and creating a fictional universe in a place that has a vivid enough life of its own.

"Anywhere," he muttered as he moved out of the line and when she did also, he guided her toward the west door and down the stairs toward Bay Street.

"That was a great ad," Rosemary said.

"Thanks."

They walked along Dundas Street toward the busy corner at University. The leaves had almost all fallen, something she remarked on as they waited for the light to signal that pedestrians could proceed. Sometimes it took two changes to cross the wide lanes of University with statues and benches in the middle, but they scurried to the opposite side just before it turned red again.

"What about the art gallery?" Rosemary asked.

He grimaced, but continued to keep stride with her in the direction of the gallery. Inside they manoeuvred through the line and into a lounge where she saw an empty table with two comfortable chairs at one end of the room.

"Let's sit over there," she said.

He nodded and lowered himself awkwardly into the chair closest to him.

"You have quite an imagination," she said.

"Why?"

"You know." Surely he knew what she meant. "That ad."

He shrugged. "I asked my buddy to write that for me."

"You're kidding."

"Why would I do that?"

If she'd asked a friend to write an ad that brilliant, Rosemary was quite sure she would not tell anyone. Least of all, would she tell a stranger. Someone who could not string a few words together was a poor candidate for her consideration.

"Who's your buddy?"

"What do you mean?"

"The one who wrote the ad."

"Oh," he said. "Nick's the man."

Nick might be of more interest to her than this buffoon, Rosemary thought, hoping her time would not be entirely wasted. A server arrived to place the coffee and a dessert she'd ordered on the table between them.

"I like the work of the Group of Seven," he said. "It's good outdoor stuff."

"Um," Rosemary nodded. "I am a fan of Matisse and Picasso."

He shrugged again. After he added some milk to his coffee, he sat back in his chair and looked at her through narrowed eyes and pursed lips. "So you have an investment portfolio," he said.

"I read *Report on Business*. I can carry on a conversation about investments."

He brushed that aside. "I had a girlfriend," he said. "She was married to a wealthy guy. They were going to court over the settlement. They're likely still haggling about it. I lived with her for a while."

"Let's try the dessert, " Rosemary said, taking a slice of her pie. "And leave the past history for later." Obviously they were both old enough to have a history and she would rather learn about that gradually.

He swallowed a mouthful of his carrot cake, and ignoring her request, talked through the crumbs about an ex-wife who would not speak to him. "I have two sons I don't see much," he said, wiping bits of icing off his chin. Typical, she thought. He was disappointed, angry, bewildered. Out of touch with his children. She had answered many ads over the years and she had become cynical. There was nothing fresh and new about this date. She ought to have known better. But, oh well, she had managed to get to what she referred to as "the interview" and she was free to dismiss him at any time. And it had only taken fifteen minutes to write the letter. If she could write a story that quickly, she might actually get something published. She thought of all the years that had passed of imagining stories in her head, but never writing them down. Her conversations with Brent at the church had made her feel she could write them. But when would she find time? She had written a poem once when she was very young that her grandfather had published in a small newspaper in Stratford. Her name had appeared after the title: "Snow," by Rosemary Willis. But since then, she'd more or less only talked and thought about writing. "Too much else to do," she imagined saying to Brent or some other listener. "What with working at the library, some travel, going to art exhibitions, it's all I can do to make it to church on Sundays."

Still, she read everything that she could manage, choosing from anywhere in the Dewey decimal system. She did not have an investment portfolio, even though she knew quite a bit about investing from frequently reading about money. So she knew, for instance, that the millionaire next door was just as likely to be a self-employed, first-generation businessman with a modest life style as the high flyer on the street who drove a Mercedes or BMW.

"Why would you get someone else to write your ad?" she asked now

"I don't do words," he said. "I do music."

"What about Nick?"

"Oh, he owns the horses I ride. I'm an exercise rider. And he has a bar with an upstairs patio open to the stars. There's music on the lower level. Nick's a smart guy. I hang around the pub when I'm not working at the track. Sometimes on weekends, he lets me play music I've mixed."

Rosemary thought she'd like to meet Nick, but knew better

than to say so. "What kind of music?"

"You know. Popular stuff. U2. Blue Rodeo. I dunno. What do you like?"

"Oh pretty well across the spectrum. Rush. Beethoven."

"That drummer," he said, and his eyes lit up.

"Do people dance at Nick's?"

"Not really. They drink. Eat pretzels and stuff. Talk."

Rosemary did not think he'd said anything yet that interested her except maybe what he would have said about Rush, the drummer, if she had not cut him off so quickly. Still, she wondered what would have kept Linda engaged so long in conversation with him. Maybe Linda loved horses, not something Rosemary had ever heard her talk about though.

"I like Grieg. Handel," she said now, knowing she was testing him, that she was even being snooty.

"Singers?"

"No. Composers."

"Don't think I know them."

"Not likely. They're dead."

"Dead?" He eyed her with a baffled look. "Well, I like Duke Ellington," he added. "He's dead too."

"I like the Duke," Rosemary said, relenting slightly. She did not have to see this man ever again, this man who was dense enough he might not even have understood the nuance in his own ad, written not by him but by his employer. But she would like to meet Nick, she thought. How would she wangle that?

"Maybe I could drop by the bar some time," she said. "And meet your employer?"

The man shrugged. "I don't know why you'd want to."

16.

A T THE END OF THE DAY, Detective Cosser was exhausted. All he wanted was to have a hot shower and fall into bed. As he drove toward his apartment on the main floor of a house just up from Bloor Street in the Annex, he realized he was also hungry and he picked up a pizza at a corner shop. When he arrived, he ate mindlessly in front of the television set. Suddenly he lurched up and headed for the telephone. He wanted to hear Jaime's voice.

He missed his daughter. Not seeing Jaime every day, not tucking her in at night, not reading her stories left a huge void in his life. He savoured every moment she was with him. He knew that not all divorced fathers were like him. Deadbeat Dads were numerous in situations he encountered and sometimes existed even among his colleagues. The failure of his marriage made him feel deeply sad. It bothered him that he had not been able to salvage his marriage and that his angel lived with her mother, although his former wife was a good mother, and he never doubted that his daughter was in good hands.

Since the divorce, he'd felt a deep need for spiritual solace, and he had tried a Unitarian church, the Quakers, even once a Roman Catholic Church. And then he'd stopped that quest and started to visit art galleries where he'd stand and gaze at paintings for hours. Sometimes he could lie in bed and visualize the ones he liked best—the bright colours of van Gogh and Cezanne, the twisted figures in Picasso's works, the blues of Matisse, and the Chagall windows of the cathedral at Chartres with its deep blue stained glass, as well as some of the American moderns. He liked the starkness of Wyeth's paintings. And there were Canadians among those he visualized, too—Colville's horses, guns, strange haunting themes. These existed along with his own disturbing images—a plastic bag lying in a corner still had the power to awaken him from a deep sleep. The memory of the child's body in that bag in a rooming house floating unexpectedly to the surface. It was not easy to confront mortality on an ongoing basis, but more than that, such a young life wiped out represented the death of hope, of potential.

It was after that discovery that Cosser had visited a number of churches on subsequent Sundays. The image of the child's small, naked body, her head twisted by her killer, never left him. Every new case reminded him. Every happy-go-lucky child reminded him.

When he opened the plastic bag in his nightmares, it was Jaime he found. He'd awaken screaming. He thought he ought to see a counsellor, but he could not reconcile that need with the expectations of being a man, a strong man, in this society. And more than that, he could not reconcile it with being a cop.

He thought of the church where the woman, Margaret or Marni Atchison, had been found lying on the washroom floor. Holy Trinity had seemed different to him from others he'd visited. Even the way the congregation had continued with the service while the minister was busy with the crisis had been unusual. He'd seen children laughing and moving around freely as if they owned the place. He wished he could go back there on an off-duty Sunday and take Jaime with him. But as the detective investigating the case, he could not do that. Maybe he could once they had a suspect arrested. What was he thinking? Of course he would have to go back as a detective interested in the congregation because of the crime, and he need not reveal a dual purpose. Taking Jaime would have to wait.

Indeed, when he did return to the church in his official role, it was to observe the people, and try to grasp the underlying dynamic of this community. Something had to lead to unravelling the mystery of the woman's death. He had a hunch that he was meant to be the detective on duty when this particular call came in. He might have described this to Marion as a case that had to be his, although it was too soon for him to understand why he felt that so strongly. It was not something he could talk about with his colleagues, most of whom responded matter-of-factly to cases as they arose. If he revealed to his colleagues some of the moral questions he pondered, they would wonder why he had chosen to be a cop. But he knew why. He believed in the motto, "To Serve and Protect" and he knew he was a good cop. Although he and Reid had never had this conversation, he thought, hoped maybe, that his colleague might well share some of these opinions.

The woman whose body was left in the church had not been any older than either of them. A life full of possibilities had still been ahead of her, not least of which was being there for her sons.

When he dialed his former wife's number, Jaime answered the telephone.

"Hi, Angel," he said.

"Dad," she said. Her voice was excited. "Mom and I went to the zoo today. I saw these funny monkeys. They come swinging down in their cages and it's almost as if they're talking to you."

The sound of her voice cheered him, bringing him to a place of sunlight and laughter. Children did that for him, passed on their joy, their enthusiasm, even momentarily their remarkable innocence.

"I remember," he said.

"Dad, can we go back there some time?"

"You bet."

"Will you send me a kiss and a hug good night?" Jaime said.

"I sure will," Jack replied. "There, I just did. Could you feel it?"

"I did, Daddy. It was warm. A warm hug."

When he hung up, he opened the refrigerator, looking for a snack, but there were no apples. Not even a few grapes. It was time to do some shopping again, certainly before Jaime came the next weekend. He pulled out a couple of raw carrots and washed them off with a yellow plastic dish scrubber before eating them. Margaret Atchison, he thought. Beige clay tiles. Red shoes. Had he missed something? Something obvious? None of the people he had interviewed since that morning had shed much light on anything. Except he knew who the woman was now and he had a vague picture of her life. There were a number of avenues to follow up on even though as yet nothing concrete. He hated to admit, even to himself, that it was early times in the unraveling of a crime. He wished he had a viable suspect so that he could make an arrest and tie things up quickly. It was always frightening when a killer was on the loose. Always. Not knowing who it was left everyone vulnerable. Not having any predictable patterns to follow up on made a quick resolution difficult.

After he watched the news, Cosser took a navy canvas bag from the broom closet in the kitchen and removed his fifteen pounders. He left the television on the weather channel and lifted the weights in front of it. Traffic on all the highways around the city alternated in one corner of the screen. In another were up-to-the-minute reports on unfolding stories. There was a storm in some remote corner of the world that no longer seemed very remote because of television and the internet. He was not usually affected by any of these stories in the same way as he was by a murder in his own city. This was particularly true when he was one of the first on the scene and would see the body up close. He had thought lifting weights would remove some of these images from his head, but that only worked for so long.

Sometimes a woman would wander into the police station because she had just seen a program that had reawakened for her the trauma of an earlier assault. There had been one such woman at the station the other day, in the midst of a flashback, terrified when anyone approached her, and yet she had seemingly come to the station for protection. Ultimately, he had simply reassured her of where she was and told her if she wanted to go to a friend's or to a shelter, he would drive her there. When she came out of the flashback, she was embarrassed.

"Thanks," she'd said. "I'd better be on my way now."

She did not usually trust the police, she told him. Often they had not treated her as kindly as he had. "But it was still better than going to a hospital. Once they put me in shackles."

He thought she'd meant restraints, but he had not asked her. He had listened. He knew he was a good cop because of his capacity to do that—to listen. He knew it also made him a good father. He looked at the framed photograph of Jaime on the shelf beside him. It had been taken six months earlier at the beach. It was just before her fourth birthday. Hard to fathom how you could have your heart stolen by a child's innocence, by the slight resemblance to yourself in her features and gestures. At this moment, he could not remember why Marion had insisted that the marriage had become empty. He could tell that she still loved him. Then he remembered that he had been obsessed by the murder of the child he'd found for months and months by then, perhaps even years, and he had worked night and day to track down the killer. It had intruded on every corner of his existence, and it had cost him his marriage.

Now, he was so tired after those long weeks of intense work, and his feelings of intense sadness exacerbated everything. Some time soon he would have to talk to Marion.

17.

One Week Earlier in November

WHEN PATSY WENT TO HOLY TRINITY the Sunday after she'd learned about Marni's date, she did not see the white ribbon man who had been there the previous week.

"Mr. Almost called yesterday," Marni had told her the day before.

"And?"

"Wants to meet again."

"What did you tell him?"

"No. Clear and simple."

So Patsy was not thinking she had to look for the man any longer. Marni wasn't going to see him again. She was merely curious. In a city the size of Toronto, she supposed the same women might answer the same ads, but she wondered how often you would be apt to know that. After the service, she intended to talk to Linda, but Linda was not there that morning. Most unusual, although from time to time Linda went off to a workshop somewhere and reported on it the next Sunday. She would tell everyone about it from the pulpit when those who had something to share lined up for announcements. With Linda, it was often an attempt to enlist other enthusiasts to accompany her the next time. It was all too New Age for Patsy, although in some quintessential way she knew what Linda was talking about when she referred to workshops with crystals or some other novel approach to gaining self-understanding. But that was not as important to her as the way most of Holy Trinity's congregation were at the forefront of social justice movements. At the same time there was something rather dispassionate about their relationships with each other. Something cerebral. She knew she was influenced by the warm camaraderie of the islands, but she felt like this elsewhere in Toronto often too, she thought. She was grateful for her friend and neighbour, Marni, and the caucus for women of colour in financial services that she had joined through the Black Women's Professional Association. She knew that she was considered to have made it with her rise at the bank where she worked, but she encountered barriers at that level also. These were barriers that all women encountered. But for her, as a woman of colour, she had to prove herself even more. She remembered the days of the Clarence Thomas trial when she had been expected to explain and defend all black people. Then there had been the self-congratulatory attitude of her seniors at the bank who thought by giving her a promotion they had done her a favour. She knew she had been promoted because she was good at her job, and she had told the caucus that she was sick of the racism implicit in the comments her colleagues made about her so-called "good fortune."

So, when she left the church to head home, Patsy acknowledged the friendly gestures that always seemed restrained and headed over to the subway in the mall. She was glad that Sasha had been relatively quiet today. He had crawled around on the floor during the service, but that was common in that church. The fact that children were expected to be children there was one of the things she liked about it. It was something she had told Marni about because she knew how restrictive all Marni's experience with religion had been.

Patsy had forgotten all about Mr. Almost and his white ribbon the next time she visited the church. Even when she saw Linda on the other side of the nave, she did not remember. Marni had not mentioned him again and it seemed that he had stopped calling her.

"On down his list," Marni had laughed at one point. "I was forgotten quickly. Fortunately. He probably had so many replies to that ad, he could make dates to meet different women for months."

18.

Mid-November

COSSER AWAKENED THE MORNING after the identification of the murder victim had been confirmed, knowing he would call Linda O'Reilly before he left to take the trip to visit Margaret Atchison's parents. Or Marni, as everyone seemed to call her. He would have time only to have a quick shower and shave, and maybe grab some toast and coffee. As soon as he made contact with Reid at the station and called Linda, it would be time to move quickly into what was bound to be an eventful day. Marni's parents lived near a smaller town two hours west of Toronto, and he would be heading toward the 401 just after the worst of the rush hour traffic.

He moved quickly through his usual morning routine. First was the hot shower. He took a bar of soap from the side of the tub and lathered the hair on his chest as well as under his arms and around his scrotum. Then he stood under the stream of hot water and let it rinse the foam off his body. He dried himself with a big towel, shaved hurriedly with a black electric razor, and slipped into jockey pants before plugging in the coffee pot. When he finished dressing, he poured dark steaming liquid into a mug and sipped from it as he called Linda O'Reilly. He was relieved when she answered and agreed that he could drop in and get that interview out of the way early. It was not that he expected to find out she was implicated, but it would be irresponsible not to question someone who had keys to the church. Even if she were entirely innocent, which he assumed she was, he might pick up some information that would fit into the puzzle sooner or later. He had done enough police work to know not to overlook anything. His experience had also taught him that most cases were solved not only by diligent police work, but that chance often played a role.

It was still dark when he slid behind the wheel of his car, but gradually lightened as he headed toward the address the O'Reilly woman had given to him. A low cloud cover suggested there would be snow soon and he turned on the radio to hear the weather report. It was a relief that any precipitation was not likely until much later in the day, or early evening. Not that the forecasts were always accurate, but they were nevertheless useful as a guide on days when he found himself on the road.

When he pulled up in front of the building where Linda lived in a second-storey walk-up not far from the Art Gallery, he could see lights in a window on the top floor and some movement behind the drapes. He knew nothing about her except her appearance and he would try not to make assumptions on that basis. Well, he wished he would not, but he could not help making comparisons with Marion who would never have dyed her hair such a ridiculous colour.

The lights above went off, but another one was turned on in what appeared to be the next room. He took in a long breath of the cool November air and rang the doorbell, waiting for a sign that she knew he was there. It was going to be a long day, he thought, as he heard a buzz and the door unlocked for him.

As he stood in the hall, his cell rang. Reid's voice was on the other end.

"You know that woman you are going to interview—"

"I'm just about to see her," Cosser said. "What's up?"

"You remember the community group that came to the cops to work with us on neighbourhood safety. Hang on a minute—it was the group working on violence against women. O'Reilly was on that as one of the reps of an agency."

"Thanks, Simon," Cosser said, shaking his head. He remembered her now, the strident red head, although it had been a different shade of red at that time. It was hard now to imagine that he had not recognized her. He supposed she had been more quiet than usual during the investigation at the church as she had been tasked with staying with the woman who had found Marni Atchison's body. How that must have tried her curiosity and her patience, he thought, recalling characteristics that had come to the fore more than once in the meetings Reid had drawn to his attention.

"Hello, down there," a woman's voice hollered from above. "Are you coming up?"

"On my way," Cosser called out, looking up in the direction of the voice. He did not wait for an answer, but started to climb the stairs.

19.

Linda had awakened at just after six, as happened most mornings, and turned the radio on to Metro Morning. The host talked about a book published that year called *No Great Mischief* that had won some award. She thought she would have to read it. But her mind had drifted and she'd fallen back to sleep. Usually when there were voices on the radio, they made her drowsy, but not if there was music. On this particular morning, the next time she awakened, Randy Ferry had just announced that it was six-forty-five, and that a body had been found in one of Toronto's downtown churches. Linda reached for her remote control to turn up the volume. She shuddered, as if she were suddenly in the basement of the church again, standing at the foot of the stairway. She could feel herself at the door to the washroom and then comforting the woman who had found the body, waiting until the police wanted to talk to her.

"I went into the church to use the washroom," she heard a woman say to Ferry in a telephone interview. She was a source who did not want to be identified. But Linda knew who she was. "I didn't see anything at first because I went over to the sink. When I turned around, I saw her feet, her red leather heels. And some blood. I didn't open the cubicle. I guess I started to scream."

"The police still haven't released her identity."

"No," the woman said. "I gather that. I didn't know she

was dead. I wasn't quite sure at the time. Only that she was on the floor. All I could see were her legs and her feet. And ... she wore expensive shoes."

"Not a street person looking for a place to spend the night then," Ferry said.

What was the woman about to say, Linda wondered, drifting off again even as she heard the word "blood." She was still hearing that word as the rest of the conversation disappeared into the void of sleep. When she awakened once more, she was surprised that she had missed the rest of the interview. She had also missed the news. What she heard now was the weather report that followed the seven o'clock news. She had a shift on the crisis line at noon that day and thought maybe she would find someone else to do it. She had not consented to any interviews because she did not want her voice heard on the radio or much less for herself to be seen on television. She used a pseudonym on the crisis line at work, but she knew her voice was recognizable and it mattered that she not be connected publicly to this event and thus to her work. Otherwise she could not maintain a situation that allowed both caller and counsellor the anonymity that made it safe for many women to break their silence for the first time.

Linda remembered her father belittling her mother, and that sometimes he hit her. It was not hard to understand why she had gravitated to this work. And her two marriages to men who had ultimately betrayed her might be why she stayed there. Sometimes she would become very angry at the stories of abuse and oppression that she heard during her work hours. But surely anger was what was called for. Anger led to action and action led to change. When men were angry, they did not get accused of being hysterical or strident or whatever other names she had been called in the course of her lifetime. She had been working a long time for change now, yet society seemed to be moving backwards. A whole raft of politicians continue to call women a special interest group! she thought. What mentality could possibly think this way? It was a throwback to the dinosaurs, for chrissakes.

Yet she knew that in the suburbs and in small town and rural Ontario where she came from, and,probably even in the city, that the dinosaurs were your neighbours, even your family.

It took tremendous effort for her not to become bitter, Linda often thought.

"I'm having a little problem with my husband." She would hear that phrase repeated almost in those exact words before the day was over, likely before the first hour of her shift was over. Before the end of the call, she would know that the woman's husband had tried to choke her. Or there would be something else that was so much more than a little problem. Was the woman in the church a victim of this kind of abuse? she wondered. Although her own experience with Ross two years earlier, when he had announced he no longer loved her and planned to leave, had left her cynical, she also knew the statistics.

As she had continued to lie there, she'd pondered the assumptions we make, the stories we tell ourselves in order to make sense of our existence. And how hers, suddenly cast in doubt that day, had undermined for a long time her confidence in rearranging the pieces. She was startled when the telephone rang. She looked at the clock and thought only one of her colleagues would be calling this early. If that were the case, it would be someone trying to change a shift.

"Hello," she said.

The caller identified himself as a police officer. It was Detective Jack Cosser, the same officer she had met at the church the previous day.

"I'd like to come by and talk to you," he said. "Would that be possible this morning?'

"Can you give me an hour?"

"Certainly."

When she hung up, she leapt out of bed. The sheets were

almost on the floor and the pillows were jammed together and creased. They would have to wait. Linda grabbed a black bra and a pair of matching pants from a basket beside her bed and headed toward the bathroom. She needed to shower, brush her teeth, and put on some makeup. She might as well dress for the office so she would not have to change again. That was simple enough. Since clients could not see her, she could wear what she wanted. So much for Ross and his desire to see her in skirts. Sometimes she had worn them and still did, but she found slacks much more comfortable.

Damn Ross, anyway. "I'll be flying out in two days," he'd said after breaking the shocking news to her. And he did just that, leaving her to freeze in a spring that refused to settle in even as the days became brighter. She remembered shivering in their bed, even when she was covered by the heavy duvet. As she showered, she recalled the bright red rhododendron Ross had planted in front of the window of their lanai in Florida. Sometimes she wondered if there had been some chemical change in his brain, some imbalance. She had not been sure she would sign the papers for the sale of the condo. Why should she? He did not even ask what she might want. Long before he knew her, there had already been a pattern. It seemed bizarre that she had considered herself immune, especially with the evidence of two ex-wives—she was now the third. Yet even now she could not remember any signs that might have given her a clue of what was to come.

Her thoughts shifted to the police officer. All she had done was go downstairs and stay, as requested by the minister, with the woman who had found the body. She knew nothing.

Too bad you could not get a police officer like the one who would soon be at her door to go out and do the dirty work, tie the guy's balls in knots. She stepped out of the shower and wiped her back with a fluffy green towel. Then she dried her breasts and under her arms, her legs and her feet. Looking at her figure in the mirror, Linda saw that she had gained a few more pounds. What did it matter? Here she was, alone in her apartment on a cool November morning, one of many suspects in a real murder, albeit not a very likely candidate. It was more likely that she would have murdered Ross, given the opportunity.

She moved to the bathroom where she stood in front of the medicine cabinet, the voices from the radio blurring.

Opening the cabinet door, she was annoyed to see many of Ross' things still there. Two years and he had neither taken them, nor had she discarded them. She put on her foundation powder, covering a red mark on her forehead. Then she found a box and put Ross's razor and bottles of after-shave and cologne in it. She took an old blue toothbrush from the shelf and threw it in the wastebasket. When she went back to her room, she saw his old dressing gown in the closet and threw it in the garbage also, wondering all the while why she had not done so ages ago.

She heard Randy Ferry announce that it was time for the hourly news again. She had almost lost track of the time and that the police officer was coming. There was a slight catch in Ferry's voice that always surprised her, such a rolling, mellifluous voice, and suddenly that fraction of an instant when a cough intruded. Were there people all across the region listening from their kitchens, their cars, their beds, wondering if he had a cold again? Or what else might cause the awkward moment he always managed to move through quickly? Once again the newscaster, someone different, talked about the body in the church, repeating what Linda had heard earlier. Either the police still did not know who the woman was or they were not releasing her identity. Linda thought about the man she had recently met at the church, the man with the white ribbon; he had not come back.

Just after she'd made a pot of coffee and was about to pour a cup, the doorbell sounded. Through the intercom, the caller identified himself as Detective Sergeant Jack Cosser.

Soon the officer was at her door. She let him in and offered him a cup of coffee.

"Thanks," he said as she poured the steaming coffee into two blue mugs on the kitchen counter.

"Would you like to sit down?"

"Thanks," he said again as she gestured at the table.

She sat down across from him and waited for him to speak.

"This is pretty routine," he said. "But there are a couple of things. Such as, we have to clarify when you might have been in the church because as a warden you have a key. And, I believe you probably see more than most people. I know I've already asked you, but we have to be certain we haven't missed anything. Also we now have identification."

"Oh, the radio broadcast said you didn't know yet."

"I imagine they're reporting now that we do. Her name was Margaret Atchison."

Linda shook her head. "The name doesn't mean anything to me."

She thought the detective was a handsome man, but she observed this from behind a wall she had erected around her that said *don't let anyone in.* She wondered if one day that might change and she would encourage the interest of some man she might meet by happenstance.

"I keep wondering about a man who wasn't there yesterday," she said. "He wore a white ribbon on his lapel. He was at the church the week before."

"Do you know his name?"

"No."

Cosser asked a few more questions.

"You know, I'd forgotten I have a key," she said. "Even though I use it from time to time. Mainly it's a backup for David and Brent. I do any paper or computer work for the church at home or in the office at the church, and that's in a separate building, so I rarely use the key I have."

More to the point, she had not been around the church at

the times Cosser asked about and she could provide evidence to prove it. Fortunately she had been with friends, something that could be verified easily. He asked her if she had the key in her possession and if she knew where it had been during the past weekend.

"It was on my key chain the whole time." It had not disappeared, nor had it been in anyone else's possession.

"I may have to contact you again," the detective said. "That's it for now."

"Sure," Linda said, smiling at him pleasantly as she walked him to the door.

After he left, Linda wondered why she had not mentioned that Rosemary might know the name of the man who had worn the white ribbon. After all, she had left the church with him that Sunday. But it did not seem that important. It was not as if he had come back. And Rosemary was alive and showed no signs of distress. She could call the detective at the police station, she supposed. Like everyone else from the church, she had been given his card with telephone and badge numbers, and was encouraged to call if she thought of anything that might be useful. She thought he had looked vaguely familiar, but was not sure why. She noticed the time. She would have to leave for work in fifteen minutes. As she slapped together a tuna sandwich and gathered up some papers she had brought home to review for a staff meeting, she remembered the community meeting where he had been the main rep from the police department.

20.

R EID WOULD HAVE BEEN WILLING to accompany him, Cosser thought, but he'd asked his colleague to stay at the station instead and go through all the lists of people Marni might have known, and to make sure all the lab reports and evidence that might have turned up were there so he could check in with him later in the day.

"And credit cards and all of that, too," Reid had added.

"I'll be back mid-afternoon," Cosser had said. "In time to speak to the couple who are moving to Vancouver. Before they actually pull up roots, although by now their lives are probably so disrupted that it will be a relief to board the plane. Claire and Harry Withrow. I understand the mover is picking up their things tomorrow and they'll be flying out after a night with friends near the airport."

"All right," Reid said.

"We can talk over who we'll interview and when, especially if you turn up anyone who appears to be a person of interest," Cosser said. "And thanks for making sure someone told Margaret Atchison's parents. How was that? Do you know?"

"Charlie told me that they were very quiet almost the whole time the officers were there. Almost unnaturally so," Reid said, referring to his colleague in the area who had gone to their home and relayed the news. "Said they hadn't seen her, except once, for twenty years. The mother showed a bit of emotion, shock really, and then tears. But very restrained tears. It might be worth looking into the relationships in that family."

Cosser nodded. That was one of the reasons he wanted to visit them himself, but also because he felt responsible for doing so as the detective in charge of the case. The news about their daughter was something no parent deserved to experience and he wanted to tell them everything he could. He had not previously questioned anyone in the Jehovah's Witnesses community, so he was keen to learn everything he could from Reid prior to this visit. Reid's colleague had told him the parents had appeared at the very least hungry for more information. It was not that Cosser had more he could tell them, but there were questions he needed to ask. Would they know if anyone had resented their daughter or her lifestyle beyond the rejection of their faith? If they did, would they tell him? Such rancour could have caused Marni's murder, Cosser knew. These were the avenues he would continue to follow. Who had a motive? Who had the opportunity? Soon he would have to pose these questions to Marni's parents, her brother, and her grandmother.

In the meantime, before driving out to the heartland of farming in southern Ontario, he placed a call to Claire and Harry Withrow to make arrangements to see them later in the day. That interview might be difficult, too. Cosser thought. The older couple had both struck him as frail, but he figured the upside was that they would be cleared easily. Still, they might have seen something that may have seemed even slightly incongruous as a result of being part of the church for a long time. They had certainly seemed observant.

"I'll be around this afternoon, probably on the late side," he told them. "I have to go out of the city on connected business this morning. When I know what time I'll be back, I'll call to make sure you are there. But I do have to see you some time today."

"Yes, of course," Harry said.

Cosser drove quickly on the Gardiner after this last call,

heading north to the 401 on another major highway, his destination in mind. It was a long time since he had ventured out into rural Ontario and with snow imminent, there would be no waving rows of corn in the fields. More likely everything would look brown and dry. Even the hay stacks would have been removed and the fields would lie fallow. He remembered from his grandparents' farm that this was the time of year when there was a bit of a respite rather than tasks that began at dawn and lasted till dark as they did in the planting, growing, and harvest seasons.

When he reached the exit that would take him toward the home of Marni's parents, he moved at a slightly reduced speed into the lane for northbound traffic. It was another half hour before he turned onto the gravel road up to a house with a sloping roof that seemed to sway toward the centre. As soon as he stopped, a door opened and a man came out and walked toward Cosser's car, a hand raised up to greet him.

As Cosser hopped out onto the gravel, his fleeting thought was that this man looked ominous as he hulked down the path toward him. He would already have experienced the first shock the night before when Reid's colleague arrived on their doorstep with the bad news. This was a job no police officer liked doing, knowing they had to deliver news no one ever wanted to hear.

He put out his hand with his card. "Mr. Miller, I'm Detective Sergeant Jack Cosser," he said. "I called earlier. I'm very sorry for your loss."

He watched Victor Miller scan his card and then meet his eyes, and found himself confronted by an impenetrable steely gaze.

"It was going to happen some time," the man said. "She didn't follow the way of Truth and anyone who doesn't suffers sooner or later."

Cosser took in a long, slow breath. "I've come from Toronto to tell you that the investigation is actively searching for a suspect."

"Come in then," Marni's father said. "Come in and tell my wife. She wants to know that."

"Of course," Cosser said, looking around as they moved through the door into a mud room where a tidy line of rubber boots leaned against one wall. There was a stack of *Watchtower* magazines piled high on a stool. Cosser acknowledged this was a unique experience for him, having only encountered Jehovah's Witnesses on street corners, or occasionally at his door.

"No, thank you," he had always said. Now for a brief moment, he wished he knew more about the kind of people who tried to convince others of the absolute truth of the path they followed. He did know that they believed they had a mission to "save" people, but their certainty always astonished him. He also knew they preached that the end of the world was at hand with such conviction that it was almost frightening to hear it. If he had listened to one or two of them more closely beyond the moment of discomfort when he was ready to slam the door in their faces, he might know what to expect. All he really knew now was that the names of Marni's parents were Caroline and Victor Miller.

"Come in," Victor Miller repeated gruffly.

The mudroom was attached to a warm kitchen where Caroline Miller was clearing away dishes from a table with a dark cloth spread over it. The heat seemed to come from a wood stove that was still in use, although electricity came into the house from poles strung out along the highway. The room was dull, Cosser thought, no pleasing or bright colours anywhere, just serviceable pots on the stove and plain dishes on the counter.

Cosser also handed Caroline Miller his card, and expressed his regret about her loss. It was sincere.

She nodded mechanically, as if she did not know how she was supposed to act. He had encountered these kinds of moments in other situations and did not find her behaviour nearly as unsettling as he found the steely eyes of her husband. He wondered what might be hidden behind them and sensed it would not be easy to find out.

"Please sit down, detective," the woman said, gesturing toward a wooden chair at the table.

Not knowing how else to conduct the interrogation that he would try to keep as short as possible, Cosser stayed on his feet, merely nodding at the woman. Victor Miller leaned on the counter, silently staring at the police officer. Cosser thought he would not be surprised if the man presented him with a copy of *The Watchtower*. Perhaps, feeling some respect and consideration for the loss of his daughter, Victor Miller chose not to do so.

He might sit soon, Cosser thought, but not before he had a better sense of the room and felt somewhat more comfortable himself. "I'm sorry," he said. "But I'm going to have to ask some questions. They're fairly routine at this stage. Things like the names of people you think your daughter might have known, people we ought to question."

"For twenty years we have had no contact with our daughter. Until a few days ago, after she called us out of the blue," Caroline Miller said.

Cosser refrained from commenting that he found not seeing their daughter for all that time a bit odd.

"She left," the father said, anticipating a question. "She was disfellowshipped."

This was a word Cosser had not heard before, but he understood that it meant she had been disowned as punishment for choosing to live her life on her own terms. Good for her, he thought. Although he hoped she had not ended up dead as a result of it. "What was the occasion for her call after all this time?" he asked.

"Her husband left her."

So, Cosser thought. Surely they would have had some contact around the grandchildren. But it turned out, to his surprise, that they had not.

"We've never met them," Caroline Miller said, eyes suddenly downcast. "We were hoping to. That's one reason we went to see Marni."

"And?"

"The boys weren't there. She did show us some photos."

"Mother," Victor Miller said. "Let's not get into that."

"Why not?" Cosser asked.

"We don't want to waste your time. Your job is to get on with finding whoever did this. Your job is to catch him, isn't it?'

Cosser watched the man's fists stiffen and wondered what this body language might mean. "It's all right," he said. "One way of finding something unexpected is to ask a lot of questions. Some of them may seem irrelevant, but some might well not be."

Victor Miller looked annoyed as he turned away.

"Do you have any other children?"

They told him about Marni's older brother, Leonard, who had a small farm up the road. He had never left the community, they said. And gradually Cosser learned about Kingdom Hall where they went to meetings and how they went out with leaflets three times a week, sometimes to districts far away from their own homestead.

"Do you have any photographs of Leonard and Marni when they were children?" Cosser asked. He was not sure quite why he asked, but thought their answer might tell him more about this family. Instead of saying anything, they turned toward each other with a quizzical look.

Victor shrugged and Caroline looked away.

Cosser heard a dog bark in the distance and the sound of a cat scratching at the door post. Now what? he wondered. Their behaviour was unusual, and not something he had anticipated.

"Has he been told about his sister?" Cosser asked.

"Yes. Yes. Yes," Victor Miller answered hurriedly. "He's supposed to be here by now."

And at that remark, Cosser heard the door to the mudroom open and a tall, lanky man in overalls entered the kitchen. The father introduced his son and Cosser took out his card again and offered it, then shook the man's hand.

"I'm sorry for your loss," he said to Leonard, as he had to the parents.

The man's lips were pressed closely together and he nodded slightly to acknowledge the comment.

It was another twenty minutes before Cosser felt he had exhausted his questions, but without learning anything more. He was struck by Leonard's passivity and how he deferred to his parents, Victor Miller in particular. There did not seem to be much grief in this family, but a comment Leonard made with a sudden spark of anger in his voice alerted him to something underlying the interview.

"She always was a troublemaker," Leonard said.

"How so?" Cosser asked.

"Oh you know. Had her own ideas. Didn't pay attention to the Truth."

Cosser did not respond to this, but changed the direction of his questions and concentrated on Marni as a child.

Leonard shrugged. "Well, I suppose we got on okay when she was six or seven, but even then she was different."

By the end of the interview, Cosser did not have anything concrete to go on, but knew he wanted to talk to each of them again, this time separately.

"I wonder if I might spend a few minutes with each of you on your own," he said.

The woman nodded, but he noticed that her husband, who had until then been quite detached, looked suddenly uncomfortable. His face set and he crossed his arms across his chest. "Nothing to say that my wife can't hear," he said gruffly.

"Even so," Cosser replied. There was something going on that did not seem like collusion so much as maybe Victor trying to keep something from his wife. But what? And why?

As it transpired, Miller did not say anything that Caroline could not have heard.

When he was ready to leave, Cosser said he would be in touch again and asked them to call him if they thought of anything.

"It might help the investigation."

AS HE DROVE BACK DOWN A ROAD with fallow fields on either side to the main highway, Cosser thought that it seemed this trip had been unproductive, but he had at least fulfilled his duty. At the next stop, he would check his messages. When he pulled up at a red light, he was not surprised to find a couple of messages from Reid. No doubt he was calling to let him know what had emerged from the reports from the various teams, he thought, as he called through to the station.

"I'll be a couple of hours on the highway," he said when he reached Reid. "Anything of interest?"

Reid told him the time of death was not yet pinpointed, but that the woman could have died outside of the church. Though, it also could have happened just after having been taken there. There was reason to suppose, Reid said, that someone had disposed of her body in the church basement washroom after she was already deceased, but there was nothing that would stand up as proof yet. And the distribution of the blood suggested otherwise.

"Anything else?"

"Yeah, she had one of those date rape drugs in her system that would have made her dopey, unable to defend herself."

"Good work," Cosser said.

"What about you?" his partner asked. "Was the trip worth it? "

"I don't know yet."

"That's not like you."

"There's something weird about that family. More so than most, but it's under wraps, whatever it is."

"It's probably that religious stuff. It would make anyone seem weird. They didn't get you to Kingdom Hall or distributing *The Watchtower*, I take it."

Cosser hesitated a moment, thinking about Victor Miller. "Actually," he said "There was something else and I want to find out what that is."

"In the meantime, what do you want me to do? Are you going to see the Withrow couple?"

"Keep doing what you are doing; stay on the case," Cosser said. "I am going directly to the Withrows. We need to know about Marni Atchison's contacts. Are you making any headway on that?"

"Yep."

"Unless I need to change plans this afternoon, hold it until we talk later."

"Okay."

"It will be in the papers already, on radio and TV. Might get some tips, cranks more than likely, but all of them have to be followed up."

"Roger."

Cosser could not think of anything else to say about the case. There would be plenty when he spoke to Reid later in the day. Now he feared that as soon as the connection was broken, left alone with his own thoughts, he would start to think about confronting his empty apartment again. No warm greeting from Marion when he opened the door. And it would likely be too late to call his daughter. He did not think he would ever get used to it. He wondered if Reid felt the same way since his own breakup.

"I'm really sorry about your girlfriend," Cosser said. "Kim."

"Oh, I expect it's all okay, Jack. I've met someone else, too."

"When do I get to meet her?"

"I don't know," Reid said. "It's complicated."

"Is she married or something?"

"Something."

"Oh." Cosser wondered how complicated it could be, so much so that Reid had become uncharacteristically reticent. He was not about to place his colleague on the spot though.

What he ought to do was end the conversation.

Just as he was about to do that, Reid spoke again. "His name is Chase."

Cosser was confused. Had he asked a question that he had forgotten? Reid could be talking about a new dog for all Jack knew.

"His?" Cosser said quizzically. "Whose?" Maybe he had not heard right. "Oh," he said as it suddenly dawned on him.

"Oh," Reid echoed.

"Well." That was all Cosser could muster. He did not comment on the name. He did not have anything to say in that moment.

"Over, out then," Reid said, as if answering a question.

"Roger," Cosser said.

When he reached the highway, Cosser was still thinking about what Reid had said. That was it then, whatever it was that had been niggling away at him about his colleague. And he was confronted with a whole different picture of Simon Reid's reality. They might never talk about it again, but it was there now, out in the open. He had cut Reid off almost as soon as he'd learned that his new interest was male. He had been surprised, but knew that that was only partially why he had stopped the conversation. Somewhere, he'd had a nagging suspicion of something and rather than startle him, he now knew that his previous slight uneasiness about Reid had fallen into the place.

He did not care if Reid preferred men, Cosser thought, although he did not want to think about the details. Details such as how a man could go from having sex with women to having sex with men. But Reid was still a good cop. That ought to be all that mattered. And a friend, too, he thought. Insofar as he had friends on the force. And how would he deal with it when others they worked with found out? How would Reid? He attempted to absorb the news and put it aside so he could focus on the afternoon ahead of him, but he knew everything had shifted and innuendo at the station could lead to repercussions for Reid. For him, too, although he was less worried about himself than his colleague. It was not the first time he had known about someone's orientation and had to deal with the fallout. But he was closer to Reid and even felt attracted to him at some level. Would that change now? Would he start to monitor himself closely because he was afraid his responses might be misinterpreted? He was glad that Reid was already involved with someone and he would not face overtures that he might understand but choose to ignore. That could happen anyway, he thought, but was less likely.

It had happened in the past, not from another cop, but in a bar. He had been wearing civvies so the other man had not actually known he was a police offer. They had been chatting over a beer, he and this man who turned out to be a tourist from over the border. He thought it had been Buffalo. Trim chest and arm muscles, summer revealing all the visible ripples. He'd turned the man down, then seen him put his hand on another bloke's arm just below a band of tattoos, and lean toward him. They had disappeared soon after, arms around each other, leaving the bar by then almost empty. The bartender had leaned over and said to Cosser, "Shouldn't be allowed. The Bible says only men and women. Disgusting." And Cosser, surprised by the bartender, had gotten up and left, and never gone back to that place. Now he was unsure if that had been a negative statement about the bartender's comment or his own reluctance to encounter another proposition from a gay man. Not that it couldn't happen anywhere, but that encounter had left an unpleasant taste in his mouth.

Finally Cosser's thoughts turned to the interview with the Withrows. He would contact them and let them know he would be there mid-afternoon, which he did, and then concentrated on driving as quickly as he could through heavy traffic back to Toronto. He recalled thinking that he and Reid were both men and had the same underlying drives that led them to act in similar ways. Would that perception of his change, he wondered. Then he thought it was still true that they were the same gender even though their orientation was different. And Reid was still Reid.

As he approached the Toronto skyline, the traffic increased and the distance between him and the tall buildings ahead diminished. There were dark clouds gathering behind him and he hoped he would make it before either snow or rain hampered his return to the metropolis where he knew Reid, if he chose to, or anyone for that matter, could almost disappear into the variety of people who populated this city.

An hour later, Cosser was at the door of the Withrow's apartment. He was not surprised to see the room he was invited into was overflowing with boxes. Claire carefully navigated the area, stepping around one carton after another. There were large black numbers written on white labels to indicate what was inside each box and what room in the new place it was destined for.

"Harry is so organized," Claire said. "I ought to be used to this after all the moves we've made, but I'm always thrown by the amount of chaos and all the boxes."

She walked between the stacked piles toward the bathroom. Jack imagined it would be hard to leave an apartment that looked as if they'd lived there for many years. A little easier now that it no longer looked like a home.

Cosser wondered if Claire Withrow hoped her pain and the limp would get better. Even though over the years her body had likely changed gradually and she'd become accustomed to it each time, this felt to the detective like a different kind of change, like something that could limit her and make her dependent. Cosser hoped their plans to move west would work out. Would their children, whom he understood had been urging them for almost four years now to make the move, have the time and patience for aging parents?

"Friends from the church came and helped pack," Harry said.

"All the china, glassware, kitchen utensils, and books. All I did when they were here was write out those labels you see."

Cosser nodded. "Big job," he said, looking around.

"Well," said Harry. "If giving directions about what needs to be done next is a big job." Although, he told the detective, he'd collected piles of newspapers to protect all the fragile pieces of their accumulated years—the plates, cups, and glasses. The knick-knacks.

"Looks as if everything is under control," Cosser said. "When the movers come, they'll only have to take it all down to the truck."

The telephone rang. Harry answered it and from his end of the conversation it was clear the movers were confirming their time of arrival the next morning. When she came out of the bathroom, Harry told Claire what the arrangements were. She looked so tired, as if another session with the police would completely exhaust her.

Cosser wished he could just leave them in peace for their final day here. His presence must be rather frightening for them. Harry told him that in Canada they had never had the police arrive at their door. "It was alarming in China in the last year when we never knew what to expect. Ultimately we had to leave."

"Guns bother me," Claire said. "I'm a peace activist from way back."

Cosser thought that she could also be unsure she trusted the police any more, a common occurrence for him to hear about. One he had to work around to gain the respect of the community and now, today, this elderly couple. People who were exhausted and, he felt sure, had been inadvertently caught in the midst of the investigation by virtue only of attending their church on Sunday.

Cosser handed them his card. "I want you to know how to contact me, should you remember anything that might be important," he said.

"There's really no place to sit down," Harry said.

"You folks make yourselves as comfortable as you can," Cosser said. "I'll stand. No problem."

So Harry cleared the sofa in one corner and Claire found a chair that was not piled high with boxes.

"We have plans for dinner with friends," Claire said, confirming Cosser's hunch about their last hours in Toronto. She and Harry sat close to each other and he could stand not far away from them on the parquet floor from which the rugs and carpets had already been removed. Harry reached over and touched Claire's hand and she looked at him, her glance a testament to all the years they'd spent together. There was a warmth and comfort about it that was in stark contrast to the couple he had interviewed that morning, the reflection also of trust that had sustained them.

You must get to know someone in a lifetime, Cosser thought. At least if you were open and honest with each other. But recalling the Millers, he thought the dogmatic truth they believed in kept them from what existed between this pair.

"Then we're staying tonight with our friends," Harry said.

"In an apartment that overlooks the end of one of the runways at Pearson," Claire added.

Cosser wondered if from this apartment they would watch the lights on the planes as they landed and took off, their direction depending on that of the wind.

"And in the morning, they'll drive us back here to meet the movers and lock the door before we leave to catch our flight to Vancouver," Harry said.

He did not seem to be implying in his polite way that this was itself sufficiently taxing and now they had to contend with a police investigation. No, he was still as hospitable as one could be under the circumstances.

"I can see that you have plenty to do without this," Cosser said, wanting to alleviate whatever strain his presence created, even though it was not apparent in their demeanour. What showed was fatigue more than anything else. "It's important for the police to get as much information from you as we can before you leave," he continued. "Neither of you are suspects and we don't have to detain you in any way."

Claire scrutinized him, likely noting the wavy brown hair that was cut fairly short, a recent cut, matched his eyebrows. Or at least that was often what people he knew said to him. He could feel Claire thinking: he's young, probably around forty. Behind the pleasantries he was now uttering, would she see steel in his eyes as Marion, his former wife, had in their last months, something cold? Was he not so different from Victor Miller? No, that could not be true. But he knew he wore his own version of a mask to keep from being overwhelmed by the trauma he encountered. Still, as his ex-wife knew, there were also all the hours police officers spent in doughnut shops. Tim Horton's. One more cigarette. The long hours on the beat could be boring, and trying.

"You remind me a bit of our son," Claire said. "He's not a policeman. He's a social justice advocate for labour and human rights groups. He's been out on picket lines on the west coast. He's been arrested..." Her voice trailed off, as if she were suddenly wondering what he could have in common with a policeman.

What Cosser surmised was that it was likely he was around the same age as their son and also more immersed in a world that had become so much more complex in the last couple of decades than theirs was.

"Clive will meet us at the airport on Sea Island," Harry said. "He'll drive down from Kitsilano where he and his wife, Nancy, have a house that looks out over the water. They have renovated it slowly over the years and it's filled with mementos."

Claire nodded, directing her next comment at her husband. "Nancy seems glad we're moving out there." Her glance turned to the detective again. "If we reach the stage of not being able to look after an apartment, we won't move in with Clive and

Nancy. In this society, that's an unfair burden to place on one's children."

"But some bridges you can't cross until the time comes," Harry said, looking fondly at his wife.

"True," she said. "No one can know what will happen, whether we'll become gradually less mobile, have more pain, or even get Alzheimer's."

Harry nodded.

Cosser watched their interaction, feeling their angst at the thought of their aging. The poor woman was having enough difficulty getting around already, he thought. She might die suddenly. Or Harry might. Likely these thoughts had been on their children's minds for a while. He was glad his own parents were not that far away, just up the highway an hour, in Barrie.

"I want to ask what you can tell me about a number of people who were in church yesterday morning," Cosser said. "Did you notice anyone who isn't regularly there? And I know that there are often people who aren't, so that doesn't necessarily indicate anything unusual. Who did you notice?"

He had a pad and as they talked, he jotted short notes, then looking at the two people opposite him straight in the eye, he nodded. Anyone who had come up against him likely knew better than to cross him, although most of the time he was so gentle with these two that one might imagine small animals like squirrels had been known to hover around him.

Cosser could see a veil creep across Claire's eyes and knew the signal, one that suggested the person felt invaded as he asked about friends they had known for years. But he also suspected she knew little about the lives that most of their fellow churchgoers lived away from the church. Rob, for instance, so gentle and yet Cosser had already discovered him to be a quiet drinker. What did they know about him? Well, that was one person he suspected they did know more about than some of the others.

"He wouldn't hurt anyone," Claire said. "You can't imagine that Rob did anything."

"These are standard questions and standard procedures," Cosser said. "We have to ask about everyone. And if you think of something I've overlooked, something odd you might have noticed yesterday, about anyone or anything, I'd appreciate it if you would tell me."

"Yes, of course," Claire said. "That poor woman."

It was apparent to Cosser that Claire did not want to have to deal with this now in the midst of all her mixed feelings about leaving. It was no doubt enough that their last morning at the church had been totally disrupted.

"Yes," he said. "Thank you for your cooperation in difficult circumstances."

"You have to credit David, really," she said.

"For?" Cosser asked.

"It's amazing that the people remained involved in whatever could be preserved of the service, that the food was eventually eaten, that speeches were made."

"I see what you mean," he said.

"Although it is time for a change," Harry said, looking now at his wife.

"What kind of change?" Cosser asked.

"Well," said Claire. "Maybe for a younger minister, perhaps for a woman."

Cosser nodded as if he had known the church for a long time, which, of course, he had not. To listen to them might turn up something unexpected. And if it did not, he was still doing something for the investigation by keeping options open. He never knew what might emerge that could offer something further to explore.

"Well," said Harry. "It's hard to imagine what the bishop was thinking when he approved David for the post. Maybe he had the foresight to see David as a bridge. It is, after all, an interim position he's filling."

"That would explain the choice," Claire said. "Someone able to remain unnoticed might have been the best person to give a congregation of such activists a chance to define needs for the future."

"I'm going to change the topic," Harry said. "Something you said earlier." He was studying Cosser. "Rob wouldn't hurt anyone," he said. "Claire is right about that."

"What about the caretaker? What do you know about him?"

"Not much," Claire said. "He does his job. Mostly he remains aloof. I don't see him as a killer. He's sympathetic with some of the needier and more disadvantaged folks who come to the church. We hope he'll extend his contract. It's healthy to have someone who has other dimensions in that job and it's rare to find that person."

"Do you know anything about his personal life?"

"No."

"What about the minister?"

"Surely he isn't under suspicion," Claire said.

Harry did not say anything and Cosser figured it must be because he realized no others had more access to the church during off-hours than the minister and the caretaker. It was not that either of them would ever suspect the minister of anything, but they would understand why the police would have to eliminate any possibility that he might have been involved in some way. Until they discovered someone who was obviously guilty, or there were foolproof alibis for the minister and the caretaker, the lives of both men would indeed be under very close scrutiny.

"I've wondered," Harry pondered. "Oh no, not about David. But about that man who came to church a couple weeks ago. You know, Claire. The one who was wearing a white ribbon on his lapel, and who talked with Linda and left with Rosemary. I couldn't figure that situation out. There was something not quite ordinary about it and Rosemary is, after all, if nothing else, quite ordinary."

"Well, she's certainly quiet," Claire said. "Who's to know if she leads an ordinary life?"

Harry nodded.

"Works in a library, I think. Goes around with her head in the clouds. Always has a book tucked in her bag. Don't see her socializing much. Except for those phone calls and visits she does for the church," Claire mused thoughtfully. "The man was handsome and attentive to her, although I didn't get the impression they knew each other well. Did you see her interrupt the conversation with Linda? The man looked surprised when he saw her, as if he were meant to meet her, but hadn't known what she would look like."

"I guess everyone is going to jump to conclusions about each other," Harry said. "It's so upsetting to think of the community being filled with suspicion because of this."

"Tell me more about this man," Cosser said. He had not given people a chance to comment further on the white ribbon man and this was the first he had heard of the circumstances that included Rosemary breaking in on a conversation between the man and Linda, something apparently foreign for her, and that she was the one who left with him shortly afterward. He also noted that of all the people he had interviewed, Rosemary was one of only a few who had not mentioned him. It struck him that even though this man had not been in the church on the day of the murder, his presence earlier was so memorable that most of the people he had questioned could not resist commenting on seeing him.

"I can only describe him," Harry said. "I don't know a thing about him. I'd think Rosemary would be the one with those answers."

"We're looking for everyone's perspective."

It was like a huge jigsaw puzzle with most of the important pieces still missing. Or perhaps some of them were right in front of everyone's noses and no one had seen them yet. For aside from the caretaker, the minister, and the man with the white ribbon, what other suspects were there? Although now that they had an ID, there were more people to consider, to interview. The ex-husband already had an alibi. Was it someone else in Marni's family? But nothing had emerged from his interview with the parents or the brother.

"I hope you clear it up quickly because in the meantime women all over the city will be more nervous," Harry said.

"And they'll have reason to be," Claire said. "We all will."

"Of course," the detective said. "The primary aim of the investigation is just that, to get this solved as quickly as possible."

"Has suicide been ruled out?" Claire asked.

Cosser did not immediately answer. "The investigation is at such an early stage that those kinds of details aren't yet public. I can't really say anything yet." He chose his words carefully. "It will depend on the forensic investigation."

Nonetheless, there was a head wound and somewhere there must be a blunt weapon. There would hopefully be some telling evidence from forensics to identify a criminal, he thought, very clear himself that what had happened was a crime; the amount of blood alone indicated that the murder had more than likely taken place right there in the basement washroom of the church.

21.

Patsy's day at the bank had been eventful—markets were sliding. This had led to worried calls and, unexpectedly, a new client. Arriving at home, she found an envelope on the hall floor under the mail slot. Inside it was a message from Chris on lined paper that had been torn out of a notebook, giving her the address of his father's house. "Dean and I are here," he wrote. There was also a phone number. The note said that they had come to pick up some clothes, books, and their boom box.

Patsy pondered the note as she poured herself a cup of coffee, hoping for a rare moment of quiet before going to pick Sasha up at the daycare centre. The ongoing politics and manoeuvring of the workplace had been harder to deal with than usual because she was upset about Marni. She noticed now how quiet the house next door was. While she wanted to talk to the boys, she hesitated to call their father's home. Maybe this was the day to make contact. So she dialed the number and left a brief message on an answering machine, relieved not to have to talk to their father. She did not like anything Marni had told her about him. Although earlier in the day, she had wanted to ask him about the funeral. At first, she had not even been sure there would be one or where it would be. Or who was planning it. If the former husband were a suspect, how would that affect the funeral, where the boys would live, everything? Marni's family? Had Marni left instructions for anything like a premature death? But now Patsy knew from the newspaper that the funeral would be the next day in a church in the suburbs. That morning she had made arrangements to be off work for the afternoon. If she did not talk to the boys sooner, she would see them then. The church was the one their father went to, she gathered. She was sure this would not have been Marni's choice, nor would anything her parents might have decided been either. Patsy suspected she would rather have had a memorial celebration outdoors on a beautiful day and her ashes scattered. Now she would probably be put in a casket and buried under the earth in a cemetery she would have known nothing about. What did it matter? No box could confine Marni's spirit.

Marni had told Patsy what it was like to start to question the precepts in a fundamentalist household. How she gradually withdrew and finally left, how her family, even her brother, disowned her. "I have no one," she had said. Although it was clear that she'd had friends and that she'd been a good mother to her two bright and lively sons. All the same, she'd always been careful, aware that her family would try to lure her back, that sometimes she was watched by strangers. She'd told Patsy she was not sure if it was intentional, but when it became a pattern, she was more careful. Nothing could dampen her internal life though, she told Patsy.

"Have you ever fantasized about having sex in a church?" she asked one day when they had started to confide in each other.

"No," Patsy said. "That's one I've never thought of." She had not told Marni a great deal about her Methodist up-bringing in Jamaica, about a church founded by John Wesley where the work ethic had been such a strong component. As a participant, you were actively involved in an act of salvation. It was a surprise to her that in Toronto, the church that oc-casionally comforted her was Anglican, when her experience of that denomination in Jamaica was of something so close to Roman Catholicism that it was wholly alien to her. The community at Holy Trinity interested her with its openness and focus on social justice though. All the same, not many of the members of the congregation had dark skin like hers. There would be a great deal of work to do if they were to be truly inclusive.

"People do," Marni continued.

"What? Fantasize about it?" Patsy replied, somewhat bewildered.

"Do it."

"I don't know that I really want to know, but since I do now, let me say I know people do it in washrooms on airplanes," Patsy said. "The first time I saw two people come out of one of those tiny cubicles, I thought they must be nuts. And then it dawned on me. I suppose it's some kind of challenge."

"Maybe they just couldn't wait."

"Yeah, sure."

"I wouldn't be surprised if people even found ways to have sex on altars in churches," Marni said.

"Why not underneath them?" Patsy asked. To her it seemed more likely the act would happen under an altar covered with a cloth that went down to the floor. Either way, it would be sacrilege, but underneath the cloth, it would at least be more private.

Marni had told her this fantasy had something to do with imagining her parents together, and since she could only visualize them in religious places, she used to surmise it must take place there. "I know it's kind of kinky," she said. "They were too straitlaced to do anything that imaginative. I don't think they had fantasies. I think I imagine doing it in a church because it would enrage them. Daughter of Jehovah's Witnesses discovered having intercourse on pew in local church after minister has left for the day. Or with minister. What do I know? Find a lecherous minister and entice him into his place of work and seduce him. I mean, it happens in workplaces all over. Politicians do it, I wager. And professors. Why not in a church?"

"Yeah, but would they do it in the council chamber or in a classroom?" Patsy asked.

They laughed uproariously. This was, of course, long before any body was discovered. This was when Marni was still alive and full of *joie de vivre*. But as Patsy considered that Marni had likely been murdered, she recalled these conversations. Somehow, she was not ready to share them—not with the police, not with anyone. How would exposing Marni's fantasy life help her friend now?

Patsy sat down on a chair in the kitchen across from where Marni had so often sat sharing a cup of coffee with her. Who could have killed her? She was such a gentle woman, so devoted to her sons. So she had had a vivid imagination. It was the source of marvelous stories and lots of laughter. She visualized Marni on stage in a solo performance. Her chum could have done that. Patsy had often been doubled over with laughter. They'd been good for each other. Patsy's eyes filled, tears streaming silently down her cheeks.

The phone rang—it was the daycare centre. *Where are you?*

"Oh my goodness," Patsy said. "I lost track of the time. I'll be right there."

She went outside and walked to the curb where she had left her small white Toyota. There was a man at the bank who drove a BMW with MYPERK on the license plate. I don't think so, Patsy thought. She had wanted something reliable and not too expensive when she bought the Toyota. If she had a perk in mind, it was more likely to be a trip to Jamaica. Yes, she thought, how she would love to stretch out on one of the beaches beside the blue green water of the Caribbean. That was her fantasy. And as soon as she could take some time off, she would leave Sasha with her mother for a week and fly south with Aloha. They would go to the island that held all her childhood memories and to Stony Hill, the area where she had lived just outside of Kingston, the residents a mix of poor and affluent. It was cooler there and many of the houses overlooked the bay. At twelve, old enough to go to school at Excelsior, she had done well enough to earn a scholarship where she had boarded with the Methodist deaconesses and had gone home on weekends. When Marni told her about the Jehovah's Witnesses, she remembered that on Sundays they'd knocked on the deaconesses' door and the girls who boarded there considered it an act of total disrespect. Until she met Marni, that was her only experience of the Witnesses.

22

COSSER WALKED QUIETLY, but with determination, into the suburban United Church where the funeral for Margaret Atchison was scheduled to start in fifteen minutes. He was there to see who came that day for whatever reasons. He would watch to see if there was any strange, or unexpected behaviour among those who attended. Without a suspect who did not have an alibi, it was part of his job to attend this funeral. There was also a plainclothes officer in the church, but he was careful not to look at the woman off to the side in her modest attire, a grey check suit with a white blouse.

From where Cosser sat in an aisle seat toward the back, he had a full view of everyone who came in. Patsy's face was the first familiar one he saw, but deep in thought she did not notice him. As he continued to look over the faces of those gathered for the service, he was disappointed to see no one who appeared to be from that earlier part of Marni's life in the Jehovah's Witnesses community. Maybe they were with the family in a private room until the service began, he thought.

He watched as the stragglers arrived. Finally the minister appeared from behind a door at the side with Marni's ex, Richard Atchinson, and their two sons. The younger boy wore sunglasses and clung to his father's hand. It seemed the boys were comfortable with this man who, by now, Cosser knew had abused his wife. Marni's parents were not there, their absence still speaking to their rejection of their daughter.

Although Cosser was surprised they had not wanted to attend, if only to see their grandchildren. By now, he knew they'd never met the two boys and likely Richard did not want them to do so, so they might have tried to convince Richard they had a right to be at their daughter's funeral. Or maybe not. He did not know. Although he would ask Atchinson when he had the opportunity. He'd never been able to understand the way a rift could develop in families for reasons that made no sense to him and continued to exist for the same, or just as ludicrous, reasons.

The service started with the minister speaking from the front of the church. He had not known Marni, but Richard regularly attended this church now. So the minister talked about Marni with some of what he had gleaned from his new parishioner. And, as he said, from her two sons. He turned to include Chris and Dean in his remarks, but their eyes were cast down.

Patsy also sat in an aisle seat, in front of Cosser on the other side. He saw her reach for a tissue and wipe her eyes. He would talk to her later, although he did not expect that she would have any more information. She'd told him she would have liked to help out with Marni's boys, but there had been no way to say that to their father. He wondered if she would find a way to talk to Richard after the funeral.

"Marni told me he didn't ever hurt the children," Patsy had told Cosser in their interview. "And I believe her. But I know they would have been affected by how he treated their mother." It profoundly saddened her to think that Marni would not be around for them.

Cosser pondered these comments again. What would happen to the boys if their father turned out to be the one who had killed their mother? He hoped Richard, whose alibi thus far was unassailable, and corroborated by his sons, would not turn out to be that person. It would be irresponsible to dismiss the possibility of pressure on the boys, or some plot that the man was involved in and maybe carried out by someone else. Even though he was such an obvious suspect, Cosser thought the children would be better off with him, were he innocent, than with the Jehovah's Witnesses, even knowing that his thoughts were tinged with his own biases.

A man hurried into the church and walked by Cosser, up the aisle to a seat mid-way on the edge. Cosser wondered what connection he had with the people assembled that day. With his bald head and a tattoo of an anchor on the back of his shaved skull, he stood out from the others. Here was something he would want to look into it as soon as the service ended, Cosser thought.

After the minister spoke, Cosser half listened to the music, perking up when Richard went forward to make a short speech. He said he was very sad to lose this special woman who was such a good mother to his children. His demeanour did not suggest that he had ever hit her, but Cosser knew that was often the way with men who had abused their intimate partners. Many that he had arrested were involved in their communities with no hint that they could ever hurt anyone. It was also often true that there were those who refused to believe it even when these abusers were arrested and convicted, although public perception had started to change slightly.

After the service was over, everyone was invited for a light lunch in a room upstairs. Wanting to watch people until they left the church, Cosser stayed in his pew, taking note that the bald man also went upstairs. He noticed the minister from the downtown church file out with the people who were leaving. He had not seen David speak with Patsy and now, as the minister glanced in her direction, Cosser noticed she was talking with the ex. Cosser wondered if the minister had spoken earlier with Richard, then assumed he must have. When the rest of the people had moved off down the steps onto the street, Cosser followed those who had gone to the lunch. He moved quietly over to where Patsy was standing by trays of sandwiches.

"Oh, hello," she said.

"Hello."

"Do you always go to funerals of victims of crime?" she asked.

"No. But not infrequently."

"I thought someone in Marni's family might have come."

Cosser acknowledged her comment with a nod. He noticed that she had not asked him why he was there. Maybe it was obvious that when a case was still open, a funeral might turn up information, even leads.

At that moment, Richard approached them and Patsy turned toward him.

"I wondered if we could talk again for a moment," Richard said to Patsy.

She nodded and they moved slightly away from Cosser. Aware that he could still hear them and that he wanted to keep them within earshot, Cosser turned toward the table and picked out an egg salad sandwich. It was difficult to remain within the range of their voices as others also chimed up around him.

"I spoke to the boys," he heard Patsy say.

"Yes," Richard said. "I want to thank you for that. It matters a lot to them."

Patsy looked surprised, as if she found it hard to believe this was the same man who had hurt her friend. "They're welcome to come and visit. I know Sasha would like that, too."

Cosser noticed the boys were coming up behind their father. Both of them nodded hopefully when they saw Patsy. She leaned forward to hug them. "Miss you," she said. "Love you."

"Maybe next week?" Richard said.

"Would you like me to call you to make arrangements?" Patsy asked. "I don't get home till after five most days, but if that isn't too late, maybe they'd like to come after school."

Cosser thought they might not go much longer to the school near the house where they had lived with their mother. If he were their father, he'd want them closer to his home, but maybe not until the next school year. They moved away then and he could not hear any more of that conversation. He looked around to see who was left in the church and noticed that it was almost empty now. He went upstairs to look for the bald man with the tattoo, but he was nowhere in sight. He watched the washroom door, thinking this man might emerge, but when the door opened shortly afterwards, it was someone else who came out. It was then that Cosser noticed another staircase and dashed toward it. The man with the tattoo was pushing an exit door at the back, but it seemed to be stuck.

"Hang on a minute," Cosser said, holding out his badge.

"What's up?" the man asked.

"I have a couple questions for you."

"Yeah, okay. What questions?"

"Do you have a reason for being at the funeral?"

The man shrugged, his eyebrows rising. "Yeah. Sure. Of course."

"Did you know her?" Cosser asked.

"No," he said.

"So you came because..."

"She was a friend of a friend."

"And that's it?"

"Yeah, that's it."

"Your friend could not come."

"Out of town. Wanted to pay her respects. Asked me."

The man started to push on the back exit door again and went hurriedly through it, heading toward a row of cars in the parking lot. Cosser watched until he saw the tail end of a BMW move quickly round the corner. The man did not fit any description the investigation had thus far gathered, but Cosser regretted not asking the man for his name.

He went back to the reception to look around before he left to see if anything else might give him some insight into what had happened to Marni, but all he saw were a few remaining people eating sandwiches and chatting quietly. No one from the Jehovah's Witnesses community seemed to be there. It was time for him to slip away and get on with the information he had already gathered. All he had found out at the funeral was that the walls Marni's family had built by excluding her were so pervasive that they extended even beyond her death. It continued to surprise him that they were not trying to create bridges with their grandchildren, but from what he had gathered thus far, their father was not about to change his mind about that.

As he went toward the stairs, Cosser acknowledged the plainclothes officer with a quick gesture. If she stayed longer, he could go without missing anything. Although he suspected there was nothing further to learn there.

23.

PATSY REMEMBERED MARNI'S VOICE as she talked about a time when her husband had tried to choke her. "I would give anything not to know what it feels like to have my eyes almost pop out of my head," she'd said.

After the separation and divorce, it turned out he was not one of those men who harassed a woman from the moment she left, who followed and threatened her. Surely he was not the person who had followed her into the church in the centre of the city, down into the basement where the washrooms were. If they did not know already, the police would find out soon enough that Marni had left her marriage because of all the times her husband had hit her. Though she suspected that might be the reason for the detective's presence at Marni's funeral.

She thought of Richard's efforts to see that Chris and Dean visit with her and Sasha. He'd even said before she left the lunch after the funeral service that he had not been a good husband and he regretted that, but that he would be a better father. It was clear that he loved his boys. She hoped he would get whatever help he needed to deal with them. She was not altogether confident, knowing how her own ex had apologized and promised to change, but once she forgave him, the abusive behaviour began again not long afterwards.

"I just can't do this. Why does this have to be my life?" Marni had said one day when she was certain she was being followed again. It could have been the ex-husband, but Marni had not thought so. More likely it had been someone from the Jehovah's Witnesses community, because by then it had been going on for years. But who? And why? She never saw anyone she recognized. That earlier experience had controlled her life as much as her husband had. Yet Marni had been sure that she would escape and she had rarely succumbed to despair. Patsy missed most of all the times they had laughed together. She was about to go and see if Sasha was awake when the telephone rang.

"Hi Patsy, this is Rosemary. From the church."

Patsy did not know Rosemary very well, although they did greet each other in passing at the peace when people shook hands or hugged. It was a time of sharing what Christ offered that preceded the gathering around the altar for communion when the prayers of the people were also offered.

Perhaps she was on a telephone tree that Rosemary had been given to call, Patsy thought. The church community had taken on the aura of being a family, but at this moment she did not trust it.

"I didn't have a chance to talk to you last Sunday," Rosemary said. "It wasn't a happy time to be there. I hope you'll be back next week."

"I don't think so." Patsy did not want to be in the building where Marni's body had been discovered. It might make it impossible for her ever again to be part of that community.

"There's going to be a memorial for the woman who was found here," Rosemary said.

"But that's bizarre," Patsy said in a spontaneous response to what to her seemed ludicrous. "Marni wouldn't want that. Not in a church. I assure you."

"I don't understand. The woman's name was Margaret. And no one here knew her."

"Well, I did. She was my neighbour. She lived on the other side of the semi I live in. And she was my friend as well. And to her friends, she was Marni."

"I see," Rosemary said. "Does David know that? Does anyone at the church?'

"I wouldn't know. Although David was at her funeral and he probably saw me there. There was no chance to talk with him then and he didn't stay for the reception. All I can say is you might want to let someone know that Marni wouldn't have gone into a church by choice and she wouldn't want anyone remembering her there."

"My understanding is that the intent of this service is not to publicize it as being for a particular person, but as a healing ceremony for the congregation. It was very difficult for everyone to go through the discovery and the police presence. It still is."

"I can imagine."

"So, will you come?"

"No."

She suspected Rosemary would be even sorrier to hear she likely would not go back at all, but she decided this was not the time to tell her. All Patsy knew was that it would be a while before she could go anywhere near the place. She could visualize the washroom. She could visualize Marni's body being carried out on a stretcher. She wanted to know who had killed her friend and how she had died. She wanted the case to be solved. She was nervous, too. How could she be certain that whoever followed Marni did not know that she was a single woman also, that she lived alone and was vulnerable? She tried to focus on Sasha.

"Could someone come and visit you at your home?" Rosemary asked, interrupting Patsy's train of thought.

"Pardon?" Patsy said. Her mind far away by then—she had forgotten that Rosemary was still on the other end of the line. She rather liked Rosemary. She would not mind knowing her better, but she did not want to see anyone from the church for a while.

"Not for the time being," she said. "After the police get through with all their questions. Maybe then. I don't know."

Sasha started to holler.

"I hear your child," Rosemary said. "I'll let you go, but either I or someone else will call again. All right?"

"I guess so."

Patsy went to Sasha's room, picked him up and held him against her. She breathed deeply. This child gave her joy and some sense of normalcy. He struggled in her arms. She knew he was both wet and hungry. She laid him down in his crib on a towel with colourful owls on it, the word *Who?* written underneath each owl. She unzipped his navy pyjamas and removed his diaper. He'd made another huge poop. She reached for a wet cloth to clean up his bottom, but she was not fast enough and a stream of urine hit her in the face. The baby laughed as she grimaced and wiped her cheek.

"You rascal," she said.

She heard someone at the door, but ignored the knocking as she cleaned Sasha and powdered his bottom, then attached a new diaper. She heard the knocker again.

"Oh, go away," she muttered. But she lifted Sasha out of the crib and went down the stairs. Through the curtain over the front door, she could see the detective who had also been at the funeral. "Oh, not again," she murmured. What did they want now?

"Detective Sergeant Jack Cosser," the officer said. "Sorry to trouble you so soon again."

Yes, yes, she thought. Just get on with it.

The detective was with the same officer who had been with him when he came to her house before, but he left the questions to Cosser.

"Do you know how Mrs. Atchison had planned to spend that weekend? Or anything about what she actually did?"

I wish, Patsy thought. For all she knew, Marni finally had her wish to have sex with someone under the altar of a church, but she was damned if she was going to say so. What seemed likelier was that Marni was shopping and had to go to the bathroom, that she had known there was a washroom in the basement of the church, that someone had followed her there. But all that was speculation.

"We had coffee on Thursday after her boys left to visit their father. That's the last time I saw her. Although she was going to pop in on the Sunday; she obviously never did."

She was irritated at being asked the same questions over and over. Were they any closer to an arrest? It did not seem likely or they would not be asking her about Marni's final movements. Most of all, she wanted them to leave.

"Thursday," Cosser said.

"Yes," Patsy said. Would they have her go on repeating herself? She was distracted enough. She was on the verge of tears now. And she would have to work at the bank each day as if nothing had happened. It was enough that as a black woman she had risen to a managerial position. If she became emotional or if they ever found out she was lesbian or bisexual, she suspected any career aspirations she might have would be demolished.

She answered the rest of their questions politely, but tried to remain calm and somewhat removed from it all. It was almost time to feed Sasha again before putting him down for the night. She was relieved when the detective thanked her and both cops left.

Patsy dialed Aloha's number. When her lover answered, she started to cry.

"What's the matter?" Aloha asked.

"Can you come over?"

There was a slight hesitation on the other end of the line before Aloha said she would come.

Patsy fed Sasha some pureed green beans that he tolerated, followed by some squash that he loved. Then she gave him a cup of milk with a small spout on the top he could drink through. She had nursed him for a long time, but now that her maternity leave was over and he went to the daycare centre, she had weaned him. He gurgled contentedly and put his hand in the bowl that she, distracted more than usual, had not removed. Soon the tray on the high chair and his face were covered in green. In another frame of mind, she might have taken a photograph, Patsy thought. But the camera was on the upper floor and she would likely have many opportunities like this.

She lifted the baby out of the high chair and carried him upstairs where she ran a tub of lukewarm water and set him on a blue bath mat in the middle. When the rubber duck she put in the water floated toward him, he laughed loudly and splashed with his arms and legs. She laughed with him and covered his stomach with water, then took a cloth and wiped his face and behind his ears. Soaping the lower part of his body, she leaned him over her arm while she splashed water on his bottom. When Aloha arrived, he was clean and dressed in pale blue pyjamas, clutching the bunny her colleagues at the bank had sent when he was born. That had surprised her. It was an undemonstrative group and she knew her rank was often resented.

Aloha held Sasha while Patsy cleaned up in the bathroom. She could hear Aloha crooning and talking to the baby. Aloha was around often enough now that he no longer acted as if she were a stranger by screaming for his mother. She hoped this woman would be around for a long time, although the thought of what that might mean was almost too frightening to contemplate. Living alone suited Patsy.

"So what's the matter?" Aloha asked as soon as Patsy returned.

"Let's go downstairs," Patsy said.

When they were sitting at the table in the kitchen, Patsy asked if Aloha had eaten.

"There you go," Aloha said. "Looking after me instead of yourself. Are you going to tell me now why you sounded so upset when you called?"

So Patsy told her about the police officers coming to the house on Sunday looking for Marni. "Margaret they called her." And finding out that her friend was dead.

Aloha sighed. "Oh my," she said. "I wish you'd called sooner."

"I thought you were away."

"I check my messages."

"I didn't think of it. I just kept wondering why you didn't call me. I wondered if I'd said something."

"Nothing that was significant. It's just that you try to take care of me all the time. Almost as if I'm another Sasha. And I want an adult relationship. I don't think it's a big deal, Patsy. I just think it's something we need to talk about." Then she asked which church they found the body in.

"It's been all over the news. Haven't you heard about it?"

"Oh," Aloha said. "In that downtown church near the shopping centre."

"That's the one. The one I go to."

Aloha looked momentarily surprised and then speculative. "Sounds like it might have been the ex-husband, don't you think?" she said.

"I hope not, for the sake of their boys. Maybe the cops don't know that she was possibly being followed by members of her family's religious community, because she'd left it. It sounded almost like a cult, you know, with strong admonitions about everything being dangerous unless you adhered to the tenets of their beliefs and were an active participant. On the other hand, although she told me a lot, she didn't like to talk about that very much. But she did worry about being followed."

"I can imagine why, can't you?"

24.

COSSER DRANK A QUICK CUP OF COFFEE at a Tim Horton's. Something was niggling away at him, so he called the station.

"Bad news," Reid said. "One of the boys has gone missing."

"One of the...?" Whatever he had called about, Cosser quickly forgot.

"The younger one," Reid said. "I have someone on it. The father is frantic."

"You mean one of Marni Atchinson's boys? But I just saw them."

Reid confirmed he did mean that, as if it were the only case he could think about. And that was true for Cosser, too. Immersed in a case, it often was his only preoccupation until either something broke or the trail went dead. Suppose whoever had murdered Marni was not finished with her? Could that person be behind the disappearance of one of her sons? Or had he just run away after the funeral service? Wasn't that something a young boy who was very upset might do? Now he recalled also how the man with the tattoo had disappeared at the end of that service and wondered if the two events were connected. Up till then, he'd assumed it was women who needed protection and the reassurance that this culprit would soon be in police custody. But if the boy had been kidnapped, this criminal had other things in mind besides meeting women through ads and harming them. This made Marni a victim who had been targeted rather than caught up in a random situation. Could her father, Victor Miller, have orchestrated all of this somehow?

"We are going to have to announce something," Reid said.

"Wait on that," Cosser replied, thinking that he would like to check a few obvious possibilities before fanning public fear. An alert could be mounted within an hour if talking to the boy's father led nowhere. He knew from a history of police work, like the gruesome discovery of the young girl that still haunted him, that there were cruel and twisted people out there, but he hung onto the hope that they would find this young boy within an hour or two. It was not uncommon for a child to disappear for a short period.

When he picked Reid up at the station, his colleague was humming a tune Cosser did not recognize. "C'mon Detective," he said. "What is there to sing about?"

"Sorry," Reid said. "I didn't realize I was."

He grinned and wanted to tease Reid about his love life obviously going well, but suddenly remembered that Reid now had a man in his life, so he did not want to go there. As he pulled up in front of Richard Atchinson's house, they both became quiet.

"If the guy is innocent, and thus far he appears to be, this is just too much for one person to bear," Reid said.

"Well, let's find out," Cosser said.

The door flew open before they could knock on it.

"Have you found him?" Richard asked, his eyes darting back and forth between the two police officers.

"Not yet, no," Reid said.

"Any ideas where he might have gone?" Cosser asked.

Richard slowly shook his head, and let out a long sigh as he motioned for them to come inside.

The other boy peered at them as they moved into the hall.

"Did he say anything to you?" Reid asked him.

Chris shook his head.

"You are Chris, aren't you?" Cosser said.

The boy nodded.

"So where do you think Dean might have gone?" Cosser asked kindly.

The boy shook his head, holding back tears.

"Let's suppose he did just decide to go somewhere that felt safe to him," Cosser said. "Where would that be?"

Reid watched with an expression of respect on his face. He knew that the way Cosser dealt with people was what garnered him such good results. Often he discovered things that in retrospect would turn out to be somewhat obvious.

"Patsy," Chris said.

For a moment, Cosser looked bewildered and then his face brightened. "Ah," he said. He gestured to Reid. "That's where we go next."

"What about if Chris and I go with you?" Richard asked.

"Sure," Cosser said.

They would find the boy at Patsy's or they would not. And if not, all other avenues would be explored, including broadcasting a description and asking for information from the public.

Chris slunk along beside his father as if he needed protection or, at the very least, moral support. At the curb, he climbed into his father's car. When the cruiser pulled away, the two followed closely behind. When they drove up and parked in front of the semi, Cosser immediately spotted a figure slouched down on the front steps of the boys' home. Before Cosser could get out of the car, Richard was running toward his son. Cosser hoped he did not admonish the boy and was relieved to see the tall man sit down on the steps and put his arms around the teenager who collapsed into his father's arms.

For the police officers, the relief was also palpable. There were so many other scenarios that could have played out and cause even more tragedy for this family.

Cosser stood at the foot of the stairs.

"Thank you, sir," Richard looked up to say.

"Hello, Dean," Cosser said. "I guess Patsy isn't home from work yet."

The boy's eyes turned toward the door of the other semi. "I didn't knock yet."

Richard kept his arm around the boy and drew Chris beside him, too.

"Do you want to try now?" he asked.

Chris nodded.

"I just want to go to my room," Dean said.

Both boys wanted to do that, it seemed. And Cosser knew they must ache for their mother. Nothing was going to be easy now, especially for the two teenagers.

25

DAVID WALKED UP AND DOWN In the hall outside his church office, wondering who he could talk to about his dilemma. How could he explain the sleepwalking and that it made him a possible suspect in a murder? Well, that was not entirely true. His wife would be able to clear him, had already done so. He was grateful Anne knew he had not been anywhere that night. But it would still be a problem for the bishop and he had to decide what and when to tell him. He looked out the window at a bright sunny day in Toronto, a surprise so late in the season. He thought of Claire and Harry and that these two wise souls might be able to give him the advice he sought. Both of them were of keen mind still. Going through a list of parishioners, David was relieved to find he had added their Vancouver number. There were three rings before someone picked up. He was thankful to hear Claire's familiar voice.

"Oh, David. What a surprise," she said.

The conversation began with the usual sorts of exchanges, David thought. What was the weather like in Vancouver? Rain was falling there, he learned.

"There's scarcely been a day since we arrived when we haven't been surrounded by grey clouds," Claire said. "Our apartment is near English Bay and looks toward the mountains on the North Shore. We've scarcely been able to see them so far." It was one dull, grey day following another.

"Oh, what a shame," David said, visualizing them walking, arm in arm, along the sea wall. Harry was a little taller than she was, even a little more so since her operation when she maintained another inch or so had been removed from her height. Claire had once told him she dreaded the day when some upstart intern or resident would talk to her son as if she did not exist anymore. Or shout at her because someone would assume that she could not hear because she was old.

"Often the clouds and fog are thick enough that we can scarcely see the ships that are right in front of us. At other times, we can make out the grey hulks, but aside from tiny lights shining through, that's all."

David had a vision of these ships, sitting ominously on the waves.

"We hear from our Toronto friends that it was sunny and warm into late November there."

"Yes," David murmured.

Silence followed. David was grateful Claire was still there, presumably waiting for him to go on. He felt suddenly on the verge of tears.

"I have to say we are mystified by the amount of suspicion we gather has occurred since the recent tragic event," Claire said.

"So you've heard,"

"Yes, we get letters and phone calls from our friends there."

David supposed they'd also heard he'd become less open, more introspective. Although he knew he had not been all that open before all of this suspicion had erupted, before the murder. It pained him as much as his parishioners that the trust and laughter of the community was eroding and he felt helpless to do anything about it.

"It's hard to be so far away and to hear this news," Claire said. "But at this distance, we have to be content with being kept informed."

She kept on talking into the silence and David listened, wondering what to say. How would he raise his reason for calling, David wondered. Finally he just blurted the words out quickly. "I'm afraid the bishop will soon have doubts about my ministry." He paused, and then continued with his voice slightly more controlled. "I'm not under suspicion as far as the police are concerned, but the bishop might have no other option when he learns about some personal problems."

Claire was quiet at the other end.

"It's this sleep walking thing," David sputtered, as if Claire knew all about it.

"I don't know about any sleepwalking thing," Claire said.

"Well, I sleepwalk, but there's no question that I was at home the night the murder occurred. Anne has attested to that. They're still calling it a murder, by the way. And the police don't know about the sleepwalking. But I think the bishop will soon. I don't know what to do. Whether to tell him or to wait until he finds out."

"I don't know either, David. Did you expect me to?"

"I guess I didn't. But I thought you would likely think it should not impair my ministry."

"Have you talked with the community?"

"No. Not yet. You see, I feel embarrassed. I only know about these episodes from third parties. Strangers I've met in doughnut shops who have returned things. Like a lost wallet. And Anne says there have been Tim Horton's bags and crumbs in the kitchen and normally I'd never set foot in one of those places. It's all too bizarre, but—"

"Would you like to talk to Harry?" Claire asked.

"Yes, I think I would."

There was a moment when Claire must have filled Harry in quietly on what he, David, had just revealed. He wondered why he thought they might know what he ought to do. He felt mortified for putting these two gentle souls on the spot. What had he been thinking? At that moment, he heard Harry's voice.

"Hello, David," he said kindly. "So how are you?"

David sighed, then started to talk almost incoherently before he sorted out his thoughts enough to repeat what he had
started to tell Claire. Surely God was there somewhere. It was
not lost on him that he, as a minister, ought to be offering
solace to this elderly couple rather than burdening them with
his problems. He hoped nonetheless that Harry would have
some words that presently eluded him.

"Look David," Harry said. "I understand it's a real dilemma,
but it sounds like it's something you need to talk over with the
bishop and perhaps with the community. Maybe you need to
tell them about the sleepwalking. You shouldn't have to hang
on to a secret like that yourself."

"Yes," said David. "I've thought of that." But the moment
he did, the police would pounce on him.

"You said Anne says you weren't out that night."

"But suppose it didn't happen that night."

"When else could it have?"

"I mean, they don't know if she was murdered there or
brought from somewhere else and left there. Anyone could
have done it."

He could hear Harry's deep intake of breath at the other end
of the line. David shuddered. He should not have called, he
thought. It felt as if instead of clarifying what he ought to do,
he had further muddied it. He hoped they did not think that
he wanted them to try to influence the bishop. His head in his
hands, David knew that serious allegations could flow from a
condition that left a minister unconscious of his whereabouts
for large segments of time.

With a chastened voice, David thanked Harry, wished him
more clear weather and hung up. He felt almost as if he could
hear their conversation now, his imagination vividly recreating
it. They had been around him long enough to know his foibles.
He'd even found Claire staring at him one day in the cafeteria
when he was chatting away to himself in French. "Bonjour,"
he'd said, at first not recognizing Claire, so immersed was he

in planning a homily for the next service. But she would not have known that.

"It's all very strange. But then, he is a bit strange," Claire might be saying. "Although not incompetent. Quite competent. And likely a good interim appointment for that church. But did you ever hear him talking to himself? Oh, I know, not uncommon, we both do it. But I heard him in the cafeteria kitchen chatting away in French. He seemed to be quoting poetry. When I went in, he blushed profusely although he didn't seem to recognize me."

"On the other hand, we sometimes spoke Chinese to ourselves and each other for many years after we came back from China." This was something David knew because they had told him so.

Harry had been clear about what David ought to do. It was advice David knew and had been afraid to follow, but he had no choice. It was time for him to pull himself together, he thought, time to call the bishop and begin to deal with his situation.

26.

Mid-November

ALMOST A WEEK AFTER Rosemary had spoken to Patsy, she once again made calls for the Congregational Care Committee. She had managed to reach only two people and was glad Ardith was one of them. For the rest, she left messages on answering machines.

"I'll come by after work on Friday if you would like," she said to Ardith. "I could bring something to eat. What about chicken?"

An enthusiastic "Mmmm."

David had told her that Ardith was having a difficult time of late. Sometimes he was quite astute and noticed who needed special attention. He would sometimes ask Rosemary to forego the order of her list and highlight a particular person. Right now, she starred Patsy's name with a red asterisk and left it till the end. She was surprised to hear Patsy's voice and not another answering machine.

"I wondered if we could meet for coffee," Rosemary said.

"All right," Patsy agreed.

They discovered that the bank where Patsy worked and the library where Rosemary worked were not far apart. "What about lunch instead of coffee?" Rosemary suggested.

They both liked a small restaurant on the east side of Yonge Street not too far below Bloor.

"Wednesday would work for me," Patsy said.

So, on Wednesday, Patsy came north a few stops on the subway and Rosemary walked down from the reference library. This was the first time they had met outside of the church.

"Thanks for suggesting this," Patsy said.

"I've missed seeing you on Sundays. This seemed like a way to maintain contact, even to get to know you better," Rosemary said.

"So, you're a librarian," Patsy said.

"Yes."

"You know, Marni met a man at the library not long before she died. A man who had placed an ad in the newspaper. We laughed about it at the time. He called himself Mr. Almost and described himself as having two left feet."

If she'd been more observant, Patsy would have seen the blood drain from Rosemary's face. Rosemary felt dizzy and images began to swirl, as if the earth were turning. Patsy's face seemed to be going around in a circle. She had not mentioned that man to the detective. If she had not told him about the ad, why would she say anything about his call? At the thought of being interviewed by the detective, Jack Cosser, Rosemary felt even dizzier. Why would she have said anything about the stranger with the white ribbon though? How could she have known that something as inconsequential as her letter to a stranger would have anything to do with the body in the church? Now there was no doubt, she thought. The dead woman had also met Mr. Almost.

"What's the matter?" Patsy asked.

"Well, he's a possible suspect in her murder, I think. But not because anyone knew she had met him. He was in the church one Sunday. You see, I answered that ad also. The place I suggested we meet was in the church. I asked him to wear a white ribbon so I could identify him. I thought that if he looked really sleazy or, you know, like someone I wouldn't want to meet, I wouldn't have to. As it turned out, he talked to Linda for quite a while, or she talked to him, and I had a chance to observe them and decided to take a chance. We went to the

Art Gallery and then for some Chinese food over on Spadina."

Patsy nodded. "I saw him at church that day, too. His name is Patrick Sloane."

"No, his name is Michael Sloane."

"Well, the man Marni met told her his name was Patrick."

"Do you suppose he's the same man?" Rosemary asked.

"Sounds like it. It was a pretty unique ad."

"I think we'd better get in touch with the police," Patsy added. "It seems suspicious that he would use two different names."

Rosemary hesitated. Why had she remained silent, appearing now either to have concealed something from the police? Or lied to them? Now she would have to expose herself, but there was really no choice. "Surely they'll have figured it out by now."

"Do you know, they may not have. I'm not sure anyone knew about Marni meeting with Mr. Almost except me," Patsy said.

"He didn't strike me as dangerous."

"Well, what can you tell from one meeting in a public place? He may have figured out that you weren't vulnerable and decided to move on to someone else."

"Oh God, that makes me sick. Do you suppose he placed the ad to lure women with the thought of murdering someone?" Rosemary was again nervous. You could not tell from his appearance, Rosemary thought, but she ought to have known better. He could have been creating a hit list with the women he met through his ad.

"I don't know how people like that think. I just know Marni's dead and so far as I know, they haven't found the killer. There were people in her life to be suspicious about and this guy may be completely clean. But I would hate for even an abusive former husband to be charged with murder if he didn't do it. Or for Marni's family to be subjected to an investigation that might be unnecessary. Even though she was estranged from her family, they didn't sound like bad people, only misguided ones."

"What do you mean?"

The waiter came toward them and asked if they were ready to order. The menus lay on the table, still unopened.

"We might need a little longer," Patsy said. "I'm not sure what I want yet. Something simple. What's the soup of the day?"

"Carrot and leek," he said.

"Sounds good to me," she said "I'll have that."

Rosemary ordered a sandwich on multigrain bread. Then she turned to Patsy. "What do you mean?" she repeated.

"Fundamentalist religion. Zealots. They disowned her because she left home to get away from all that. She called it 'disfellowship'. They'd disfellowshipped her. But she actually missed her family. And I think in spite of everything, she loved them. Especially her grandmother."

"But you don't imagine that they would go so far as to kill someone simply for leaving the group."

"You know, I *don't* know. I know there are ritualistic cults where it could happen. But, no, I don't really think she was in fear for her life. Or had reason to be."

Rosemary sighed. This was becoming so complicated; there were so many overlapping strands, and she wanted to figure it out. Not only because she might be in potential danger, but if she were writing a story, she would need to know. She'd never had an overall picture of what writing a novel, or even a story might entail, only a character or an incident that would set her mind racing. She would have to sit down some time and run with an idea to find out where it led. In this instance, this was a job for the police. Although it *would* make a good story. And she could count on Brent to support that idea. Of course, she could not mention the idea of writing about a murder in the church to Patsy, she thought, who was mourning the loss of a friend. To Rosemary, the woman had been, after all, a stranger.

The waiter arrived and set their food down in front of them. Patsy tasted the soup and nodded. "It's very good," she said.

"Shall we call the police after lunch?" Rosemary asked, not quite ready to reveal her duplicity.

"We ought to do it now," Patsy said. "We can use my cell."

"Let's eat a bit. Another half hour isn't going to change things."

"You never know. And I think I'd rather get it over with. I have a card they left with me."

The two women compared the cards they had been given. The officer's name and badge numbers were the same. Detective Sergeant Jack Cosser. Patsy pulled her cell phone out of her purse. "Do you want me to call? Or would you rather?"

"I'll call," Rosemary said.

Patsy handed the phone across the table. Rosemary pressed in digits and waited. When someone answered at the other end, she asked for Detective Sergeant Jack Cosser. It felt like a long time before he came on the line. She told him what she and Patsy had just discovered.

"I didn't tell you I met the man through an ad," she said. "I'm sorry. I was embarrassed and it never dawned on me that it might turn out to be important."

"I'll want to talk further with you," the detective said.

It appeared the police had not given priority to finding the man with the white ribbon. Until this phone call, there had been nothing to connect him with the murdered woman. The detective sounded matter-of-fact, but Rosemary sensed an underlying tone of urgency in his voice. Maybe this would be the information that would help crack the case wide open. Rosemary visualized the detective sitting at a desk down on College Street in the large new police building, his every antenna up and vibrating, furiously taking notes. She thought this might be the very information he had been waiting for.

"Are you somewhere that I could meet you now?"

"Well, we're both on lunch breaks." She looked at Patsy who indicated that she could call her office. "We can call and extend them." She told him how to get to the restaurant. He was there in less than ten minutes.

"This man with the white ribbon. Did he give a name, Rosemary?"

"Yes."

She and Patsy started to talk, almost in unison. Cosser took notes.

27

NOW HE HAD TWO NAMES and a better description of the man, Cosser thought. And the knowledge that the dead woman had answered a personals ad placed by someone who had actually been in the church on an occasion that preceded the discovery of her body there. Before the end of the day, he knew the man had placed the ad in the personals section of the morning newspaper. He had a lengthy description of him and knew that he went by slightly different names when he met different women. Rosemary had given him the date the ad had appeared.

He went to the newspaper offices and discovered neither Patrick nor Michael Sloane had placed that ad. It was paid for by a Nicholas Duncan. It seemed likely to Jack that all three were the same man.

He obtained phone and credit card numbers for Nicholas Duncan and with that information found an address easily. It did not take long to drive to a house in the midtown area that had been converted into apartments. He rang the doorbell with N. Duncan under it, but there was no answer. A neighbour in the upper apartment came to the door. "You looking for someone?" he asked.

"Nicholas Duncan."

"Could be at the pub."

"Is he a drinker?"

"Well, not really. He manages the place. The Fiddler. He also spends a lot of time at the track. Watches his horses race. Or just checks in on them."

"What does he look like? Any distinguishing features that make him easy to recognize?" Cosser asked.

"Just shaved his head. Has a tattoo on it."

Cosser raised his eyebrow. "Okay thanks," he said. "That ought to do it." It sounded as if the man he'd spotted at the funeral would turn out to be the same man who had paid for the ad in the paper. Was he also the white ribbon man so many people in the congregation at Holy Trinity had remembered? But that man had red hair. Had he shaved it off?

"In some kind of trouble?" the neighbour asked.

Cosser shrugged. He was going to find out. "Thanks, buddy."

He climbed back into the car and headed for the pub on Bloor Street mentioned by the neighbour. A man with a bald head sat at the bar on the second floor. Cosser watched him butt out a cigarette in a heavy glass ashtray and simultaneously light another. He approached the bar and leaned toward the man who peered up at him, dark eyes behind thin-rimmed glasses. It was the same man. Had he not already met him at the funeral, the bald head and tattoo would have been enough for him to recognize him. "You again," the man said. "Like a drink?"

"Thanks, no," Cosser said. He took out his card with name and badge number on it that he had shown to the man as ID the day they first met. The smile on the bald man became a straight line across the lower part of his face.

"So? Forget something?"

"I'm looking for someone who placed an ad in the *Globe and Mail* in the Personals column," Cosser said. He showed Nick the ad.

"I can't help you."

"Aren't you Nicholas Duncan?"

"Yeah, that's me, all right."

"Well, I believe that you *can* help. Apparently you paid for the ad."

"That could be," Nick said. "I like to help my friends. I've paid for things for them when they ask. So it was an ad, was it? I'd forgotten."

"Did you place one for anyone recently?"

"Yeah."

"Who would that be?"

Nick looked toward a man with the bright red hair Cosser had expected Nick Duncan might have once had, but Nick's dark eyebrows suggested otherwise. This man was wearing earphones and swaying to whatever music he was listening to. His head moved in rhythmical motions and Cosser took the measure of the red head as Nick continued to talk. The fellow looked bright enough, but totally preoccupied.

"Paddy over there," Nick said. "My exercise rider. Sometimes drops by the pub when he's finished with the horses. He's a good man. He's never been in any kind of trouble."

"Well, he may not be now." Although Cosser could see that this Paddy fit the descriptions he had been given of the man with the white ribbon. It would be hard to miss that hair. He felt a small sense of satisfaction, even of elation.

He approached Paddy, who looked up as the detective presented his card. After going through the routine once more of saying why he was there and pulling out the ad, Cosser asked, "Are you the one who placed this ad?"

"Yeah." Paddy said simply, but you could hear the 'so what?' in his intonation.

"Well, I need to ask you some questions. You're going to have to come into the station."

"I'm on duty here tonight," Paddy said. "I get paid for keeping the guests happy even though it isn't a regular job."

"When are you off?" Cosser asked, not convinced this Paddy could not ask to leave what was at the moment an almost empty bar. But he thought he might learn something by watching for a while and did not press the issue.

"Couple of hours."

"I'll wait."

"What's this all about anyway?'

"It's about the man who placed this ad, who this man met, and what happened to the women he met."

Paddy looked over at Nick. The detective followed his gaze to the newly shaven head that gleamed under a light over the bar. Nick filled a glass with draught from one of the taps. He was talking to the bartender and to people at the table next to him. "Nick's a friendly sort," Paddy muttered. "Doesn't talk about much besides horses, golf, and women, but sure knows them, I tell ya'."

"How long have you known each other?" Cosser asked.

"Twenty years now," he said. "We help each other. Tell me, mister, how does putting an ad in the Personals lead to a police investigation?"

"We can talk about that at the station," Cosser said. He noticed something in the man's eyes then, a look that said he remembered something. Perhaps he had seen the news on television or in the newspaper about the woman who had been discovered in the basement of the church.

"Oh," he said then. "Does this have anything to do with a downtown church?"

"It could," Cosser said.

"I sat through a service in that church, that's true, because I was going to meet Rosemary something or other. The librarian. Phew. Church stuff didn't mean a thing to me. I was raised Catholic. I thought Anglican was something like Catholic, but not that church. It was so modern that you'd scarcely recognize anything." He suddenly realized that he was talking a lot. He changed the position of his earphones and poured more beer into his glass. "I didn't pay much attention," he said. "Kept wondering who would come and speak to me afterwards. Or whether the one who'd suggested the church as a meeting place would take off after she saw me, you know, like—"

"Um," Cosser said, nodding just enough to encourage the man to continue.

"But listen to this. You wouldn't believe it. Some woman came and started to talk to me and she wasn't even the one who answered the ad. She had a thing about the white ribbon. I tell ya'. Almost gave myself away, thinking she was this Rosemary lady. Turned out she wasn't. Too bad because she turned me on more. I was about to suggest we go to lunch, Linda was her name, when this Rosemary came along. Never saw Linda again. Too bad."

"And?"

"Phew. That Rosemary ate almost nothing in the restaurant and I was starving. I tell ya', she was boring. A librarian who was going to write a book someday, but she didn't know when. She had some ideas; she liked having the ideas. Never seemed to get going, though. Not my type. I didn't call her again and I didn't have the other woman's number."

"So you moved onto someone else on your list?"

"Yeah. So what? I've never met anyone I wanted to see again. Those ads are a crap game. And anyway some nut case must have been following me, or her, because I could see the guy in the shadows—when I moved so did he, and I didn't want to get involved in some woman's divorce case. You know, the ones where if there is a lover or something, they can blackmail the husband or wife. Why else would anyone be following me?"

His face and eyes became veiled. Cosser could read into them he'd seen the news about the body in the church and now he did not know how much to say about it.

"You can tell me the rest at the station." Cosser went over to the bar and sat beside Nick. They did not talk to each other. The detective ordered some mineral water and sipped from the glass. He watched Nick's movements from the corner of his eye.

"Seen the garden upstairs?" Nick asked.

"No."

"Why not have a look see?"

"I might." Cosser did not budge for half an hour and by then he had a sense of the style and movement of both men. He also had a picture in his mind's eye of the bartender and had listened to the banter between him and Nick. They had talked about an upcoming race at Woodbine, about a cottage, a hockey game. He thought he might just as well go up the stairs at the far end of the room. When he did, he was surprised to find a roof top patio full of young people and, even in November, open to a starlit sky. You could come back in a week and find this place covered with snow, Cosser thought. Better idea to wait until the summer to drink a beer here.

He went downstairs where Paddy nodded at him and they walked together out of the club to his car. When they arrived at the police station, they sat on opposite sides of a desk there.

"So where were you on the night of November eleventh?" Cosser asked.

"At the pub."

"You have someone who can verify that?"

"Oh yeah. No problem."

"How about on Sunday morning?"

"Don't remember. Probably sleeping."

"Well, you'll have to figure that out and have someone who can corroborate your story."

"Come on."

"Listen, Mr. Patrick Sloane, or Michael Sloane, whoever you are, there's something serious here. A dead woman was found that morning and we have reason to believe she was one of the women you met as a result of your ad."

"What was her name?"

"I can tell you that, but the fact is she may have given you a false name. I'll show you a picture." The detective reached into a file and pulled out a snapshot that came from a family album.

"I do know her." Paddy looked shaken at the thought he had actually met the woman who had been killed. Or maybe shaken because he had thought he would never be discovered,

Cosser thought. You don't know what's going on under someone's outward appearance. Until you do, it's like having an elephant in the room that no one acknowledges, he mused. It's there and it's very disconcerting, even unnerving. For a police officer, it requires uncovering. But how?

"So, you're Mr. Almost."

Paddy nodded, still nervously. He apparently did not like the connections. But, thought the detective, who would, guilty or not? Although someone not guilty might be more convincingly so, not this sea of uncertainty Paddy seemed to have turned into.

"That's Marni," he said. "Liked her. But—"

"But?"

"Did want to see her a second time. There were not many I bothered to call again. Something about her. Great legs. But something else."

"Mr. Sloane, where were you on that weekend?"

"Don't remember."

"I think you'd better start remembering. You're a suspect. You need to know that." The police officer cited Paddy's rights to him.

Paddy looked down at the floor. "Christ," he muttered. "I should have known that the first time I placed an ad, it would backfire."

"Pardon?"

"I want to talk to my lawyer," Paddy said. "But hey, there won't be a problem. I was at the lake."

"How far is the lake from Toronto?" Cosser asked.

"Two hours."

"So you could have come into the city and left again. Was anyone with you?"

"Yeah, yeah. My girlfriend."

"Let me understand this. You have a girlfriend and you placed an ad?"

"Yeah, yeah, so what?"

So maybe the girlfriend could have been jealous, Cosser

thought, but that felt too unlikely to pursue at the moment.

Paddy pressed the numbers on the telephone to reach his lawyer. He muttered that he had never had to contact Irv before about a criminal matter, but that he knew the man well by now. "If Irv doesn't handle this kind of thing, he'll know who does." It seemed Paddy needed to talk aloud, but maybe it would have been better if he kept it to himself. Cosser thought that it might be an occupational hazard for an exercise walker who probably muttered to the horses all day. Maybe he talked so much in an ongoing patter to keep the animals listening to him that when he was elsewhere, he simply continued doing so. Now he looked up at the detective.

"Can I call Nick, too?" he asked. "Or do I need to ask Irv to call him?"

Cosser shrugged, conveying that it was okay with him. *Go ahead. If you need to.* He could see there was still no answer to the first call and Paddy hung up and waited before punching in another number.

"God, I wish I'd never placed that ad," he muttered. "Never even met anyone worth seeing more than once. Except that one in the picture. Marni. And she ended up dead. Christ."

Cosser watched him, and listened to his mutterings. He was developing a strong sense the guy was innocent. Maybe because he was so flustered in all the ways he would not be if he were guilty. It took good intuition and lots of investigative experience to pick up on something like that. This "Almost" guy seemed too guileless to be the guilty one. He seemed more worried that his girlfriend would now find out about the ad he had placed and be more furious than worried that he himself might end up in the slammer.

"Too much," Paddy said with an inflection that suggested he was beginning to recognize the gravity of his situation.

"We're going to have to question you further," Cosser said. "You'll need to be available."

"I'll tell Nick," Paddy said. "Kind of friend a guy needs.

He'll see that I can still do my job with the horses. Good man, doesn't ask questions. You know, he knew about Marni. I told him. Showed him her photograph. He looked a bit surprised when he first looked at it. He said he'd like to meet her. He could have, he had all the numbers. He saw all the letters first. He threw out the losers."

Paddy seemed to be telling the police officer this as a matter of interest. Cosser did not think he had any idea he could be implicating his friend. He wondered where he came from, some small town somewhere, some backwater.

"Where is this lake?" Cosser asked.

"East," Paddy said.

Cosser thought of the Maritimes, but you could not drive there in two hours.

"Where east?"

"Peterborough way. East of. Why? You need to go there."

"Maybe."

28

WALKING BACK TO THE LIBRARY, Rosemary could not stop thinking about the interview with the police officer. After she and Patsy had connected enough dots to realize they had to do something, Rosemary wondered again if she were at risk. Somehow, in the bright daylight, it didn't seem likely. Especially since the detective now had the information the police needed.

Unlike Patsy, she felt removed from the actual tragedy even though it might affect her more than she would like to think. And at the same time, she envisioned herself as somewhat of a sleuth. After all, a librarian knew how to find information. And she had been handed the guts of a remarkable story. At last she would write her novel. When she arrived back at her desk, she placed a call to Brent. She wanted to talk to someone. When she left a message on his machine, it struck her that it had not occurred to her to call the minister.

Rosemary suspected David had some secret that would surprise everyone. There was always something just slightly off kilter there, as if he were not quite the same person as he had been the last time. Once she ran into him on the street and he had not seemed to recognize her. It was rather late and she had not been sure it was David at first. He had walked by her almost as if he were sleepwalking.

What a hook that would make for a novel, she thought, a minister who did not know what he had done for the previous twelve or thirteen hours. Imagine not knowing whether he had been out strolling on Bloor Street or gone back to the church. She did not realize that she had stumbled onto something that would take the detective somewhat longer to discover.

She heard a voice and looked up to see a client with a request form for a copy of *Writers' Markets*. She found the book and asked for identification that she filed in a drawer under the counter. She thought it might be unwise to tell Brent very much at this juncture. Everyone was still implicated and she did not think she should be passing information back and forth. Anyway, it was her book now, her mystery, and this one she might actually write. If she said anything she might sabotage herself. Still she might talk to Ardith who saw and heard more than anyone ever suspected. Usually, people did not have the patience to listen to her. As a member of the Congregational Care committee, Rosemary could find reasons to call almost anyone and was glad she had arranged to see Ardith on Friday. What about Polly? she wondered. She spent a lot of time in the church, practising with the choir or playing the piano, and she could also ask Brent some questions without divulging anything. There was also Jim, the ancient mariner as Brent had so aptly nicknamed him. He would have some theories to propound.

"Excuse me, ma'am," a voice said.

"Yes," Rosemary replied to a man who had just approached her at the desk.

"I'm looking for an issue of the *Canadian Forum*," he said. "An older issue. I understand you have bound copies."

"Right over there," Rosemary said, pointing to shelves across from them. As he turned away, she carried on with some paper work. It was hard to believe that she had grown up in a town without a library and come to the marvelous world of books shelved in large numbers for the first time at university. Her parents had both been avid readers and her father read to her as a child from books with leather covers that were lovingly shelved beside the fireplace. He must have brought those volumes across two continents because there were, as well as Charles Dickens, Samuel Johnson, and Sir Arthur Conan Doyle, books he'd had as a child in South Africa. She'd always loved the one about a dog named Jock with the title, *Jock and the Bushveld*. When it was snowing outside and onto the windows of their company house on the mine property in northern Quebec, her father had read descriptions of faraway times and places to her. When she walked into the library in Montreal where she was a student, she had known right away that she wanted to work in such a place, surrounded by books. She had wanted to have the facility to find what patrons were looking for. And she had wanted to select and organize books for a collection. Everything about libraries had interested her. But underlying it all was the desire to write something that would be shelved in a library for others to read. She could almost visualize her own book sitting on those shelves. Here was her chance. "Mr. Almost." Would someone look for a book with that title? Surely it was sheer folly to imagine that her book would stand out enough for anyone to ask for it. But she knew if you had a dream, you had to follow it. You had to believe.

"To dream the impossible dream. To fight the..." she hummed.

"Rosemary, there's a call for you," her colleague said.

"Thanks." She picked up the line. "Hello, Rosemary Willis speaking."

"Hi there. It's Brent. You called me."

"I did. I wondered if you'd meet for coffee or lunch sometime. Sooner than the next church service."

When Rosemary hung up, she began to shudder, a visceral response that at first made no sense to her. Then the thought that had been there all along manifested itself again. The man who had called himself Mr. Almost could have met her character, the woman who was found dead in the church. She could have met him through the newspaper. Mr. Almost was more than a title. He might be a killer. And she too might have been his prey. She had been careful. He did not know her last name or where she lived. She had met him in a public place. He had seemed harmless. But what could she tell in one meeting? Maybe she was just lucky. He could have followed her. She could not remember if she had told him what library she worked at.

"What's the matter, Rosemary?" her colleague asked.

"Oh, excuse me," Rosemary replied. "I felt a little dizzy."

"Do you need a drink of cold water? Is there something I can do?"

"It's all right," Rosemary said. "If you don't mind though, I'll take a short break."

"Go ahead. Take your time."

Rosemary went to the washroom and patted cold water on her cheeks and forehead. She freshened her lipstick. What could Ardith, Polly, Jim or Brent tell her? They could talk about the congregation, but the murder was another matter. It did not belong at the centre of the community, but on the periphery. Surely it came from the world outside the church and would be solved there. All the same, if she could find out more about what each person had observed, it would help her develop her ideas for the novel. She noticed that two people she had not considered were Linda and David. Nor had she considered Rob. The first two she had never felt comfortable with. Rob might be useful though. He usually had an unexpected slant on life. And he had seen the scene of the crime.

29

THERE'S SO MUCH THAT PEOPLE KNOW about each other that remains unspoken, David thought. Yes, secrets abounded in any community, usually with no reason to surface. Take his sleepwalking, he thought. He figured Polly and Eric knew about it. He did not know, of course, that Rosemary had imagined it. Now Claire and Harry knew because he'd told them. David thought he should speak to the bishop before he told the congregation. It would be too much if it got to the diocese from someone else or was the subject of media coverage. David was embarrassed that he had not spoken sooner. What would a sleep disorder matter if there had not been a murder? All the same, someone who had another life he did not know about could be a liability to the church. He could already hear the bishop.

"But this is my life," he murmured. A life he had managed to live for enough years that he was on the verge of retirement. At just under sixty, he could retire now. What would he do though? It did not occur to him that he might be found guilty of murder and spend the rest of his life in prison.

"There would have been blood somewhere," he continued when the thought crossed his mind. He found that reassuring. And then he remembered that there had been blood, plenty of it. Why would he for a moment imagine that there had not been?

His appointment with the bishop was made quickly when

he revealed the urgency of the situation. The next morning he was in the incumbent's office.

"Good morning, David," the bishop said from a comfortable armchair across from another where the minister was perched awkwardly. "You asked to see me."

David was surprised at how nervous he felt. He was older than the bishop, who appeared to be a rather ordinary man, but David knew he had garnered this position because he was known as a diligent theologian and a skilled mediator. He was known also for his writings and his pastoral care. On previous occasions, David had felt quite comfortable.

"Yes," David said. "Ever since the murder, there's something I've felt I needed to tell you. I probably should have before this, but it never struck me that it would be a problem."

"Why does it appear to be a problem now?"

"Well, you see, it could cause adverse publicity for the church. I walk in my sleep and sometimes I don't know where I've been. My wife can tell you I was at home the night of the murder, but if it were to get out now, I can just imagine all the speculation."

"Yes," the bishop said. "It's a made for a media frenzy, isn't it?'

Does he know already? David wondered. He did not seem the least bit surprised. Maybe Harry or Claire had decided to tell him. But surely they would not have done that. They would have waited for him to do so. Did someone else know his secret? Did he or she pass it on? You never knew in a parish who knew what and what they might do with what they knew. You wished they would talk to you, but often they did not. Often there were little pockets of gossip that developed for a while, until someone brought things out in the open. It seemed such a waste of energy, particularly among a community that so diligently pursued issues of social justice. Why waste one moment on such miniscule concerns?

"That's what I'm afraid of," David said.

"Have you sought medical advice?" the bishop asked kindly.

David felt his face getting hot and supposed he was flushed now. "Yes, I've been through a sleep clinic and I see my own doctor regularly."

"It might be worth checking in with your doctor now, just for any reassurance there might be from a medical perspective. What do you think? I'm concerned that you are out at times without knowing you've been somewhere. Anything could happen."

"Yes, of course," David said. "I'll do that, of course. I'm glad you suggested it. I haven't been thinking entirely clearly."

"As for what to do, I think I need a little time to think about it. On the other hand, perhaps you would be more comfortable if you took some time off. At least until this is over. Actually, I think that's likely the most prudent course in the interim. For your own sake really."

"It could take a long time to find the murderer," David said.

"Yes, it could."

"Oh dear," David sighed.

"We've talked a bit about early retirement before this even came up," the bishop said. "Would you give some thought to that also, David? You'd have your pension and we could look at the situation if you were to take it early."

David sighed again. He wondered why he had not figured out that there really was no way the question of retirement would not be an obvious issue in such a delicate situation. He did not feel ready for it, but it seemed he had no choice but to consider it seriously now. And likely it would be better simply to acquiesce gracefully.

"So I could ask for early retirement," he said. "Yes, you have intimated as much." David's face turned red. Since he had never run into trouble as a result of his night wanderings, he had not considered the ramifications. It seemed impossible that he could have ignored them. But the truth was that it had only been recently that he realized the extent of his travels. Before that, he thought he might go as far as the curb at the front of the house and possibly into the backyard, but never out onto the streets, even into doughnut shops.

"Yes," the bishop nodded.

David lowered his head. "What about waking up in the Humber River?" he muttered.

"Does that mean you have some doubt yourself?" the bishop asked.

"No, not really. That was a while ago. All the same, I find myself wondering." You never knew what you might be capable of in some kind of state or trance. Was everyone capable of murder under some particular set of circumstances?

"David, I think we need to pray," the bishop said.

Shortly thereafter, David departed. They had agreed that he would no longer conduct the Sunday services and that a replacement would be sent shortly. In the meantime, the wardens would tell the parishioners what had happened and the congregation would be asked to take over. It would not be too different from when David took holidays. There were enough ordained ministers to officiate at the Eucharist. There was no need to worry that this church would not be able to carry on until an interim minister was appointed. Even then, the minister would have little to do as far as directing the business of the church or implementing services. He would have to follow the direction established by the congregation. David did not imagine that the next incumbent might be a woman. Not until Linda mentioned it to him.

"Oh yes," he said. He was picking up his personal belongings from the church office. "That's quite possible." Times had changed and even David could see that. But it galled him to have Linda remind him.

"You know, David," Linda said. "I don't believe for a moment that you could have done it. And I'm sorry we've had so many difficult moments."

She would not go so far as to say he had done anything for their parish, he thought, but she had made some internal sacrifice to speak at all. "Thank you, Linda," he said, feeling she had meant what she'd said.

When he left his keys with the secretary, she had tears in her eyes. "It's all right," he said. "Once the police investigation clears me, I'm sure everyone will feel more comfortable."

"I'm sure that's so," the secretary said. "But you're the one I'm thinking of. And of how much we'll miss you."

When he walked out the door, David felt as if he were leaving home. As a minister, one church or another had been his home and his refuge for over thirty years now. He was apprehensive about telling Anne and this was what preoccupied him on the trip north on the subway to Bloor and east over the Don Valley Parkway. What would she say?

When he arrived at the house, Anne was in the kitchen. She called out a greeting as he moved down the hall.

"Come and have a cup of coffee," she said. A talk show was playing on the radio. She listened to political and cultural commentary, the radio always in the background somewhere in the house, usually the kitchen. As company, she'd said. She must have spent many lonely moments as the wife of a minister. He did not like to think that his vocation might have altered the course of her life in ways she might regret, especially with the news he was about to give her.

"I went to see the bishop this morning, Anne."

"Thank heavens for that."

"Why do you say that?" It had never crossed his mind that she would express profound relief.

"I've been worried," she said. "But I haven't known quite what to say to you. Or how. I had faith you'd find your own guide, your own direction. I'm relieved you have. I suppose he's said you have to relinquish your post."

"No, actually he didn't," David said, suddenly angry. "Is that what you wanted?"

"No, of course not," Anne said. "It's just what other option is there when you get right down to it?"

"But you believe I'm innocent."

"David, I know you're innocent. This isn't about innocence and guilt. This is about perception. It's about health. It's about many things. But it's not about anything criminal."

"I'm sorry," he said. "Of course you're only thinking of what's best. As was the bishop. He was exceedingly kind. Suggested I seek medical advice, that I take a break. He did raise the question of retirement, as he actually has previously, and this time I agreed with him. With some difficulty though. I don't feel ready for it. But the time seems to be upon us, my dear."

"Mainly that's what I'm thinking of, too," she said. "What would be best. Although there's a small selfish part as well, I must admit. I'm ready for retirement. It's been a long, difficult haul. Perhaps it's different when you're the one who actually does the work, but as your spouse it hasn't always been easy. Parishioners place great demands on partners even when that partner doesn't become a part of the community."

David took the cup of coffee she handed to him and added a spoonful of sugar. "You know, this is so much better than Tim Horton's."

"I thought you didn't know about your visits there."

"Well, you don't think I wouldn't check in to taste the coffee some time when I'm awake to see if it's as bad as I always assumed it was. It's not, you know. It's quite good. And I've become quite fond of their apple fritters."

"Oh David, you are something else. I guess that's why I married you."

She reached out and embraced him and he let himself sink into her arms where he let the tears that surfaced fall onto her shoulder.

"We'll manage," she said.

It did not seem fair that the telephone rang and that he still felt compelled to answer it, although he let Anne pick it up.

"Yes, he's here." Anne put her hand over the mouth of the receiver. "Police," she said. "That detective you told me was at the church on Sunday. Jack Cosser."

"Oh yes," David said tiredly. "Him."

Anne went over to the table and sat down as he took the receiver.

"I was about to call you," David said. "Yes, you can come over. I'm not going anywhere."

30

Rosemary made a list of characters, adding some of their idiosyncrasies as well as their physical attributes. It was the first time she had sat down at her computer, not to surf the internet or to check e-mail, nor to do her banking or reserve a book at the library, but to make notes that might lead to a story. Even a novel. Mostly she was interested in exploring the sleepwalking proclivities of her putative killer, the minister. She was sure someone would tell her that the minister as villain was all too obvious, but at this point she did not care. Although, as this unusually quiet man conceivably assumed the proportions of a monster when he was out in the middle of the night, she began to think perhaps she should alert the police officer who might not yet be aware of David's sleepwalking to have considered such a possibility. Jack Cosser, the detective, was an attractive man in some ways, she thought. Not with the charming good looks of a film star, but there was a ruggedness about him, a few distinctive lines on his face that appealed to her. And his thick neck was unusual, the way his head rested on it as if all the strength in his body was there just beneath it.

The card the detective had given her was still in her purse on the other side of the room. She went over and pulled it out and studied it. This was hardly the right time to call him, but when was the right time to call a police officer? Maybe he was working an evening shift. Maybe he had a wife also. This thought had popped into her mind unbidden. Why should it matter to her if he were single or not? she wondered. Even if it did not, she was quite sure that in her story the detective would be.

When he returned her call, Cosser said he would meet with her, possibly toward the end of his shift since she lived on his route home.

"Have you thought of something that you didn't tell me?" he asked.

"Well," Rosemary said. "Not exactly. But there is something I need to talk to you about."

"All right," he said. "I'm not surprised."

"What do you mean?" she asked.

"Well, many people who were in church on Sunday have begun to have nightmares." She noticed he did not add that the thought that someone might have been out on a date with a possible killer would leave most people reeling.

Rosemary changed into a pair of tight blue jeans before the detective arrived. Maybe he was right. Maybe she was nervous and needed reassurance. Or maybe she just wanted to see him. It was her day off, in the middle of the week, and she rather enjoyed that he would be there soon. She put on the coffeepot. There was beer in the refrigerator, but she supposed it would be improper for her to offer, much less for him to drink it. In her vivid imagination, she foresaw the opportunity would arise in the not too distant future. She also knew that she had been making up stories since she was a small child and that this could be yet another. What a dull life she led on the surface, but if anyone had access to what she conjured up to amuse herself, they would know she was not as uninteresting as Mr. Almost had found her. He would rather have gone for lunch with Linda, she thought. But when she had become aware of that, she, Rosemary, had seen that Linda did not get that opportunity. After all, she was the one who had written to him. Now she felt that inadvertently she had done Linda a favour. Linda might have ended up dead. On the other hand, if the villain really was their sleepwalking minister, there might yet be more bodies.

When the bell rang, Rosemary peered out the door where she could see the detective on the porch. How attractive he looked through the glass window with the streetlight in the background. She had always liked men of about his height and with his craggy features. She recalled that he did not wear a ring, but also knew that in and of itself did not prove anything. She opened the door, disappointed to find another officer was with him.

"Hello, Rosemary," Cosser said. "May we step inside?" He introduced his colleague, Simon Reid.

"Come in and have a cup of coffee," she said.

That she scarcely knew either of them did not cross her mind. Cosser was about to go off duty, but his presence was nonetheless official. It was a response to her call. Reid, it seemed, was on duty until later.

They sat down at the table across from the counter where the coffee pot brewed. There were white tiles behind it, with a few randomly inserted hand-painted blue and green fish. On the wall was a large framed poster of a Magritte painting. It was the one with the rock that almost filled the room. It spoke to her of mystery, of something bizarre, yet something that made her chuckle. She did not know what it was that intrigued her, just that she had always been attracted to works of art and literature with a tinge of the odd, even bizarre, about them.

"Nice place," Reid said.

She could see Cosser was also looking around, taking in her environment. What she had wanted to say to him, she did not want to say to this other man. She did not even want him to hear it. But what else could she do? Except not tell them and that might leave them open to missing something.

"Thanks."

"You mentioned that you wanted to talk to me about something to do with the case," Cosser said, looking at her now.

"Well, yes, you see I decided to write something about it and in my story the minister walks in his sleep."

"And?"

"Well, that makes him capable of doing things he wouldn't do if he were awake, things he probably doesn't even remember."

"Did someone tell you this about the minister or is this something you've made up to fit your story?"

"Well, I am just imagining the possibility," Rosemary said, blushing. "But I thought it was worth mentioning just the same."

"Under the strain you've been dealing with, it's not surprising your imagination is running rampant. And I don't mean to be rude," Cosser said. "But that's not the way police officers go about their job. I suggest you make up what you like, but don't imagine that you're solving an actual murder."

"No, of course not," Rosemary said, noticing that the other officer had a lopsided grin on his face. She did not like being fodder for their amusement. "I'm sorry. It's just that I've made up stories forever and this is the first one that I've actually begun to write. I started to believe it, I guess."

"Well, the people who are having nightmares believe those, too, until they have a chance to walk out into bright sunlight or to talk to someone to rid themselves from the stress of knowing there has been a murder."

"You don't sound like any police officer I've ever met," Rosemary said. "You'd fit nicely into a British mystery story."

"It's from the Scottish side of the family likely," he said more kindly. "My mother gave me a name that she thought would fit also, but my father changed it from Alistair to Jack."

"Do you mind if I use Alistair in my story? I like that name."

"He might," Reid said." It depends on what you do with his character."

"Oh, he'll be a decent sort, you don't need to worry."

Cosser laughed at that and stood up. "Thanks for the coffee. We'd best be getting along."

"Oh," she murmured. "That's too bad."

"I have a dog that needs to be walked and fed," he said. "And no one else to do it."

Reid watched him closely, as if he suspected something.

And no wife? Rosemary thought. She did not dare ask. But what did it matter? Her mother would have called it poor manners, but good manners had not provided opportunity. It was a ruse to keep children in line she'd decided long ago, an admonition that being polite on all occasions would have its just rewards. Where were these rewards, though? She was a mousy librarian living alone in a large city and she knew that was what people thought of her, including Mr. Almost. Almost suited her as well. Almost intelligent did also. Almost a nonentity might fit, too, and she did not want it to. Not that there was anything wrong with being a librarian, but she was not involved in her profession beyond the routine of it. Her mind was always wandering.

Rosemary looked at Reid who had a broad smile on his face now. Glancing at his partner, Reid started to move toward the door while Rosemary and Cosser stood awkwardly, measuring each other. "My daughter is too young to walk the dog," Cosser said. "Anyway, she lives with her mother."

"Oh."

"Her name is Jaime. She's four years old."

"Oh." She walked with him to the door, catching up with the other officer. "Would it be against policy," she hesitated, then continued, "for me to call occasionally to ask if you can verify if certain police-related details in my novel are plausible?"

Cosser looked attentive, so Rosemary continued.

"Maybe we could chat over a glass of wine. Or a cup of coffee." She was surprised that she managed to get the words out, hoping that Reid could not hear her. Or that it would not matter even if he did. She felt her body tense as she noticed Cosser's features freeze into a mild frown of disapproval at the mention of wine. Or even coffee.

"For now, while the investigation is still ongoing, it's not a good idea," he said and she could see Reid nod in agreement.

Embarrassed, she closed the door behind them. She should not have mentioned the wine, she thought. He would think that she had made up a way to lead him on and to—oh, she thought too much about everything. This time she would put her energy into trying to write something. If he ever called her, that would be a bonus.

31

WHEN COSSER, ACCOMPANIED BY HIS PARTNER, rang the doorbell at the minister's house, a woman came to the door. "Hello," she smiled warmly. "I'm David's wife. Anne."

"Yes," Cosser said. "This is Detective Simon Reid. We're both working on the case. Sorry to trouble you again. Your information that your husband was here all night during the hours of the murder is not in question. But I gather he has something to tell the police."

"Come in," she said. "David is waiting for you. He's in the living room."

When the two police officers entered the room, the minister rose to his feet and beckoned to them to sit down. As they did, Cosser introduced Reid.

"I gather you have something to tell us," Reid said,

"Yes," David said, turning to look at Jack Cosser. "This is embarrassing and I'm not sure what impact it will have on your investigation."

Cosser nodded and both police officers waited for what the priest would say next.

"You see," David said. "I walk in my sleep."

Cosser's eyelid twitched, but he did not otherwise show how he felt about this so-called revelation. What kind of game was that woman, Rosemary, playing? He was furious, but aside from his face reddening and his lips tightly pursed, there was no other indication of his consternation.

David proceeded to tell the officers about escapades he actually knew nothing about except from his wife. And sometimes told to him by complete strangers.

"That doesn't change anything really," Cosser said. "Your wife stands by her story that you were having dinner, watching television, and then sleeping soundly during the hours in question. I imagine though that it might be difficult for your ministry."

"Yes, well," David answered slowly. "I have handed in my resignation. Well, not quite that. I actually said I would take early retirement. "

"I see," Cosser said.

The three men sat silently for a while, David fiddling uncomfortably with his hands. Finally David spoke again. "This has all been very upsetting for the community. The murder. The suspicion. And now to hear my story, which if anyone doubts me would lead them to wonder if I might really be involved."

"Yes," Cosser said. "I understand all of that. "

"Are you any closer to an arrest?"

"I hope so. But I can't really say more than that for now," Cosser said, feeling some confidence in the police work thus far, but not clear that it would lead to an arrest as quickly as the community, or he, would like. They needed a break of some kind—a few pieces that were still missing, floating just beyond reach.

"We'll keep you posted," Reid said.

David nodded.

SITTING OUT IN THE CAR in front of the minister's house, Reid looked at his superior. Cosser turned the engine on, his face inscrutable. "Any new thoughts, Jack?" Reid asked. "Seems odd that the woman we just saw would suggest that we should look more closely at this sleepwalking minister."

"Well, it doesn't move us any further ahead, does it?" Cosser asked rhetorically. The minister had his alibi, and he certainly didn't arouse any other suspicions, despite his unfortunate sleep-walking problem. He looked over at his partner and thought the other man looked about as confounded as he, Jack, felt.

Reid sighed. "What about the victim's father? Have you decided not to interview him again? You seemed to think there might be something there."

Now it was Cosser's turn to sigh. "I think he's hiding something, but I don't think he or his son had anything to do with the murder. Or knew anything that might have prevented it. I suppose we might question him again, but I'm leaving that until we check out some other avenues first."

He could feel Reid looking at him, waiting for him to say what those were. But he did not know yet. He just had a sense that something was about to open up a crack that would widen to create the crevice the killer would eventually fall into. These sensations came to him at a certain point in an investigation before he could clearly articulate them. So it was now. He had nothing, but felt as if he had most of what he needed.

"So is it a deep dark secret or can you tell me? I can't see any way through what we've discovered so far."

"No, not quite yet," Cosser said. "Let's get on with it."

They drove in silence for a couple of blocks.

"Do you suppose that woman made it up?" Reid asked. "Or did she know already?"

Cosser let out a long, low sound. "What a nuisance she could prove to be."

"I thought you liked her. It looked that way."

Cosser laughed. "Well, I thought I did, too. But now I might be thinking better of that." He sounded annoyed. "Actually I need to call her." He pulled into a coffee shop where they sat in the parking lot. He looked for Rosemary's number and dialed it.

"Why didn't you tell me that your minister actually does walk in his sleep?" he asked right after he identified himself. "Why did you make up the stuff about writing a mystery?

You should have come right out with it. Don't mess around with our investigation. We need everyone to tell us the truth."

"I did tell you the truth," Rosemary insisted.

"Well, it seems pretty suspicious."

"I didn't know. Are you telling me that David is actually a suspect and that he does walk in his sleep?"

"I'm telling you only what is known now. Also, I want to make it clear that you must stay out of the investigation. It only confuses things. I'll have questions for you, but for heaven's sakes, don't go around trying to solve a murder and spewing theories you actually know nothing about. You could hurt the investigation, or worse, cause harm to yourself."

32

EVEN SOMEONE WHO DID NOT WANT to write about the death in the church might want to figure it out, Rosemary thought, especially if sufficiently at risk. Having dated the man she met through the ad, wasn't she entitled to seek information that might lead to the killer? No one knew yet what role Mr. Almost might play in all of this.

What a shame, she thought. For the first time in her life, she had a book she might write and she'd just been told to leave it alone. From now on she would write it without telling anyone. Least of all would she tell this police officer whom she suspected would never ask her for a date even when the investigation was over.

When she called the church to ask the secretary which parishioners might need a call from the Congregational Care Committee, Rosemary learned that David had decided to take some time off.

"Why?"

"Well, it seems that he told the bishop that he has occasional sleepwalking episodes, and he and the bishop decided that it would be a good idea for him to take time off even if he is not in any way implicated in what happened at the church. And he isn't, you know. He has an ironclad alibi. But it could create a lot of ugly publicity. And apparently he has met some rather unsavoury people in his night wanderings. Can you imagine? What a bizarre twist to things."

"What next?" Rosemary muttered, troubled. It had never dawned on her that David could hurt anyone. Certainly not kill someone.

"I think Ardith would appreciate a call."

"I've arranged to see Ardith."

"Oh, good. Possibly Rob then. And Polly."

"Polly?"

"When she's here, I can tell she's having a difficult time these days. Those are the folks I'd suggest you contact, Rosemary. If there are any emergencies, we'll take care of them from the office."

"Thanks." Rosemary was grateful that the people identified were among the ones she wanted to call anyway. She would not have to pretend to have a reason.

On Friday, at six o'clock, she rang the bell at Ardith's apartment. "It's Rosemary," she announced to the intercom and waited for Ardith to buzz her in.

She walked to the elevator and then down the hall to the door of Ardith's apartment. This was not her first visit, so Rosemary was familiar with the way everything was carefully installed to make moving around in a wheelchair possible. The kitchen counter was low as were cupboards that Ardith could reach easily.

Ardith nodded happily and gestured for Rosemary to make herself comfortable. She said hello and wiped the back of her hand across her face. Rosemary took the bag of takeout food she had picked up at the Swiss Chalet to the kitchen, and placed it on the large plastic plates Ardith had left out. As she put the plates on a table on the other side of the counter, Ardith wheeled over and took her place. She grinned at Rosemary, who sat down on an old oak captain's chair with a striped cushion on the seat.

"Bless this food," Rosemary said.

Ardith nodded. "Amen."

Ardith was slow eating her food and Rosemary tried to pace

herself. When they were finished, Ardith looked at Rosemary with tight lips. "What's the matter, Ardith?"

"Body."

"Somebody."

Ardith shook her head. "Body."

I don't get it, Rosemary thought. Body. What body? "Oh," she said suddenly. "You mean the body in the church."

Ardith nodded as if Rosemary were very clever. "What about the body?" Rosemary asked.

"Saw her."

"You saw her?"

Ardith nodded again. Rosemary knew the other woman could tell when someone began to figure out what was going on in her head. Usually people did not have the patience.

"Man."

"Man."

"Woman slump."

"Did you see the woman outside the church, Ardith?"

"Ahhunh."

"With a man?"

They were getting somewhere, Rosemary thought. How could she ask if it were the man with the white ribbon? Well, she could just ask, couldn't she? So she did.

Ardith shook her head. No.

Rosemary felt her jaw relax, unaware until that moment that she had been hanging onto tension so profound that it had become a part of her body. If the man with the white ribbon was not the man who had taken Margaret Atchison into the church, she, Rosemary did not have to worry quite so much. No more than any other woman did, knowing the killer was still on the loose. At that thought, she felt a hint of panic. After all, the killer still *was* on the loose. She breathed deeply and slowly.

"Have you told the police?'

Ardith shook her head again. No, she had not.

"Did someone come to see you?"

She nodded in the affirmative, but from the troubled look that crossed her face, it was apparent she had not been able to make herself understood.

"Would you like me to call the police officer now and let him know you want to talk to him again?"

"Ummm." This time the nod was in the affirmative.

Rosemary took out Cosser's card. He was not at the station, so she left a message that Ardith would like to talk to him, that she had seen something before the service on the morning of—

Ardith interrupted her and started waving her hand in the air. "No," she managed to utter and shook her head.

Rosemary had no idea what she might be talking about now. She ended her message with Ardith's address and phone number. When she hung up, she asked Ardith a few more questions, but still could not grasp what she was trying to say. If only she could tell that surly detective something useful without him concluding she was trying to run her own investigation. She hoped he would be patient enough to get all the information he needed from Ardith and that it might help the police to finally identify a suspect.

33

POLLY SAT AT THE PIANO in the nave of the church. More and more young people had been coming to services until the murder happened, and she thought the music, more contemporary but consistent with the liturgy, must play a role. She wanted to find a way to draw them back and thought even more emphasis on music their generation liked might help do that. The word would spread through youth who had remained despite the suspicious atmosphere that had descended on the community. One or another of them always stayed around to talk to whoever played the flute or drums or guitar. Eric had said he would play his guitar at the next service. He said the kids wanted to know about the music and if he wrote the songs. They seemed surprised to discover that some of the music was actually from a previous century.

"Man, you're kidding!" Their eyes lit up.

"Like cool."

Eric was good with them. He always showed them a few notes and then steered them to her for lessons. Polly felt an underlying sadness about the tense atmosphere that had existed in the congregation since the murder, but she always brightened up at the thought of Eric. She was surprised to see Linda cross the wooden floor toward her.

"Hi, Linda," she said.

"Hi," Linda said. "I came to talk to you about being in the choir. Although I'm not sure I can carry a tune." Then she lowered her voice, although there was no one else there. "What do you think of David and the sleepwalking bit?"

"You know, Linda," Polly said. "I think he's a decent man. I'm glad his wife knows he wasn't out that night because I'd hate to see him have to go through a trial when he's innocent. It would likely kill him. That's really all I have to say about it."

Linda looked disappointed, as if she were hoping for some juicy gossip. You have to know, Polly thought, that Linda never liked David. She had been adamant that he was the wrong person in the wrong place at the wrong time. Likely Linda would not be able to see any time when David might have been the right minister for this parish. He was staid and quiet and somewhat behind the times. Odd that she had been named a warden when everyone knew her opinion of the man.

"I know what you think of him," Polly said. "But all the same, he is a good man and there are some that spout all the right jargon and political stuff who are jerks."

Linda sighed. "Yes, of course." But she did not look convinced. "Maybe that's why we need a women's group here. To help define how to deal with whatever the other gender comes up with. Men have always had networks and clubs and meetings where they've been able to discuss things. We need to create our own."

"Sure," Polly said.

"And we need to work at getting a woman as the next minister of this parish."

"I think it's not a bad idea to start thinking in those terms for the future, but David's been gone less than a week. I think your timing is premature."

"Well, we could get the group going."

"We?"

"I'm starting to talk to people. Don't you think Patsy would be a great advocate?"

"Patsy may never come back to the church."

"Why ever not?"

"Don't you know that the woman who was murdered was her friend?"

"You're kidding."

Polly did not reply to that. She looked at the songbooks strewn across the floor beside the piano. Her work was only partially done at this stage, although she had learned that part of what she was expected to do as well was to deal with parishioners. That was how she knew a little about David's character, and that he was a gentle and caring man under a rather austere exterior. Many times she had seen him drop everything when there was an illness or a death or when someone wandered in off the streets and needed to talk. She had even seen him make coffee and sandwiches for some of the homeless men.

"I guess you're not," Linda said. "In spite of the work I do and what I hear on an ongoing basis, I'm still often surprised by the absurdity of life. How do you know that?"

"I guess Rosemary figured it out. Rosemary does make calls, you know. Patsy must have told her."

"Funny, she's never called me."

Polly could see Rosemary coming up beside them, but Linda had not.

"I've been meaning to," Rosemary chimed in. Linda jumped and her eyes shifted, as if she were trying to focus. "I'm sorry," Rosemary said. "I didn't mean to startle you."

"What about going for a cup of coffee?" Linda asked. "And leaving Polly to her work."

"It's okay about the choir, Linda," Polly said. "Come to the next rehearsal." The two women walked out together and she was relieved to see Eric at the door not too long after. Her life felt so fragmented on days when she did not see him. She would be glad when they had finished moving all her belongings over to the island.

"Hi, sweetheart," he said.

"Hi."

He kissed her lightly on the lips. "Do you have time to go for a walk?" he asked.

"I said I'd be here for anyone who comes in to look around the church today while I'm working on the music for next Sunday's service. Maybe we could just sit here and chat."

"What about on the steps just outside the door?" he asked. "It's beautiful out. The sun is strong enough that you'll be warm wearing just your sweater." He picked up the multicoloured cardigan that she had knit for herself the previous winter and draped it around her shoulders. "Let's go," he said.

When Eric was around, she could feel herself get taller and her heart start singing. It was as if someone had come along and painted sunshine across her day. "Okay," a broad smile lit up her face.

On the steps, he pulled out a brown paper bag and offered her a bagel. "It has all your favourite things on it. Cream cheese. Smoked salmon paste. Tapenade." Although it was hard to imagine eating all of them in the same mouthful, she knew she would. And lick her lips and think she was in heaven.

"Thank you, sweetheart," she said.

"Only for you."

Polly thought of the many times he'd told her that she had brought music into his life on a daily basis. "You can't thank someone enough for that," he'd said then. "You have to do things for them that remind them they're special." And she had discovered he was a man of large gesture, of generous propensity.

Not long after what Polly thought must have been a very short coffee break, she saw Rosemary pull out a blue helmet and get on a bicycle near the restaurant, a clunker by the looks of it. Would Rosemary have agreed to a women's group? She and Linda were so different from each other, Polly thought, and there was always some underlying tension when they crossed paths.

"Soon we'll have to start to plan our wedding," Eric said.

"I'd like to wait until the police investigation is over," Polly said. "Because I'd like to be married in this church. A small wedding though."

Eric nodded. "Will we ask David to officiate?'

"I'm not sure if we can now. I suppose we could ask the bishop whether it's appropriate."

"Why not one of the priests in the parish?"

"That's a thought." She tried to figure out who they might ask. "I still have nightmares sometimes about that woman," she added.

"What woman?"

"The one who was killed."

"Would you rather be married somewhere else? Outside maybe. In a park."

"No. For one thing, we'd have to wait too long for the good weather. I think the church is a good idea. I think it needs to have celebrations take place in it. A wedding in January or February would be cheerful. Right when everyone needs something to celebrate. And right in the middle of winter. We could simply invite anyone in the congregation who wants to come. Perhaps we could tell them the reception will be a potluck. You could ask your family and—"

"You're always full of good ideas" Eric pulled her close and whispered in her ear. Then he stood up. "But the crime might not be solved by then."

"That's true," Polly said. "But can't we keep talking about the wedding so we can go ahead as soon as it is."

Eric nodded skeptically and she thought maybe he did not want to say what she was also thinking: what would they do if the case was not solved soon?

When Eric left, Polly went back inside the church. She gathered up all the sheets of paper and the books she had strewn around the piano. She did not hear Linda come back in and stand waiting for her to turn around, so, she was startled when the other woman cleared her throat.

"Oh that Rosemary," Linda muttered. "Such a cork up her—"

"Linda, please," Polly said.

"She's obsessed with that damn murder. She says she's going to write a book. That woman has been going to write a book ever since I've known her, but she all she does is talk endlessly about it. Now she has fastened herself onto this murder and makes up all kinds of things about people. Did you know she was painting the minister as a sleepwalker before it was public about David? She made it up, that's what she says. I think she feels that she's created the truth, that David did not sleepwalk until she said so. Such a bizarre sense of reality."

"I don't know," Polly said. "She seems quite down to earth to me."

"So you don't think she's slightly off?"

"No, not really. I think she's a bit shy and maybe also lonely, and sometimes gets carried away by her own imaginings. But off? No, no more than the rest of us."

Linda turned around abruptly and started to walk quickly toward the door. Polly was mystified, had she offended her? Then she was just as surprised when Linda turned around again.

"Did you know that the man with the white ribbon is a suspect in the murder?"

"What man?"

"You mean you didn't see him?"

"Oh, yes, of course I did. You just caught me off guard. How so?"

"Well, he placed an ad in the newspaper. That's why he was here. Rosemary answered it."

"But that doesn't explain the murder."

"The woman who was killed could have answered the same ad."

"Oh, that's so terrible," Polly said. "Rosemary could have been murdered."

"I might have been too. If she hadn't come along that day in church and headed off with him, I think he was about to ask me to go somewhere with him. I think if she hadn't interrupted, he would at least have asked for my phone number."

"Oh, that's so frightening," Polly said again. "You aren't safe anywhere anymore."

"I don't know," Linda said. "I like to live with the illusion that there are places where I am, but you sure have to be careful. Especially if you're a woman. Men don't understand it."

"Some do, I suppose. But they don't live with the fear all the time, so how would they?"

Linda looked triumphant. As if she were playing some kind of game and she had just scored.

34.

BEFORE MOVING INTO HEADQUARTERS, for a long time Cosser had worked out of a downtown station. You got to see about everything in a division like that one, he thought. There were more bodies than he cared to remember—car accident victims, domestics, street fights, a woman in a field who later turned out to have been sexually assaulted as well as strangled. He had seen many grim things in his day. He tried to blank out the children, always the most upsetting, whether in mangled cars at accident scenes or somehow caught in the middle of a domestic. Why he remembered now, he did not know. Maybe it had something to do with that woman, Rosemary, trying to write a mystery novel. She came up with the damnedest scenarios, but he knew that she could not come up with anything more strange or sinister than what he had actually experienced during his years as a cop. There was the time he and his partner were out in a squad car when they received the call he was thinking of. Marlene was driving. She was still around, but working out of another division now. When they arrived at the apartment, an old woman had answered the door.

"I didn't do it." She had to lean on a cane to walk across the room.

"You didn't?" Marlene had said. "You didn't do what?"

She and Cosser winked at each other over the woman's head. Slightly senile, the wink said. You knew that would be the case when an old woman called in some story about a body that was upside down in one of her closets.

"You take that one, Jack," Marlene said, heading toward a closet on the other side of the room. He could hear her open it and gasp. "Never mind," she said. "I've found it."

"I didn't do it," the woman said again.

Neither of them said anything. They were not winking now. You for sure do not say, "Of course you didn't," when you have just discovered a body, a body they actually thought was nonexistent. They both stood looking at the grotesque angle of the dead man. It took a while to discover he had a number of drugs he regularly took and had failed to get his prescription filled, then he had somehow become confused and accidently locked himself inside the closet. How he ended up in that position was never determined, but it did not take long to figure out the woman, his wife, really did not have anything to do with it.

And yet Rosemary had managed to confound him with the suggestion that the minister in her story walked in his sleep. He had never encountered a murder committed by a sleepwalker and he believed the minister's wife; otherwise, he thought, Rosemary's version could have been a plausible theory. It was utterly ridiculous at the same time, but then some things were stranger than fiction. He knew that was a cliché, but how better to describe it?

It bothered him—the hard-boiled cop, or so he imagined she described his counterpart in her manuscript—that in her story the blood on the clothes worn by the dead woman that would be used as evidence in court one day could have anything to do with the minister. Of course, it would not be used that way if it were not the minister's blood. And he had already corroborated that with forensics. Although it did not clear David entirely, and Cosser knew he should not presume anything at this point. Maybe David's wife was lying. Yet he suspected she would not protect her husband if she thought he might be culpable. Cosser had since examined the photographs taken at the scene more often than he cared to remember. He was still troubled by the suspicion that there was more involved in this case than the murder of a stranger. There were signs he sensed were there that he could not decipher even in the graphic details the photographer had created. But what was he missing? If he was indeed missing anything. Detective Constable Donald Simmons had been in charge of collecting the physical evidence at the site as a member of the force's forensic identification unit. Cosser thought it was time he talked to Simmons again.

The photographs showed the position of the woman's body: face down with her feet splayed behind her. Her head was touching the bottom of the toilet, her legs in sheer stockings and her feet in fashionable red leather pumps—suggesting this woman had some money—were sticking out from under the door. Her head rested in a small pool of blood and there were also spots of blood on the front of her jacket. You could not see the front of the jacket in the photographs, but Cosser had seen it. Nor could you see the spot where some object had struck the front of her head until the body had been moved, after Simmons and the others had thoroughly studied and photographed her, and made notes about the scene.

All of this would be evidence, but only if they found the killer. He decided he should speak to the minister again. It intrigued him that a librarian who seemed to go around in somewhat of a fantasy world could dream up what could be a plausible solution to an actual murder. For that at least had been established. This had not been a suicide. The way the wound was inflicted left no doubt. They had not found the murder weapon. It had to be something with a blunt edge – maybe a brick the killer found in his kitchen, holding down a piece of vinyl. Cosser thought of this because he had such a brick in his own kitchen. Other items that crossed his mind quickly that were features of many lives were a piece of driftwood brought back from Algonquin Park or a sculpture of some kind, maybe even an Inuit sculpture. Not poison. Although the forensic report had indicated she had some substance in her system that would have made her sleepy. Maybe a metal tool, something like a hammer, had killed Marni. Perhaps the killer had used a pillow to keep her quiet while he choked her and then to make absolutely certain, he hit her over the head. Or maybe when he dragged her body to the trunk of his car, the wound opened. Maybe he dated her and came back to her place unannounced, picked up a rock on her front porch and used it to break the window. No, that would have been far too noisy. And there had been no broken front window. His mind was running wild because he was trying to use his right brain as he thought Rosemary must have to come up with some of the story lines she'd suggested. There was creativity in everything, he thought, including police work.

He picked up the telephone to call Rosemary. He did not know what day she was off or what her hours were and so was expecting to hear an answering machine. He was surprised when she answered.

"It's Detective Sergeant Cosser," he said. "You called."

"Yes," she said. "You got the message that Ardith wants to speak with you, did you?"

"That's right."

"You know, I've been thinking. Maybe the murderer was a female. Maybe it was her mother, programmed to kill her daughter rather than see her religion defiled."

"Rosemary, I called to see if you could tell me anything about Ardith before I arrange to see her."

"Oh, I'm sorry," she said. "But I thought you'd questioned her once already. What would you like to know?'

"Tell me again what you know about her. I didn't get much information when I saw her."

"Most people don't understand her so they don't see that she's incredibly observant and sees many things that we might miss. She has cerebral palsy and she struggles to get her words out."

"I see."

"You have to be very patient. It takes time to figure out what she's saying."

"And what was it she said that led you to call?"

Rosemary told him about her earlier conversation with Ardith. What she'd understood Ardith had seen, about the body.

"The police will follow up on it pronto."

"Well, I'm glad to hear that. Are you aware you didn't answer my question? Did you consider the possibility it might not be a man after all?"

"You know, Rosemary, the police consider every possible avenue. And actually, we haven't ruled out anything. But I'm not at liberty to discuss it further."

"But she wasn't sexually assaulted, was she? So it could have been a woman."

"How do you know that? Or are you making it up? We need more evidence than imagination to go on."

"The news reports, "she said. "And, oh yes, you've made that clear. All the same, I'd hate to think you ruled something out that would find a suspect."

"I don't intend to rule out anything," Cosser said. "Every lead will be checked out." He didn't say anything about having been hasty in dismissing Ardith earlier as someone who could not possibly have seen anything. It was his failure not to have understood the woman, her garbled speech such a barrier to communication that he'd decided a more complete interview with her could wait until he had talked to most of the others who had been in the church that Sunday.

"So," Rosemary said. "I'll thank you when you've charged someone."

Cosser shook his head and let out a sigh as he walked across the office and picked up some papers. The woman was determined. He liked that about her, but it also made him uneasy.

He also knew he walked a fine line with her. Whenever he was in contact, however official the reason, he was either attracted to her or angry at her. If he were not careful, she could mess up everything.

35

A S SHE WALKED TO THE LIBRARY, Rosemary thought about the bits of information she'd picked up about the murder. She continued to ponder through most of her day, no matter what else she was doing, from sorting through the paperwork at her desk to cleaning something when she arrived at home again, to cooking or having a shower, on how these fragments could fit together. The detective had said nothing she could base her story on, but the whole city knew a great deal from the media. The rest she filled in for herself. Sometimes she wrote paragraphs in her head. Of late she had taken to carrying a notebook and she jotted in it while sitting on subway platforms, on the benches in the Eaton Centre, or anywhere she stopped for a cup of coffee

MARNI WEARS A BLACK DRESS *for the second date with Mr. Almost,* Rosemary wrote, leaving the names for now as those of the actual people. *She rather likes him, in spite of her disparaging remarks to Patsy. She does not know quite why. Perhaps because of the rhythm that always seems to course through him. A slight hint of music anywhere and his shoulders and head start to move and he taps his fingers. If he's standing, even on a sidewalk filled with people, he does a few steps. Whatever she dislikes about him, Marni finds his sense of rhythm disarming. She's embarrassed to tell Patsy she's decided to see him again after all. But when she goes to meet him, it is not Mr. Almost who turns up, it's someone else, with dark hair and equally dark glasses, who says Sloane could not make it.*

"*Who's that?*" *she asks.*

"*You know, Michael Sloane.*"

"*So why didn't he call himself to tell me?*"

"*I couldn't tell you, ma'am.*"

"*So he sends a stand-in? What kind of jerk is he anyway?*"

"*Too much,*" *the man says.*

"*I think I'll be on my way.*"

"*Oh c'mon, Marni, let's have one drink, eh?*"

"*So you know my name.*"

"*Yeah. Sure. Of course. Sloane told me.*"

"*You know what, whatever you name is—*"

"*Pete Cameron.*"

"*Pete, I don't know what this friend of yours would do and I'm less interested with each passing moment.*"

They walk along Queen Street West, heading toward the core of the city, and pass a pub on the south side just after they cross Spadina. Marni does not know why she continues to walk with him or what they have to say to each other. She supposes she is caught off guard by the unexpected and is curious. Otherwise, she could hop on a streetcar easily.

"*What about this pub?*" *Pete says.*

"*Sure, why not?*"

Seated at the bar on a tall stool, she leans forward and orders a beer. Although she's stopped smoking, she lights up a cigarette. She cadges them from friends until she realizes it's not working, that she has to start buying her own again. She does not know what to make of this man who has come along as Mr. Almost's proxy. Why would he bother? Maybe so many women answered the ad that he's setting his friends up now. Maybe he's running a mini-matchmaking business. She's surprised when she starts to feel dizzy after a few sips of the beer. She wonders if Pete has slipped something into it and if he's up to something. But what? When? She's been sitting here the entire time. She cannot even remember turning her head away, but then she remembers that every time she blows out smoke she turns so as not to exhale the smoke on him. He's had more than enough opportunity. She leaves the beer on the bar and tries to keep her eyes from crossing and her head from spinning, but she cannot seem to manage it.

"You okay?" Pete asks.

"Um, um, yes." She cannot get any more words out and she feels herself falling over against him. She's aware of wondering why he would want to hurt her. She's read about men who dope women and then rape them. She wonders if she can scream and get some attention, but her voice will not rise above a whisper and her words are unintelligible. She hears Pete tell the bartender that she's had too much to drink again and that he's going to have to get a cab. Again, she thinks. How would he know that? Anyway, she never drinks more than a beer or two. She has not been drunk for years now and it's certain she's never felt like this before.

In the cab, Marni falls against the man, not conscious of anything. He tells the cab where to go and drags her up to an apartment over a store a few blocks away. He drops her on his bed and takes her clothes off. Then he climbs on top of her. After he's done, he thinks he'll have to kill her. She'd be able to identify him. This is going a step farther than he's ever gone before, but he's angry with Sloane for cutting him out of the action, and he's going to see that if anyone gets caught for what he's now contemplating it won't be Pete Cameron.

ROSEMARY MAKES A MENTAL NOTE that she's changed the point of view in the story and might have to reconsider, but she goes on writing. She'll have to come back later and figure out how to handle that she wants to develop both characters and that could mean setting up separate chapters for each of them. She'd have to check in one of the how-to-write fiction books at the library.

After all, it was Sloane who asked him to place the ad and the replies had come to him, Mr. Peter Cameron, because he'd also paid for it. Sloane had asked him to read all the replies as they arrived, so he was the first to screen them, throwing out the boring ones. He had only kept a couple of names for himself. Now he has with him the woman who'd seemed the most interesting, although he'd handed her letter on to Michael Sloane in the beginning.

"You know, if this one doesn't grab you, I'd like to meet her," he'd said.

Rosemary wished she could tell the detective how her story was developing, but she knew by now it would just annoy him. What did she know? But her story felt so real that it managed to convince her that this was the explanation the police needed to be able to proceed.

Now here she is in his apartment and he's raped her and is thinking of murdering her. But he does not know where to do that or where to leave her and escape detection. Maybe in that church where Sloane had gone to meet one of the others who'd replied to the ad. She'd asked him to wear a white ribbon on his jacket. Certainly he himself has never had any connection to a church, so no one will have any reason to suppose he has anything to do with this woman's body being found there. Question is how to get into the church, commit the murder, and get out without anyone seeing him. The woman was not going to come to any time soon, so he'll tell a cab driver she's been drinking, and ask to be taken to a spot near enough to the church to slip in when there is an opportunity. He knows it is a church that is often open because he sometimes walks by it when he is downtown on an errand of some kind. Somehow he does not think he'll be able to carry it off, but he thinks it is worth a try. What does he have to lose? The woman is not dead yet and if worse comes to worst, he will not kill her. She'll have a hard time proving sexual assault since she was not even conscious.

So this was how the body of the woman came to be in the basement of the church in Rosemary's story. The man was lucky in accomplishing what he had set out to do. The woman was unlucky. Rosemary might have once again stumbled on at least some portion of the truth. She ought to let the detective know, she thought again, but Cosser had told her to keep her nose out of it. At the very least, she would call him. Even if he did not like it, if she'd come across something, he ought to know. But when she did, he shrugged off her comments and changed the subject.

"You can read what I've written if you want," she said.

"Why would I do that?"

She was quiet, embarrassed,

"Look, if you want me to read something for accuracy of the police work, just ask. You know, techniques, etcetera, I'd be glad to do that. I won't be able to discuss any details of actual cases with you, but I think you know that now."

"Sure. When you have time, let me know," Rosemary had replied. "I would love for you to look over the parts that deal with the police."

So not long afterwards, in fact only a few hours later, she had a call from Detective Sergeant Cosser who said he would be passing through her area shortly and would drop by. So when she heard a step on the front porch fifteen minutes later, she moved toward the front of the house and peered out the window. There was a Honda parked on the street so she assumed he was driving his own car.

The bell rang and she let Cosser in through the door to the living room. He sat down on a wood chair with a straight back, his actions stiff and formal.

Rosemary continued to stand, feeling awkward, as if she might find a rip in her clothes if she looked down or that something had come askew. She picked up some pages she had printed out and handed them to him.

As he began to study her manuscript quietly, not wanting to

hear a sigh of disapproval or witness an expression that was also dismissive, Rosemary backed out of the room. She would go to the kitchen and put on the coffee pot, she thought.

Once she heard him laugh and wondered if he'd found something funny, or more likely ridiculous. When she went back into the room, carrying two mugs of coffee, he grinned at her. "This is good," he said. "You write well. And you cover police work accurately thus far. In Toronto though, it's not a precinct. It's a division."

"Oh, thanks. I read all the crime reports in the papers and watch stuff on television. About real murders, not the television series. But a lot of it is American."

"Well, as I said, you're a good writer."

"Thank you," she said again, hoping she did not sound like a prim and proper librarian. If such a species still exists, she thought.

"Well, carry on with it. If you have questions about police work in general, don't hesitate to ask."

"This is fiction, of course." Rosemary said, then paused. "Some of the names I used are of the real people, but I intend to change them."

"Of course. You said you pay attention to the media. You probably know they speculate a lot before they know anything for certain. It sells more newspapers. And more ads on television as well."

"That's so irresponsible. Women all across this city are terrified."

"Actually I think the media has been fairly responsible around the murder at the church. And there has been a murder, so people do need to know that."

"Yes, of course. There's no doubt we do," she said, thinking of the headlines and television banners that screamed the horror of everyday violence on paper and screen. "I'll go on with the development of my own plot though. That's what writers do." Or, as she had now discovered, she actually took many of her ideas from the news and added them to her own emerging story.

"Good luck." He sipped some coffee and then put the mug down on a glass table near where he sat.

As he got up and headed to the door, she followed him. "Good luck to you, too," she said.

36.

WHEN COSSER ARRIVED AT HIS APARTMENT after another long day, he thought about Rosemary. How she'd irritated him. Likely because he was also attracted to her, something he had been careful not to convey. Any indication of that now would compromise his investigation and cross the line of what was reasonable conduct. He also felt uncomfortable as he still felt allegiance toward Marion. He reached for the telephone to call his former wife, relieved when it was she who answered and not the ubiquitous answering machine.

"Got a minute?"

"Sure. Jaime's already asleep."

"I thought she would be by now. Don't like to miss that good night hug over the wires, but tonight I wanted to talk to you."

"Oh yes. About?"

"Could I drop around?"

"Won't the telephone do?"

"I'd rather see you. And when Jaime's asleep."

"Okay," she said. "Do you want some coffee? I can put on a pot."

"What about tea? Do you have any chamomile?"

"Herbal tea?" she asked, a note of surprise in her voice.

"Yeah." Some time he might tell her that he now also meditated and practised yoga.

"Hmm."

"So, I'll see you in twenty minutes."

"All right."

Cosser went into the bathroom and as he combed his hair back, he noticed a few new strands of grey. Some of the women on the task force on family violence had labeled him male privilege personified. He could see it in their eyes and faces. It had been satisfying to see their perceptions change as they had worked together. He had been open to learn and to change and had tried to ally himself with their concerns and see how he could make inroads in the bureaucracy of a large police department. He had recognized Linda as one of the women who spoke to the task force, but after acknowledging that when questioning her, he hadn't referred to it again. He brushed his teeth and swirled some green liquid around in his mouth. He felt as if he were preparing for a first date, he was that nervous.

When he arrived at the house, there was a light on in the porch. The house seemed smaller than he remembered, across from a fire station. Just as he arrived, one of the big trucks drove in, back from a call perhaps. No sirens on the return trip. Many nights they had been awakened by the sound and Marion had talked of moving. But it was convenient to live this close to downtown, to be able to walk out to Bloor Street in the evenings. She had loved that.

When he lifted the brass knocker he recalled installing some years ago, Marion opened the door before he let it drop.

"Shh," she said. "Let's not wake Jaime."

"All right."

He followed her down the hall into the kitchen where there was a teapot on the table and two mugs. Not much had changed in the kitchen since he had moved out, but he could see a newly-mounted poster depicting colourful red, orange, and yellow flowers hanging at the far end beside the door out to the back garden.

"What's this all about anyway?" Marion did not sound angry, confused or surprised maybe.

"I wondered if we could—"

"Maybe I'd better tell you about—"

"I still love you, Marion."

"I'll always love you, Jack, but—"

"I'd like to get back together," he said. "I know what happened and I can't say that doing police work can ever make for an easy family life. But I know now there are things I can do to reduce the stress and that I could make more time and—"

"Oh, Jack," Marion said. "Jack. Jack."

"What's the matter, dear heart? You just said you still love me, too."

"I always will. You were my first husband. You are the father of my only child. We didn't divorce because of lack of love. In many ways, it was a tragedy. But I love someone else now."

"I see." Jack's body became rigid and his face was flushed. "Have I just made a fool of myself or what?"

"No, my dear. I'm flattered and touched. I'm glad we can still talk and that we are good parents and good friends."

"But now you'd like me to leave."

"No. Finish your tea. Tell me about what you've been doing. How was your day?"

"Interesting." He wished he could tell her more. She would have read about the woman who was discovered in the basement of the church. Murdered. But he refrained from any comment at all, necessary in his kind of occupation. The boundaries that were part of being a policeman, and the ones for someone in charge of a homicide investigation, were stringent. It did not make life any easier, he thought, but it would become chaotic otherwise.

"Um," she nodded.

"One funny thing, I think you'll find it funny anyway," Jack said. "There's a woman who is trying to become a writer and she keeps on making up stories for a mystery that parallels the investigation. She only has the media to base her stories on, but she comes up with some very plausible situations."

"And you've taken a bit of a shine to her, haven't you, Jack?"

He looked at her, his expression portraying utter confusion. What was she talking about? "I don't know what you mean, Marion. I've always loved you."

"I know that, Jack. But it sounds as if this writer interests you."

He sighed. "Perhaps," he said. "But what that made me realize was that I—" He stopped.

"It's all right," she said. "Now you know about my situation, why not follow up on whatever it is?"

"Not that fast," he said. "Maybe in time."

"Maybe you wanted to check with me first because of familiarity and habit. But it's okay to let go of that now, Jack." There were suddenly tears in her eyes and as she wiped them away, Cosser eyed her thoughtfully.

"Tell me about the man you're seeing," he said, an encouraging smile on his face.

"He teaches. In Peterborough. That's probably why you haven't been aware of him, because I haven't wanted to bring him into Jaime's life to any great extent until a few more things are settled. He's a professor at Trent. I go up there on the weekends Jaime's with you."

"What's his name?"

"Colin. What's the name of the woman detective?"

"She's not a detective."

"Well, the writer who fancies herself able to solve mysteries then."

"Rosemary."

"Nice name."

"Glad you think so."

"Good luck, Jack."

He shrugged. How could he have luck with someone it would be improper even to invite for coffee? Unless he had some reason connected to the case. Surely he could find something that would fall within the line of duty. Sooner or later he hoped he would be able to approach her as a woman with whom he would like to spend some time.

He started toward the front door, and then turned to look at the woman he had shared his life with for seven years. "Do you mind if I hug you?"

"Thought you'd never ask."

PART IV

37

End of November

JUST AFTER THE SERVICE HAD BEGUN, David came in through the west door of the church. As quietly and unobtrusively as he could manage, he walked to a pew toward the back. He knew that to continue to go to a church where you were taking a rest from the ministry, or had retired from that ministry, was not done. Yet he felt the congregation would be comfortable if he continued to attend. He understood they could discuss it at Parish Council and ask him not to, but he did not expect that. It was only the bishop he worried about, but how would he know? And, of course, since it was taken for granted that he would not have come back, the bishop had not raised it.

Anne had not liked it when he told her what he wanted to do. She certainly had no intention of accompanying him. She had made that clear. But then, he felt that she had not liked this church from the beginning. He had not told Anne that one of the parishioners had even said she hoped he would come. To his surprise, it had been Linda.

"Hello," Brent said as he came through the door. And as David sat down, Ardith smiled at him with the lopsided grin he'd always found so wrenching and appealing. He could see Polly look up from the piano and smile when she suddenly caught sight of him. It made him sad that Anne could not see that for him this parish had become a community. When you struggled as hard as he had, either you gave up at some point or gradually you began to belong in spite of the conflicts. He was not sure that he had had this sense of belonging at any other parish, this sense of being recognized as a man with his own interests and failings. They had taken him seriously both as a minister and as a person. They had accepted his information about his troubled sleep with equanimity. If there had been some doubt in their minds that he might be implicated in something immoral or illegal as a result of it, they might not have been so accepting. On the other hand, he had seen many people come and go in this church who might not so easily be comfortable elsewhere. They prayed for each other. He had noted this in the journal he'd begun to keep when he realized he'd started sleepwalking. He'd also written down his observations more generally and begun to probe his past more deeply. It was taking on the aura of becoming a memoir of sorts although he did not imagine the ramblings of an aging minister would be of much interest to anyone.

"Morning, David," Linda said as she slipped in next to him.

This friendliness from Linda was one of the major surprises of recent days. There was a lull in the service and she leaned over and told him that she was going to a tango lesson afterwards. When he looked baffled, she just smiled. "Maybe you'd like to come some time."

Now, surely, he thought, she would not be making a pass at me. She knew he had a wife and a grown family. "I don't think so," he said. "But thanks for thinking of me, Linda." If he were to leave his wife and take up with another woman, he would have to look into something like Viagra. And he would have to answer to the bishop then for sure. No, he did not have to keep the bishop apprised of what had no bearing on his work and was of a purely personal nature, he thought. Maybe if he found a way to get more sleep at night and stopped wandering, he would find he was able to sustain an erection.

David was a little shocked at the direction of his fantasy. He would have to continue what he had started of late: long brisk walks every morning and visits to a naturopath about his sleep problem. He would continue to go to church where he could find reassurance in the familiar Christian teachings, in the community here that he felt included him. He did not imagine he was about to take up the tango. Or any other dances either, although he remembered when he used to go swing dancing when he was a young man. That was so long ago and not something he wanted to repeat. He would not leave Anne and become involved with anyone, certainly not Linda, although maybe he would consider the Viagra. He had to admit also, if only fleetingly, that he did find Linda's new attitude fascinating. From his fresh vantage point as a minister without duties here, he sensed he was no longer a threat to her. As an aging white male who had fallen into disrepute, he had no power. It surely heightened his awareness of some of what Linda had previously been so angry about, but he wondered if it were necessary for him to have fallen so far to be able to do so. And if she were not just a trifle condescending now. He detested that what he saw in her was his previous attitude.

At the time for the peace, still early in the service, Linda hugged him warmly. He felt her breasts touch him through her sweater and his shirt and he turned hastily away. They had never hugged before. He had never been aware of her in this tactile sense that was heightened by her talk of the tango. To him that was one of the most sensuous dances he had ever watched, not something he ever imagined as part of his repertoire. As he moved out of the pew, Rob thrust his hand forward and they shook hands.

"The peace of Christ," David said.

"Peace," Rob murmured.

People moved freely around the church. There was even a certain gaiety to this interaction, although the words were often no more than the passing of the peace. David liked that about this church, that they saw this opportunity for warmth and let it go on far longer than was likely intended.

As he completed his circle around the pews to greet people, David wondered if he might sit with someone else now. But he did not want to do anything conspicuous. Better if he merely took his seat next to Linda and moved off among the throng for communion. So he did, sitting through the homily with seeming rapt attention while he observed the people across from and around him. Did any of them believe that he had something to do with the murder? Were they suspicious of each other? Was he suspicious of any of them? Brent had had all the opportunity, but David thought himself a good judge of people and he thought the younger man lacked the imagination for crime. Some of the women did not, but surely a man must have killed the victim, leaving her dead on the floor. The whole scenario struck him as altogether too unlikely for a woman. He wondered again why at first he had remembered the scene as if there had not been any blood. His thoughts were interrupted as people moved forward into the circle for communion.

As he followed, David felt uneasy. He saw looks that suggested his presence was unexpected. It was clear he'd made a mistake. Why had he thought he could return here and take up a role as an ordinary parishioner? Sometimes he realized he was a fuzzy thinker, relying on Anne to know what was appropriate. And as she was so often, Anne had been right about this. He would have to find a new place to worship. He hoped they could find one together. Although he thought he would like to come back to this church once more. There was something he felt was unfinished, even though he did not know what that might be at this particular moment.

AT THE END OF THE SERVICE, David went over to Polly who had closed the piano and was gathering her papers. She was at the front of the nave, near the microphone.

"I hope I will be able to announce the wedding soon," she muttered, turning to pick up her coat.

"Sorry, but I overheard that," David said. "When you're

ready, you could ask to have it put in the service sheets for the next week."

"That's a good idea," Polly said. "And when the time comes, Eric could come with me to invite people to celebrate with us."

David was surprised to hear her talking about it as if it would happen soon, but refrained from comment. "When are you planning to get married?" He had not wanted to leave the parish without knowing this.

"As soon as the murder is solved," Polly said.

She fiddled with the microphone, mouthing words. David figured she was probably rehearsing. "We invite you to join us." Or maybe she was trying to get used to making it public. She was a very private person, even though she was involved in the church in a way that made her visible to everyone.

"Suppose it isn't solved. Some cases drag on for years. Some are never solved."

Polly sighed. "Yes, of course. I guess we ought to have a Plan B for some time in the spring. Somewhere else."

David nodded. "I hope it can be here, Polly, because this is your family now, this community."

"Yes, of course," she said, starting to button up her coat. "And you know how grateful I am for that."

"I'm very happy for you," David said.

"I'm sorry you can't be the one to marry us. You're the first person I thought of."

"You could check with the bishop," he said. "I don't think there's anything that says I couldn't." There was a quick change in his expression. "But feel free to do what you think best. Nothing would have made me happier than to be the minister to officiate at your wedding. But Polly, I'll be very happy to be there to celebrate with you, whatever you do. In the meantime, I want to be the one to tell you I'll be going to another parish on Sundays. I think Anne has found one we can go to together. It really isn't appropriate for me to come here where I've been the minister, so it's time for a change."

"I have a thought."

"You know that I'll come to the wedding."

"I guess I just assumed you would," Polly said. "But I'm glad to hear it from you. For a moment, I even thought I might ask you to give me away, if I didn't find that practice so archaic."

"As I said, just let me know what you and Eric decide."

"You've been such a wonderful friend to me," she said.

David noticed people lined up for soup, others putting on their coats. Preoccupied with Christmas for now, after that when winter stretched out endlessly they would be glad of a wedding.

"Why don't you stay for lunch, David?" Polly asked.

"If you are."

"Well, I wasn't going to, but if you will."

He supposed he did not look the least bit uncomfortable, but under the brave veneer were the doubts and fears of anyone who has been a suspect in a murder. And who has had to leave his job as a result of that.

"It must have taken courage to come back here. I admire you, David. I also understand that you have to go to another parish now."

"No one here has even given the slightest hint of not trusting me. And this has been my home for a while now."

"It grows on you, doesn't it?"

He nodded, thinking of people who had moved to the farthest reaches of Canada—the west coast, Newfoundland—who still wanted to receive the church newsletter and when they came to Toronto, they came to service.

"Have you heard from Claire and Harry, by the way?" she asked.

"A note. They were very supportive. I called them when I couldn't figure out what to do. I can't imagine now that I could have done that. It wasn't something to approach parishioners about. I thought I would burst with the tension. And then when Harry said something about talking with the bishop, I knew that was the only thing to do. Actually, I knew it before I called them, but you know how you hope the unthinkable can't be true." He knew the moment he spoke to Harry, he said, that he would not be able to continue, although he had not let himself think about it until his talk with the bishop.

"I wish Claire and Harry could be here for the wedding."

"That would be something."

"But winter isn't a good time to come to Toronto. Still, I'll let them know when the time comes."

"You're a good woman, Polly."

"I miss having a family here," Polly said again. "But then, there's Eric and this community and with all of that, I hang on."

"And your music."

"Thank you, David."

"Let's go and get some soup," David said.

"Yes."

When they arrived at the counter where a woman stood ladling out portions of minestrone soup, there was only a little left at the bottom of the pot.

"But enough for two more," the woman said.

When they sat down on a pew along the side of the church, Polly looked at David speculatively. "You know," she said. "Patsy hasn't ever come back to the church. I wonder why."

"Didn't you know that Margaret Atchison was her friend?" David asked. "They shared a wall in a house. You know, one of those semis. And apparently they went back and forth a lot. It was almost as if they did not have a wall between them at times."

Polly looked troubled by this piece of information. "I wish I'd called her sooner. Now I scarcely know what to say."

"You could invite her to the wedding," David said.

"It's almost as if you knew what I was thinking," Polly said.

"No extrasensory perception. Although walking in my sleep might make some people imagine I have unusual powers."

"Some days anything seems possible," Polly grinned.

38

COSSER ARRIVED AT PATSY'S WORKPLACE and could see her waiting for him through the glass door of her office. He wanted to show her a photo he had found of the man with the bald head and tattoo before he had shaved his hair. Perhaps she had seen a similar photograph at Marni's and could offer an explanation of how this man might have been connected to her. Cosser did not think Marni's murder had been a random act, and he knew this was a lead he had to follow.

Patsy waved him into her office, and he sat down in the chair across from her. There was nothing new for him to tell her and she was not in any way a suspect, but once he'd discovered she'd been Marni's friend, he felt she deserved information. And if there were any way to offer her protection, well, that was also something he wanted to make sure the police did for her.

The phone rang and he gestured to her to answer it.

"It's probably a call from a colleague in another department," she said. "I asked him for some information."

It surprised him to see such a baffled expression cross her face as she realized it was not the call she anticipated. "Oh, hello, Polly," she said. "I didn't expect to hear from you."

Cosser realized it was Polly from the church on the line. Patsy pressed a button and suddenly Jack could also hear the conversation. He wondered why she had activated speakerphone, whether she thought there was something he ought to hear.

"I'm calling to tell you that Eric and I are going to get married," Polly said. "We won't have an actual date until the police finish their investigation and hopefully come up with a suspect. But when it happens, we'd like to have it in the church and we'd like it if you could be there."

Both Patsy and the detective could see through the glass doors out into the area where the tellers stood behind the counter.

"I don't know," Patsy said.

Cosser knew that she had a client coming in the next half hour. When he'd called to ask for a few minutes of her time, she'd mentioned that she did not have long to spend with him as her client had booked over a week ago to look over his portfolio with her and make some changes. She knew he would ask about margin trading again. For his level of experience, this was not a wise option. And she'd also mentioned it had taken a while for this client to trust her. The first time he had come in and found her as his adviser, she could tell that he had not been prepared even to enter into discussion. It happened so often, Patsy had said, that she'd become tired of it, but, she added: "I know my work and I know the things that win clients over. They want to know you are authentic. They want to know you 'get it' when they talk about their situation."

So often though, the client simply could not see beyond her colour. Sometimes it was her gender as well, but more often than not she was convinced their feelings about her were based on the colour of her skin. And Cosser had no reason not to believe that.

He could imagine her addressing the issue very directly and he had no doubt she would be very professional with all her clients. "I've looked over the information on your accounts and I would suggest that first you tell me what there is about the situation that you need to discuss. That will help me to come up with any recommendations, if any are needed, that are of the most use to you. As you mentioned on our phone call, you have a financial plan we put together early on and we can see if it still fits. A review at regular intervals is always good policy."

The man, sometimes the woman, would sit down then. A receptionist or secretary would come in with a tray of ice water and some coffee. If it was in the afternoon, there might be a plate of cookies. The client would likely begin to relax a little, but not altogether. Her colleagues had told her that this happened to them also, but she knew that she still had to prove herself in ways they would never imagine. No one ever asked them where they came from. Her education was Canadian and so was her work experience, but she did not tell these doubtful people that. She merely smiled nicely, as Canadians are wont to do, and if she answered the question, her response was brief.

"Toronto." That was where she lived now and she did not intend to elucidate further. Although she was proud of her Jamaican roots, this was not information they needed. She knew how to perform and make decisions and offer advice in a variety of situations. That was all they deserved from her, she thought, not a lengthy explanation of her ancestry.

Patsy had said this quite heatedly to him in one of their earlier interviews, Cosser recalled and he smiled ever so slightly at the memory.

"Eric and I would be very happy if you would," Polly said.

"I'd like to," Patsy said. "But I don't think I can go back to that church."

"I know that Margaret Atchison was a friend of yours. I'm really sorry. And I understand why that would make it difficult. I wish I'd known sooner and had contacted you then."

"It wouldn't have made a difference."

"Well, you might not have come back to the church, but it would have made a difference to me to know that you were having a hard time and that I had let you know I was there. It almost seems too late now. But I'm here if you'd like to get together. Even if you don't want to come to the wedding if it's in the church. "

"You're really kind," Patsy said. "Could I think about it?"

"Of course."

When she hung up, Patsy went back to the file folder in front of her and the information on her computer screen. Cosser could see the effort she was making to concentrate.

"I thought if you heard the conversation with Polly, I wouldn't have to go over it with you. If there was anything to go over," Patsy said.

"I see," he nodded.

"There's so much to fit in. I start the day by dropping Sasha off at the daycare. Then I come to work and remember that I haven't checked in with my partner. And she's been worried about me of late. I can tell."

Cosser nodded again, and then took out the photograph and asked her if she had ever seen this man.

She looked at it closely and shrugged. "No," she said. "Why?"

"He was at Marni's funeral."

"Really? I didn't see him there." She looked thoughtful. "Although there was someone who looked a bit like him. A bald man with a tattoo on the back of his head. I wondered who he was because I had no idea. Of course, Marni knew a lot of people I didn't know."

AFTER COSSER LEFT, Patsy could not shake thoughts of what would happen to Marni's boys. She managed to get through the business of the day, but as soon as she left the bank it all flooded over her again. There were the grandparents, but they had been able to cut off their daughter and grandchildren and that, in some way, ultimately cost her friend her life. But this had nothing to do with the church Patsy went to where she felt at home. She could not fathom why Marni would have gone there, least of all been murdered there.

She could tell from Polly's call that in spite of their suspicions, the people were doing everything they could to draw together as a community. She wondered why she felt she had to cut herself off from that when it might be the best way to come to grips with her own life, to become part of whatever healing they were going through. Later that day, she began to conceive a plan. She would ask Polly and Eric to come for dinner. They could play with Sasha and see her pictures of Marni. She would give them a gift then. Maybe she would ask Rosemary to come as well because Rosemary kept calling her. She did not know yet. She visualized Sasha crawling around on the floor of the nave during communion. Maybe she would simply take him and go to church the following Sunday. As it happened, when she mentioned her plan to Aloha, her lover asked if she could also come to the service.

They sat at the table after Sasha had fallen asleep upstairs in his crib.

"I hear it's a church where lesbian relationships are honoured," Aloha said.

"Yes."

"Then that sounds like a place for us to consider going."

"I didn't know you would even consider a church community," Patsy said. "After all the bureaucracy, the hierarchy, the history of the church's treatment of women. Not to mention gays and lesbians." But Aloha was, as often happened, a step ahead of her.

"I know, I know," Aloha said. "But we have to start somewhere, Patsy. We need a spiritual community. Oh sure, we have the lesbian one, but we need others as well. And ones that are more diverse. You know, for Sasha's sake, he needs to see people and families of all sorts."

Patsy began to soften. She would not be able to go down into the basement of the church for a long time. Maybe she never would be, but she could go back to the church itself. "All right," she said.

"What about this Sunday," Aloha said.

When Sunday came, Patsy put Sasha into his snowsuit. "Goose," he said, giggling.

"He thinks he's going to the daycare, doesn't he?" Aloha said.

"I guess," Patsy said. "He loves it when they read Mother Goose."

"Goose," Sasha chortled again.

Aloha put on her jacket and handed a bright red one from the hook in the front hall to Patsy. They went out into the December weather together, Sasha in his stroller. It looked as if it might snow later and it was cold enough, but there was not a trace of it on the ground yet. Aloha had brought her car, a red VW. They put the stroller in the trunk, drove downtown, and parked in the mall where they could get a reduction in their parking by getting the ticket validated at the church. Walking through the labyrinth of stores, Sasha kept peering around at all the bright colours. He pointed at a huge teddy bear in a store window.

"Sasha," he said.

"I don't think we need one that big," Patsy laughed. "But just you wait, sweetheart. You're going to have a wonderful time at Christmas."

"Isn't this the year they go for the wrapping paper and not the gift?" Aloha asked.

"Yes, I think so."

As they entered the church, Patsy saw Polly notice her and smile. She walked over to the piano. "Thanks for calling me"

She introduced Aloha. Then they found a place to sit just as the service began. Rob came over and started to play with Sasha.

"I missed him," he whispered.

Patsy had never noticed that Rob was particularly aware of Sasha, but she knew that he could have been. She smiled at Ardith as the other woman wheeled along the edge of the nave and took a place where she could participate fully and yet not block anyone else from moving. As Patsy looked around, people nodded or smiled when their eyes met. She wondered if they knew how ironic it was that her friend's body had been discovered in this church, a place Marni would only have been in under duress. She wished Marni had come here with her. She did not know what might have changed, but she thought it might have made a difference.

"Hi, Patsy," a male voice said.

She turned to find Brent standing behind them. "Hi, Brent," she said. "It's good to see you."

"And you."

"Boy, that little guy of yours sure has grown. What's his name? I'm sorry, I've forgotten. I'm not great with names."

"Sasha."

"My girlfriend's pregnant."

"I hope that's good news."

"Me, too."

Polly started to play the piano. The strains of "Morning Has Broken" filled the church. Linda stood at the front, ready to welcome people and to begin the service. It seemed strange to Patsy not to see David, but she realized he would not be able to come here now that he was no longer the minister. And would he want to as long as there remained that cloud of suspicion that would hang over anyone who might on the flimsiest of grounds have committed the crime? She hoped someone would be arrested soon. None of the people who had been caught up in this situation would be able to rest, for one reason or another, until someone was apprehended. She started to shiver, surprised that at the same time that her visceral reaction was still so strong, she could feel the words of the song—"*Praise with elation, praise every morning, God's recreation of the new day*"—reverberate through her. After a bar or two, with Sasha now reaching for her earrings and Aloha smiling at her, she began to hum.

39

THE TWO POLICE DETECTIVES, Jack Cosser and Simon Reid, met Ardith at her apartment, a building Cosser knew as one with suites that were accessible for people with disabilities. She answered the door in her wheelchair and gestured for them to come in. She was wearing a bright red cardigan with small black elephants in a line down the front.

"I should have returned sooner," he said, as both police officers gave Ardith their cards. "I had intended to come long before I got Rosemary's message."

Ardith nodded vigorously.

"You saw something, didn't you, Ms. Martin?" Cosser asked. "What was it?"

The interview was laborious. Ardith flailed her arms as she struggled to answer his questions and to tell him what she had seen before the service the morning of the murder.

"Something." A man with a woman he was almost carrying...

Cosser sat on the edge of a dark wooden chair, listening carefully to every syllable Ardith uttered. It was hard for him to understand what she was saying, but he sat quietly. This was important and this woman deserved his attention and respect. Occasionally he nodded. More often, he tried to repeat something to see if he had understood. Sometimes Reid would lean forward and as he caught something he would turn to repeat it to Cosser.

They went into the side door of the church, Ardith told

them. The man had trouble getting the woman through the door. His size, gait, and the colour of his coat matched those of Nick Duncan, the man who had shaved his head after the murder. Although the fact that this man had paid for an ad did not establish that he had met any of the respondents. It was a difficult connection to make. He knew that the victim had met Paddy, or Patrick, Sloane. Sloane had never tried to deny that. But there was no indication that Nick had met any of the women Sloane had met through the ad. And unlike Nicholas Duncan, the man Ardith described had dark hair.

"You're sure about the colour of the hair."

Ardith nodded with certainty.

"Not a bald man?"

"No." Shaking her head vigorously.

"Could he have been a bald man wearing a dark hat?"

"No."

Cosser supposed the bald head could be an attempt on Nick's part to change his appearance, in case anyone made a connection between him and the woman. A cab driver, for instance It would be easy to find out when Nick had shaved his head. Now that he was becoming more convinced about the identity of the killer, Cosser suspected Nick had probably shaved his head shortly after the murder. Maybe it had been foolish of Nick to give himself something as distinctive as a shaved head with a tattoo on it. But whatever he had done, sooner or later this bungled crime would have caught up with him.

"Thank you very much, Ms. Martin. This has been very helpful."

Ardith beamed as the police officers stood up to leave. She nodded.

On the street, Cosser shrugged. "I don't get it," he said. "Why would Nick Duncan have murdered a stranger?"

"Yeah," Reid said. "It's a puzzle."

"The initiative for placing the ad came from Sloane. It's not as if there was premeditation on Duncan's part about that. I want to check all our information to see if there's any connection with Margaret Atchison before we go out to arrest him."

When he went back to the station, Cosser checked the computer file on Nicholas Duncan again. There was nothing to link him with the victim. Except that he had gone to her funeral. There would have to be a reason for that. Cosser was going to go out and get him, and bring him in on suspicion of murder. But before that he was going to talk to Marni's father again. He gestured to his colleague and they headed into Cosser's office where he told Reid about his suspicion that there was a link between Nick and Marni's family. Why would he have been at the funeral otherwise?

"What are you thinking, Jack?"

"I'm not quite sure," Cosser said slowly. "But there's something about her father I wonder about. I don't know what it might turn out to be, but we need to know. And I found a picture of Duncan at the races when one of his horses won a couple of years ago. It will be interesting to see how Victor Miller responds to that."

"So we're going out there?"

"I think we have to, but we need to bring Duncan in first because I don't want him to slip through the cracks and disappear on us."

"Do you think he'd do that before the end of the day?"

"I guess not, as long as he doesn't suspect we're on to him."

Reid headed toward the door. "Let's get going to see Miller," he said.

"Right," Cosser said. "This time you're coming with me." All he had to do was to make sure Miller was at the farm before they set out and to let him know they would be there within a couple of hours.

"So," Cosser said when they were out on the highway, speeding west toward the London area. "You never did tell me about this new man in your life, Simon."

There was a surprised low chuckle from the passenger seat. "You don't mind then?"

Cosser glanced briefly at his colleague, saw a handsome man who was his friend by now. And one of the best cops on the force, he thought. "Well," he said." I sure don't envy you carving out a path in such a macho environment. But you're a damn good cop, Simon. Now tell me about 'what's his name.' How did you meet him?"

Reid looked embarrassed before he answered. "Ah well, Jack, you might as well know the whole story. Over the internet."

And so they had no lack of other conversation for a while before they began to speculate again on what they would uncover when they arrived at the farm.

"There has to be some connection between Duncan and Miller," Cosser said. "There has to be a reason Duncan turned up at Marni's funeral."

"And do you have a theory on that?" Reid asked.

"No," Cosser said, but he was going to figure it out.

When they arrived at the farm, Victor Miller was at the door. He grimaced when they got out of the car and approached him. He tossed a cigarette butt off to the side of the small porch at the entrance. Cosser nodded at him, wondering if he were smoking outside so as not to leave an odour in the house, or if he was sneaking a smoke that was prohibited by the Jehovah's Witnesses. He introduced his colleague.

"Come in," Miller said gruffly. "My wife is waiting to see you."

When they entered the kitchen, Cosser responded politely to Caroline Miller's subdued hello, introducing Reid again. He was struck once more by the starkness of the room. "There's not too much to report yet," he said. "But we hope to have more for you shortly." He turned to Miller. "We'd like to speak to you on your own, Mr. Miller."

"That isn't necessary," Miller said. "There isn't anything Caroline can't hear."

"Even so," Cosser said. "Where would you like to have this conversation?"

Miller looked uncomfortable, brushing his hand across his face.

"We could go out and sit in the car," Cosser said.

"That won't be necessary," Miller said. "Caroline, would you leave us for a while. Get the pamphlets ready. I will take these officers into the front room."

A room that was as bare as the rest of the house they had seen, Cosser thought, glancing at an old heavy sofa covered with a faded brown blanket.

"Sit down, Mr. Miller," Reid said.

Cosser took out the photograph and without any preliminary comments handed it to the other man, now seated on the sofa. He did not say anything, watching Miller's reaction closely. He saw the man's eye twitch and a slight quiver in the hand that held the photo.

"I've never seen him before," Miller said, looking up defiantly.

"I think you have," Cosser said. "He was at your daughter's funeral. Maybe he was looking for you there."

"Why would a stranger be doing that?"

"You tell us," Reid said.

There was a long silence. Miller grimaced and twitched again. "Caroline doesn't know about him," he said, looking down at his hands, now clenched against his knees. "She can't be told."

Cosser felt a momentary twinge of triumph. But he knew anything could still happen and that he needed to contain the elation that was growing. "It sounds as if you have a lot of explaining to do," Cosser said, watching the man closely, surprised that his face seemed to crumple and his body to shake.

"No one can know," Miller said, his eyes now pleading.

"I think it's too late for that," Reid said.

"Yes," Cosser said. "You're going to have to tell us for starters."

"He's my son," Miller said in a muffled voice.

"Come again," Cosser said.

"You heard me."

What followed left Cosser momentarily speechless as it emerged that Miller had had an affair early in his marriage, and the woman had a son about whom he had known almost nothing until now. Although he had made sure he knew enough to keep this son away from Caroline and the two children he had with her, he told the officers. Cosser shook his head at the thought that this man could have completely rejected his daughter for leaving the Jehovah's Witnesses and not be overwhelmed by the hypocrisy of his own situation. But his *modus vivendi* seemed to be rejection, however hypocritical.

"You're sure of that."

Miller lowered his head again. "He did contact me."

"When was that?"

"A couple of years ago."

But Miller had told him to stay away, not to try to gain a foothold in his family's life.

"So he harboured a very big grudge against you and might have taken it out on your daughter when an unexpected circumstance arose," Cosser said. "I wonder if he was at the funeral, expecting to see you there."

The man might have been in danger had he gone to his own daughter's funeral, but Cosser found it difficult to care beyond the necessity of his role as a police officer in protecting the public. He turned to Reid. "I think that clinches it," he said.

They left Miller with his head in his hands, no longer begging them not to tell anyone. He looked like a man facing Armageddon and Cosser could not help but wonder what solace would be left for him within his community now that the truth of his life was about to be exposed.

"So," Reid said when they were en route back to the city. "I hand it to you, Jack. You have good instincts."

They both grinned.

"It's been a good day," Cosser said.

40.

NICK WAS SANGUINE WHEN BOTH DETECTIVES arrived at the pub late in the afternoon and Cosser informed him that he was under arrest for the murder of Marni Atchison. He looked at himself in a mirror, like a vain man without scruples. Or was it just an attempt to appear nonchalant. "So, what about Paddy?"

It did not seem to bother him at all to have used a friend of so many years. When the unexpected opportunity had arisen that Marni, his half-sister, had answer the ad, he made sure Paddy saw her as a winner. Paddy had in fact asked for Nick's help in sorting out the respondents. And Nick had paid for the ad because Paddy had been short of cash at the time. After he had finally met with Marni, Nick had seemingly written Paddy off, as if he were a business loss on an income tax form.

"Anyway, you'll never make it stick," he said. "Because it's all deduction on your part. Far more likely for Paddy to have committed the murder, and not me."

"We'll see," Cosser said.

They would run a DNA match. They had hair samples combed carefully from the woman's clothing as evidence. He was fairly certain there would be at least a hair or two of Duncan's before he shaved his head and that would settle it. But he let the man preen for the time being. He would wait a bit longer and then tell him that he had spoken to Victor Miller.

When he did, Duncan flinched, and Cosser could tell he had

hit a sore spot. Duncan might not admit the crime yet, but his confident swagger would not return easily. Cosser wondered why the man had found it necessary to murder Marni, if she had scorned him when he revealed his connection to her. Had he hoped she would somehow be on his side and they could seek revenge together? She who had been disfellowshipped and he who had never been acknowledged. It was almost the same, wasn't it? But murder? It left Cosser shaking his head later. Sometimes the convoluted emotions that lead to crime made a person so bitter and twisted that Cosser had to fight back the urge to get outside and breathe in some fresh air. Anything to clear his head and his mind.

"So," he said.

"So, what now? What's the procedure?"

"Are you confessing?"

"No, but it seems like I don't have to."

"I am taking you down to the station for questioning," Cosser said. And he would book him on suspicion until the tests were done to validate his hunches. He had more than suspicions really. What he didn't have was a motive. Why had this man murdered Marni?

When Cosser got home later that day, he thought of Rosemary. He had to admit to himself that at times when he was coming up empty, her ideas had him think in other directions much faster than would have occurred otherwise. It was all part of an investigation, but he thought he had gained more appreciation for the imagination.

Still, there were clues Rosemary had known nothing about that he had followed up on. All the interviews he had done painstakingly, first with the parishioners. Until he came across the first witness of anything that had happened: Ardith. And damned if that was not also because Rosemary had alerted him. He would have gone to Ardith again because he'd obviously missed vital information on the first round. But Rosemary had been one step ahead of him. It seemed her intuitive sense and sheer luck had combined, and he almost wished she were a cop with whom he could discuss the case openly. He would have liked to be able to tell her in person what he'd discovered before it appeared in the media. But he knew he could not do that. In any case, he would have to wait until DNA proved the case conclusively.

Cosser was impatient, but later when he had all the information, what he suspected turned out to be accurate. Unlike the cop in *The Last Detective*, he had used technology as much as possible, but he was not averse to using his imagination either in trying to assess situations. As a detective, it was actually a useful asset just as it would be to Rosemary as a writer.

It was then he picked up the telephone. "Can I see you?" he asked when Rosemary answered. "Are you free later?"

"As it happens, I am," she said.

They arranged where and when they would meet. Across from each other in the coffee shop (he would suggest dinner at some later date, he thought, with cutlery and glassware atop a white tablecloth), he grinned at her. "I have some big news today, Rosemary."

She waited expectantly.

"You were right about the murderer," he said. "We've arrested a man not unlike a character in that novel of yours and he's in custody."

"Really?" Rosemary said. "Really? And you're not annoyed with me for imagining it."

"Actually, no. You were helpful because you know the community so well. You know how to talk to everyone. I think we would have cracked the case just about now, but your mind was racing and it couldn't help but make me think, too. Certainly the evidence that we've discovered is crucial to any conviction."

"So, you're saying my story was what suggested that someone as seemingly unlikely as the person who's been arrested could be the man."

"Not exactly. Now that we have arrested someone, it just

strikes me as interesting that your character has some similarities to him."

"Does anyone else know you read some of my manuscript?"

"No, do you mind?"

"Well, what will they think when I publish my novel?"

He could not help chuckling. "Probably that you're basing it on what you read in the newspapers. Because the arrest will be splashed throughout the media at any moment. That's inevitable. The case is too high profile and unusual for it not to be."

"Oh well," Rosemary sighed. "My character was Pete Cameron. Any similarity in the name?"

"No," Cosser said, suppressing a grin.

"I could never figure out Pete's connection to my victim."

"I'm sure you'll find the media reports fascinating."

The waiter put two cups of coffee down on the formica table. When he is able to take her to dinner at his favourite Italian restaurant, Cosser imagines the waiter saying something like, "As appetizer, Madame, the chef has grilled portobello mushrooms with herbs tonight. Delicious." He would describe a pasta dish, then the fish special of the day.

As they walked afterwards through the nearby park, Cosser said that it was foolhardy to answer ads in the personals, "although the truth is that for many people it's the only way to meet anyone new in a city the size of Toronto." He did not say that the internet had worked out for his colleague, Simon Reid. He did not say either that this might likely become a more frequent way for people to meet, and he was not about to pass judgment.

"If you're very careful, it's usually safe enough," Rosemary told him. "After all, if I'd never answered the ad, you might never have met me."

"Actually I might have. Margaret Atchison answered it and she ended up in the basement of your church. That's where I came in. Not to investigate who'd answered a personals ad."

"Makes you wonder," Rosemary said. "Doesn't it?"

Cosser nodded, although he was not sure what she was referring to. He was tired of the investigation now and wanted
to put it aside while Rosemary was still immersed in it. But he
had to finish with any loose ends around the case.

"True enough," He did not tell her the story became more
complicated. Nor that Nick Duncan had not raped the woman
before killing her.

"Cold-blooded murder?" Rosemary asked.

"You'd think."

"Not?" Rosemary looked at him closely, eyebrows raised.

"Well, yes and no." It was all he could say for now.

She would read about it that night or the next morning. She
would know soon enough that Nick Duncan was the murdered woman's brother, actually her half-brother. He had been
born out of wedlock, as it would have been called when Nick
Duncan was born. He knew she would find it hard to believe,
knowing that Marni came from a fundamentalist family, a
family in which they'd managed to hide this secret from her.
Or that Nick was born before Marni was. Some indiscretion
of her father's that he managed to hide from his family and
his Jehovah's Witnesses community. But Duncan had always
known about Marni and her older brother, and had envied
them being part of their own family. He had vowed to himself
that some day he'd get even with his father.

He could imagine Marni saying, "What a warped way to
think."

Cosser wondered himself why Duncan had not merely told
Marni so they could confront their father. Why kill her? And
he thought, but did not say, that he would likely never know
what had gone through Duncan's mind that led to murder.
Other than opportunity. Even though he was sure there was
a whole history behind it, of which he knew only a small part
that would explain it. He would leave those speculations to
Rosemary's imagination. He knew enough now to trust that
she could come up with something credible for her narrative.

When she knew the actual situation, she could figure out what to use or discard for her story.

It was all warped—forcing kids to belong to a particular religion, cutting them out of your life if they did not. Rosemary's furrowed face showed her mind was whirling. "You know," she said. "It's far more fun and requires less effort simply to keep stories in my head. Writing them down is harder work than I ever imagined."

"Think of it this way. Your story is already so well thought out that it seems plausible."

"But it was all a lark," she said. "Pure fluke."

"So is police work more often than not."

"Yes, but I'm a librarian. We research things. The information we find is not like what police work uncovers. I got carried away."

"I like you like that."

"Like what?" Her face flushed, redness working its way outwards from her nose.

"When your imagination is roving."

"Oh," she said. "My Dad used to get annoyed, said I went around with my head in the clouds."

"And you write well."

Cosser thought he now understood better why Marion had finally suggested separation. His work was his passion. She might not have been able to comprehend, or accept, how that passion could exist and there could still be room for her. Although he knew that it had been more than that with Marion. Just comprehending this now, he realized he had never had this conversation with her. Any woman he met in the future would have to understand this and accept it for their relationship to work. The Rosemary he had met initially might not have understood, but the Rosemary who had emerged since then likely would. He hoped when he could ask her out for dinner he would find this woman emerging easily.

"How would you feel about me going to the church with

you some Sunday?" Cosser asked.

"You want to go to church?" Rosemary looked uncertain, her pale hazel eyes darting around and then looking straight at him, eyebrows drawn together in a puzzled frown. This was the first sign he'd shown any interest beyond the case, Cosser realized. He'd managed to keep it hidden quite well by the look on her face.

"You go. Why do you go?" he asked.

"Well, I expect everyone has different reasons. It's a community for me after many years of not going anywhere near a church. And I was raised Anglican. There was a little wooden church on the edge of town with asbestos shingles on the outside. I think it's a community hall now, but it was a church then. There were quite a few Anglicans in that northern town. And because the town was so isolated, a lot of activity took place there. Bake sales. Women's groups. Youth groups. You know. So, even with the inclusive language, which I like, of course, and the activist stance, the liturgy is familiar. There's something soothing about that. And where else can I seek guidance in living a good, compassionate life, a Christian life, as my father would have termed it? I don't know. At the same time, I detest hierarchies and I question most of the readings. But I still go. And sometimes I actually believe in it. Or in something. Something rings bells. And then I buy a book like *Buddhism Plain and Simple*. But forgive me, I'm rambling."

"No, I like it," he said, hoping her embarrassment would not lead her into her shell again. "I can pick out a few strains. Could I read the Buddhism book if you like it?"

"Sure."

"I don't know if I'd go more than once, but there was something about the place that appealed to me."

"Well, it would start people talking."

"Would you rather I didn't?"

"Of course not. I'd rather you did. I rather like the idea of raising a few eyebrows."

"Really," Cosser said, watching her face, trying to fathom what she would think up next. That he would likely never be sure was part of what interested him about her.

"Just let me warn you of some of the pitfalls of coming to this church, okay?"

He nodded. It was hardly apt to be that there were frequent murders there. Perhaps she was going to tell him to beware of certain women. He could imagine Linda making a play for him as he had heard she did for Mr. Almost. So he was surprised when Rosemary began to warn him about political causes and social justice. He had thought she was there largely because of the involvement of this church in those activities.

"If you seem too enthusiastic or willing, you'll be drawn into more causes than you know what to do with. And won't they be delighted to have a cop in their midst! Someone from one of the despised bureaucracies who can advocate within the system!"

"Stop, stop," Cosser said. "I'm going to leave my work behind when I go there."

"You can't."

"C'mon," he said. "Why not?"

"They won't let you. It's not because they're unthinking or devious or anything. It's just who they are. A community that has so much going on that the conversation is bound to swirl around it. The announcements are full of it. Sometimes I feel guilty because I often go to be reflective and to be soothed. I should be out there at the centre trying to convince the government of something or other. I should be on the picket line. Or demonstrating in front of an embassy about some war in a distant place. And you know, sometimes I do. Sometimes I am. Because it's not only the way they are, it's how anyone who goes there over and over is. The church, the community, and their own need to have a voice draw them. But you have to be firm or you won't get what you need from going and if you don't, you'll burn out and lose interest."

"Wow," he said. "I just liked the warmth and the atmosphere. And the way the sun shone through the stained glass windows. The altar cloth that someone must have made especially for the church. Things like that. Is that allowed?"

41.

PADDY DROVE ALONG THE HIGHWAY out of Toronto early on Friday to miss the heavier traffic at the end of the day. It was not as bad as in the summer, he thought. He turned the radio on, but when he heard the beginning of a news report he turned it off again. How many times did he have to hear that Nick had been arrested as the alleged killer of one of the women who had responded to his ad? He was more surprised and upset at this turn of events than he had ever been about anything. He had always trusted Nick. He had trusted him more than his girlfriend, more than anyone. It was Nick who owned the house he was driving to and who had hired him to maintain it. Maybe Nick would not care about that now, but he would finish at least what had been lined up for this week.

He still felt implicated in the murder in some way in that it was his ad that had attracted Marni out of the great sea of anonymity of Toronto. But Nick could have found her even if there had been no ad. He knew that now. Nick had been related to her. This was far too complicated for Paddy; that such a coincidence could exist. He did not want to think about it. But he suddenly twigged to the mysterious follower who had been in the shadows on some of the occasions when he had met women who had answered his ad, primarily when he had met Marni, and later when Rosemary had set up the meeting in the church where she had surely not known anything about Marni. He thought Nick might never have gone looking for his half-sister, but it might have become irresistible when he recognized her from her photo in the files of information Paddy had received. He must have seen lots of photographs of her before that. He would have sought them out, wanting to know something about her, and he had probably followed her, too, over a much longer period of time. Paddy now knew that Nick had always resented this woman and her brother because they had been treated as members of a family that he had felt ought to have acknowledged him also.

A truck came up on his rear and he wondered if it would pass him. He was driving slightly over the speed limit, in the middle lane, and he knew trucks were not supposed to be hugging his tail bumper. It made him uneasy, and he worried that the truck would hit him. He decided to move into the inside lane as soon as there was an opening.

When he arrived at the house on the other side of the road from the lake an hour and a half later, he noticed the paint was peeling. There was always something to do when he came here. This time his intent had been to rake leaves and bag them, and to trim a tree that cut off the light in summer. But as he walked from the car to the blue door of the house, those were the last things he thought about. He felt like holing up here and spending the winter. Except for the horses. What would Nick do about them if he went to prison? He guessed the murder was not a coincidence after all. It still seemed bizarre that Nick had planted Marni's body in a church, but he had told Nick about meeting a woman there and maybe all along Nick had the idea of implicating him. His patsy. His flunky. Nick was devious, he knew that, but he had always thought they were friends, and that Nick would never turn on him. His mind jumped to where he could find work now and guessed he would ask at the track. And then there was his girlfriend. When she heard the story of his ad, she had ditched him. He did not care. He should have broken off with her himself. It had not turned out to be what either of them wanted. Often enough she'd told him she wanted someone with money, although she had also said she liked his sense of rhythm. As for him, he thought one day he might go back to that downtown church even if he would always know Marni's body had been left there, that a man he had considered a friend had tried to pin her murder on him. And as far as the church itself, he had to admit he had not felt anything very strongly during the service. He had been more or less oblivious to that as he had observed people, wondering which one was Rosemary. But he had found Linda intriguing. He would go back simply to talk to her, maybe sooner rather than later.

So it was that in early winter, Paddy found himself once more inside a church. He glanced down at his lapel, quite aware that he was not wearing a white ribbon this time. He was conscious that the caretaker noticed he was there, but why shouldn't he be? He watched Rosemary take a seat on one of the pews, taken aback that he had not thought until then that he was likely to see her there. It also surprised him when he realized she was sitting with the police officer who had investigated the murder. Looking around for Linda, he was disappointed not to see her anywhere. He did observe the woman in a wheelchair come in and recalled that he had noticed her when he had come to the church to meet Rosemary. She was the one who seemed to pay most attention to the men he thought were street people. Then just after the first announcements were made and the epistle had been read, he saw Linda arrive and move to a pew on the other side. He would not have met this type of woman through using ads, he thought. Although he had liked the one who had ended up dead. He wished she had not been murdered. If he had not asked Nick to write the ad, Nick might never have found her. That part, his finding his half-sister, was just a fluke, Paddy thought. Or was it? Nick had more likely been following her for a long time and when he found someone who might have to take the rap for her murder, had gone ahead and killed her. Paddy shivered and let his breath out in a low sigh. He was glad he was surrounded by these people who seemed to have managed to keep a welcoming atmosphere through what must have been a very tough time for all of them.

He felt a surge of relief that Linda was now there even though she had sat down next to a man who had greeted her warmly and he began to wonder what to say to her later, and if she would even remember him. He hoped so. He thought about his car, seeing it as Linda might, not as new as she would like. PADDY on the license plate. Take it or leave it, he thought, but she did not seem fussy like his ex had been.

COSSER WAS SURPRISED TO SEE THE MAN with red hair, Patrick—Paddy—Sloane, enter the church and make himself comfortable in one of the pews. Such a guileless man, could anyone have seriously figured he could have murdered Marni Atchison? It did not matter now as the real villain was known and in a jail cell. It would be a while before the trial, something that would have to happen since Nick Duncan, although having almost caved under questioning, had gone back to maintaining his innocence. Cosser was fairly certain the case against him with all the corroborating forensic evidence would stand up in court. He, of course, did not yet know that before the case went to trial, that when confronted with that forensic evidence, Nick would lose his tough guy demeanour.

"I didn't mean to kill her," he would finally confess. "She just wouldn't let up. She kept on and on about how terrible her life had been before she left the Jehovah's Witnesses, asking me to spare her. Telling me I was lucky. Lucky? Even though she was drugged, that had started to wear off."

But that was a few weeks hence and although he hardly heard any of the service, his thoughts were all about Marion, which surprised him as this hardly seemed the time for thoughts about his marriage. How had he been so stupid as not to notice them drifting apart and done something about it? What could he have done in the middle of a demanding case? Perhaps there was nothing that could have changed that, but at the very least he ought to have talked with her about the effect of police work on a marriage. He had been oblivious. Never again, he thought. If he became involved with Rosemary, or someone else one day, the nature of his work would be something they would have to discuss early. And not forget as time unfolded. Finally he acknowledged to himself that he had failed Marion badly, something he could not change now. It surprised him that in spite of everything, he no longer felt the awful loneliness that had plagued him for such a long time. He looked up at the splendid ceiling, thinking he would bring Jaime some Sunday soon. A thought that was premature, he knew. But, why not? He wondered if some people would disapprove of Rosemary being there with a police officer. But why should they? If not for police work and computers, there would still be one more killer on the loose. He had nothing to apologize for.

When Cosser moved toward the door at the end of the service, he saw Patsy with an energetic toddler and a woman he had not met. So Patsy had returned to the church after all. That seemed like an early sign of the strength of the community to draw together, he thought. He nodded at Patsy and as he did a smile of surprise and recognition crossed her face. He turned to look for Rosemary and saw that she was talking with Brent. Maybe about that book she was writing as she had mentioned the caretaker had suggested the idea for it. He waited off to the side to say goodbye to Rosemary. She had told him that she liked to stay after the service was over to chat with people and share some lunch.

"I'd like to come back some time," he said when she appeared. "I might even bring my daughter. Children seem to feel quite comfortable here." He had been impressed with the way they walked or crawled around right through the service, not to create a disruption, but just exploring.

"Of course," she said. "If you'd like to do that, you'll be welcome."

He turned around and headed toward his car with a smile on his face.

ACKNOWLEDGEMENTS

Thanks to Ray E. Bennett for the germ of an idea that was to become this novel and for his early feedback. I am grateful to Eric Wright who, at my then agent, Margaret Hart's request, offered critique that led me to change the entire structure, a massive challenge that ultimately gave me a lot more insight into the writing of a mystery.

Thanks to Dianne Mesh for her clarity and feedback on the church. Susan McCoy, Wendy Drummond and Harry for answering questions about homicide investigations. Paula de Ronde for insight, information and comment. Jen for her insights and clarification of information about the Jehovah's Witnesses religion. And Beth Jordan for introducing me to Jen and for her curiosity and interest in the early days as the novel unfolded.

To the Moosemeat Writing Group, especially Heather Wood and David Chilton (journalist and mystery aficionado), who tried to put me on track for what it takes to write a mystery and offered critique at various junctures. To Ellen Hrivnak and Carol Findlay for reading and commenting on the next to final draft, often with suggestions. To Farzana Doctor for her comments and suggestions on the final draft.

To Carol Findlay and John Roberts (via Michele Chicoine)

for all the mystery writers they read and recommended. And to Andrea Dickinson, Ruby Trostin, Michele Chicoine, Gene Simon, Brydon Gombay, Paula de Ronde, and Stephanie (Cosser) Farnsworth for their unflagging interest and support.

Thanks also to my family and friends who have kept on believing in me as I continued to write with little to show for it for quite a long time except bulky manuscripts. And for continuing to support me as my books have emerged. You know who you are. Hey Felipo!

And, of course, to Luciana Ricciutelli, editor and publisher extraordinarie!

Photo: Dieter Hessel

Mary Lou Dickinson's publications include a collection of short fiction, *One Day It Happens* (2007) and two novels, *Ile d'Or* (2010) and *Would I Lie to You?* (2014). Her fiction has also been published in a number of literary journals, including the *University of Windsor Review, Descant, Waves, Grain, Northern Journey, The Fiddlehead, Impulse,* and *Writ,* and broadcast on CBC Radio. Her writing was also included in the anthology, *We Who Can Fly: Poems, Essays and Memories in Honour of Adele Wiseman.* She grew up in northern Quebec and currently lives in Toronto.